The Slayer

by

Brenda Huber

Chronicles of the Fallen, Book One

This is a work of fiction. Names, characters, places, and incidents are either the product of the author's imagination or are used fictitiously, and any resemblance to actual persons living or dead, business establishments, events, or locales, is entirely coincidental.

The Slayer

COPYRIGHT © 2018 by Brenda Huber

All rights reserved. No part of this book may be used or reproduced in any manner whatsoever without written permission of the author or The Wild Rose Press, Inc. except in the case of brief quotations embodied in critical articles or reviews.
Contact Information: info@thewildrosepress.com

Cover Art by *Rae Monet Design Inc*

The Wild Rose Press, Inc.
PO Box 708
Adams Basin, NY 14410-0708
Visit us at www.thewildrosepress.com

Publishing History
First Black Rose Edition, 2018
Print ISBN 978-1-5092-2198-1
Digital ISBN 978-1-5092-2199-8

Previously published by Samhain Publishing, March 2015

Chronicles of the Fallen, Book One

Published in the United States of America

"If you kill me, you'll be trapped inside the enchantments. You'll never get out."

His smoldering gray stare dipped, tracing the curve of her lips. The trembling in the pit of her stomach intensified.

Surprise, and something darker, something more sinister, flamed in his expression.

"You think to keep me trapped here? You would sacrifice yourself to protect people you might not even know?"

She jutted her chin, defiant. Resolved. "If I have to."

"Why?"

"That's my business."

"That's no answer, little human."

"My name is Kyanna."

He assessed her in silence, though he didn't back off, didn't allow her even an inch of breathing room.

"You believe I would end your life. You think I would be a threat to other humans, so you think to trap me here inside this building. But ask yourself this, Kyanna—"

His heated stare dropped to her lips. The backs of his fingers skimmed up her arm, his touch feather-light. Gently, soft as the flutter of a butterfly's wings, Xander caressed her lower lip with the pad of his thumb. "What if I don't"—his scorching gaze captured hers, and held—"kill you?"

Praise for Brenda Huber

"Thrilling, dangerous and seductive… Brenda Huber has done it again with her continuation of a fantastic plot, amazing characters and sizzling passion."

~Fresh Fiction Reviews says of THE SEER

"With danger, passion, sexy demons, and a lot of action, THE SLAYER by Brenda Huber is a new favourite of mine."

~Fresh Fiction Reviews

"Brenda Huber is an author to watch. The way she paints a scene is fantastic…"

~Catherine Bybee, New York Times and USA Today Bestselling Author says of SHADOWS

"Huber's serial killer is truly twisted, and readers will be guessing the person's identity until the last pages of the story…"

~Romantic Times says of SHADOWS

"The turbulent, fast-paced plot leaves readers holding their breath while turning the page…"

~Coffee Time Romance says of MINE

Dedication

This book is for my husband, Lee. Thank you for believing in me, and for believing in us. I couldn't have gotten this far without you. You are the one I laugh with, live for, dream with, and love.

And for my children, Luke and Faith. You are my heart and my soul, my pride, and my joy. You are my treasure. May you always follow your dreams and never let anyone tell you that you can't. I will always love you, no matter what.

For where your treasure is, there your heart will be also. ~ Luke 12:34.

Acknowledgements

Writing and publishing a book, much less an entire series, is a collaborative effort that couldn't be accomplished without the hard work and dedication of special people. I cannot tell you enough how much I truly appreciate you.

I would to like to offer sincerest gratitude to Holly Atkinson, who offered priceless advice and supportive encouragement throughout the process of shaping and shining my world of The Fallen.

Thank you to Callie Lynn Wolfe for believing in the series and giving my guys the chance they needed to win the world over.

I would like to thank my talented and patient cover artist Renee Monet for gifting us with fabulous covers for my stories.

And last, but certainly never least, I would also like to thank my mentor, Joelle Walker, who gave me my first break and stuck with me, offering a guiding hand and a steady heart.

Then war broke out in the heavens. Michael and his angels fought against the dragon, who fought back with his angels; but the dragon was defeated, and he and his angels were not allowed to stay in heaven any longer. The huge dragon was thrown out, that ancient serpent, named the Devil, or Satan, that deceived the whole world. He was cast down to earth, and all his angels with him.

~Revelation 12.7-12.9

Chapter One

Pain ripped through his chest. Breath-stealing, mind-numbing, can-barely-function-through-the-agony pain. Fiery acid sizzled and smoked, eating through his leather jacket, stripping flesh from bone. Xander gritted his teeth and fell back, ducking behind the smoldering remains of a rusted two-door hatchback. He tore off the jacket, dropped it on the crumbling, weed-choked asphalt and clawed at what was left of his shirt. Xander mopped grimy sweat and splatters of venom from his brow with the back of his forearm, inadvertently smearing the vile toxin across his brow and down one cheek. He hissed as the acidic venom burned away more skin.

Plasma balls crackled and hissed in the stillness, showering down around him, exploding in the night like grounded fireworks. With blackened sweat dripping down his face, he glared at the mangled bomber jacket that was rapidly disintegrating in a ball of noxious smoke and swore. Profusely.

He could damn Lucifer to Hell and back for his dogged tenacity, but that was pointless. He'd expected nothing less, had known what he was getting into when he'd joined forces with Niklas and the others in rebellion. That still didn't mean he had to meekly accept his place at the top of Lucifer's ten most wanted list.

A bad bit of intel had wasted the better part of his day, sending him shimmering from one country to the next. He'd zigzagged back and forth across the globe—this trip 'round the bend had taken him to Panama, Nicaragua, Algeria and a dozen other hole-in-the-wall, rebel-seething countries that had come out the wrong end of one revolution or another—only to end up back in Minnesota, less than fifty miles from where he'd started.

Would this search never end?

Xander ducked as another plasma ball whizzed past his head and exploded in the darkness in a wild spray of sparks. Peeking his head around the fender, he spied six more demons spilling from the building. Where were they all coming from? Settling on his haunches, forearms braced on his knees, he tipped his head back and closed his eyes, expelling a weary breath.

Unfortunately, the others weren't having any better luck than he was. Nearly a year of following one useless lead after another had begun to stretch their collective patience to the limit. And there wasn't much of that precious commodity to begin with. Except for maybe Sebastian. The Demon of Vengeance didn't know the meaning of the word quit.

But they all knew what hung in the balance, and that threat was the only thing keeping them focused. Who would have ever thought, after all these centuries of rebellion against Lucifer, they'd be indirectly working to keep him in power down under—so to speak. But the bottom line was, if Lucifer fell, so too would fall the boundaries between Earth and Hell. Demons would overrun the Earth. Armageddon would ensue. *Blah. Blah. Blah.*

Strange how the choices you make come back to kick you in the teeth.

He canted his head as a shoe scuffed over gravel behind him, ten o'clock. Without glancing over his shoulder, he lobbed a plasma ball, grinning maliciously at the startled screech and the telltale whoosh of a demon igniting. But a spasm of pain ripped through his chest at the sudden movement, stealing his breath and some of his thunder.

And where has all this searching gotten me?

Answer? No-freakin'-where. Again.

Well, to be precise, it had gotten him right here, lured into this cliché ambush in the back of a dark alley. One of the Sacred Relics had already been stolen right from under their noses.

And his favorite jacket was trashed.

Another plasma ball exploded against the Honda's fender, raining sparks onto his bare back. Where the hell had all these demons come from? This was supposed to be a small nest. Ten, fifteen tops. Ten or fifteen he could handle without breaking a sweat. Twenty demons? No problem.

He'd picked his teeth with the bones of twenty, belched, and then bellied up for more.

At last count, he'd already smoked twenty-seven, and more continued to pour from the back of the building like cockroaches. Maybe he should have brought Gideon with him after all. Heaven knew the Demon of Temptation could have used the distraction. Kicking demon ass would have taken his mind off whatever funk it was that he'd slid into. Lately, the normally good-natured Gideon had been as irritable and surly as…well, as Mikhail.

And that was saying something. Mikhail, the Demon of War, was the proud owner of a prime piece of real estate at the corner of irritable and surly, with development rights to the intersection of terrifying and lethal. Mikhail walked a path Reapers feared to tread.

Weary, Xander swiped his palm over his face, dashed sweat from his eyes, and offered up a prayer for endurance. A prayer that this journey for redemption would be over. Soon. So long had he fought. So long had he been denied forgiveness. How many more trials must he overcome before he redeemed himself? How many innocents must he save before he was released from exile and allowed to return to his heavenly home? At this rate, even Oblivion—the soulless death of the damned—was beginning to look like a viable option. Anything to break this monotonous stalemate.

Xander scooted along the length of the car, twisted, and peered around a shattered taillight. Twelve more. Really? Had they somehow, after all these centuries, managed to jury-rig some kind of portal directly to Hell? Flexing his shoulder, he grimaced as pain ripped through his side.

Aw, screw this.

No one ever claimed he was a patient demon. He centered his focus and splayed his hands, palms up. Rivers of heat flowed through his arms, erupting like balls of molten energy above his hands as muscles stretched and bulged and his form grew in size.

Oh, that feels good.

Drawing a deep breath, he ruthlessly beat back the dark urges seething inside him, struggled to keep some measure of control. But these horrible instincts triggered by combat—magnified whenever he changed from human form to demonic—were nearly more than he could shackle. He'd been trying his damnedest to avoid unleashing the darkness. Lately, the deck had been stacked against him. It was getting harder and harder to put the voracious darkness back in its cage.

Part of him wondered if there would come a day when the darkness would win, and he just wouldn't come back at all.

He stared at the twin plasma balls pulsing and humming just inches above his palms. Concentrating, he forced more heat, more energy down his arms and took great satisfaction as the balls grew, burning brighter, hotter. Sizzling. Crackling. Hellfire began to pour through his system and into his hands. Burning brighter, hotter than normal plasma balls. Hellfire. Harnessed by very few but feared by all. Standing, wounded and furious, Xander faced the oncoming horde. He raised his hands and gave a mighty roar. He was a nightmare come to life. He was a methodical, cold-blooded assassin. A killer who took no prisoners. An executioner who showed no mercy.

He was the Slayer.

It was time to remind them of that.

****

"How long has it been since you had sex?"

"What?" Kyanna squeaked and ducked her head, glancing around the small café. Fortunately for her pride, none of the other patrons seemed to have overheard Summer's tactless question. But that was Summer for you. Blunt, bawdy and filter-free.

A deep, masculine chuckle came from nearby.

Oops. Not so lucky after all.

Kyanna dropped her forehead to her palm and

groaned, wishing she'd left her hair down, or thought to grab a newspaper. Anything to hide her face. But no. That would have been too easy.

There, one table over. The guy with the wedding ring. The one grinning into his coffee cup, gaze carefully downcast. His wife glared holes through first Summer, and then Kyanna. Oh, and there, with one elbow propped negligently on the service counter, Mr. GQ. Angled just so, all the better to rate her with his lascivious stare, clicking her up to a solid eight on his Easy Lay Scale.

Score? Kyanna's pride, zero. Summer's filterless mouth, a million and one.

"Shh," she hissed. "Jeez, Summer. I don't think the busboy in the back heard you." She loved Summer dearly. They'd been two peas in a pod since the minute she'd walked into her dorm room at college as a wet-behind-the-ears freshman and met her new, slightly eccentric, hippie-come-lately roommate for the first time. Regardless of the uncomfortable position Summer's thoughtless—albeit well-intended—comments often left Kyanna in, Summer's heart was in the right place. Always had been. Always would be.

Summer crinkled her nose at the greasy crumbs left behind from Kyanna's patty melt. "You know, I can actually hear your arteries clogging."

"Really? Well then, that will give me something else to die from." She licked a daub of ketchup from her thumb with relish, adding, "Other than embarrassment, that is."

"You know, if you lowered your standards a smidge, and actually got a little some-some going on, your mood might improve." Summer sat back in the booth and crossed her arms over her tie-dyed peasant blouse.

Kyanna wiped her fingers on a napkin and stacked her empty plate atop her friend's dish. "I'm sorry." Ice rattled in Kyanna's glass as she sucked down the last dregs of cold, slightly bitter tea. "It's been a long week."

"Which is exactly why you need to get out more. I swear, Ky. Sometimes you act like you've got one foot in the nursing home. Ever since you opened Treasure Box, you've tied yourself to that store. You need to let your hair down. Have a little fun. You remember what that is, don't you? Fun? A little woohoo? A slap and tickle? A game of hide the—"

"Yeah, yeah," she hurried to interrupt before Summer warmed to her subject. The poor married guy at the next table had to set his cup down and grab for a napkin as he choked on his coffee—or maybe it was laughter?—while his bearded face turned beet red. His wife kicked him beneath the table, sending a severe, judgmental frown in Summer's direction. Kyanna wanted nothing more than to crawl in a hole somewhere. "I get the picture," she mumbled.

As far as Summer—or anyone else for that matter—would be concerned, that would be the normal thing for a single, healthy woman her age to do. The logical thing. Go out. Date. Find an attractive, single man and enjoy a healthy, "normal" relationship.

If only it were that easy.

In her world—in the real world that other humans rarely ever found out about firsthand—dating was a complication. Relationships were temporary. Angels were real, not-so-beneficent beings. And demons were more than one-dimensional creatures itemized in the Bible, more than cautionary tales told to frighten children into good behavior.

Angels were a potential threat. Demons were real.

And boyfriends were collateral damage.

"So why aren't you, then?"

Kyanna studied the crown moldings as she nibbled her lower lip. She hated this. Hated keeping secrets. She'd always shared everything—well, everything else—with Summer. But this was more, a legacy her family had honored for generation upon generation. This secret was something she couldn't tell anyone. Not even her best friend.

"I recognize that look, Ky." Summer leaned forward, a frown forming between her brows as she dropped her hands to the table. "What's bothering you? You can talk to me, you know. Was it Jack? Did he—" She went silent for a moment, visibly struggling with her conscience, then blurted, "Did he do something?" Summer reached out, clasped Kyanna's hands. Her voice dipped, whisper soft as she peered at Kyanna with concern. "You never really told me why you cut him loose. That's not like you. You tell me everything."

Another stab and twist of that guilt-crafted knife.

"Jack didn't do anything. He just wasn't for me, Summer. It was me, not him. So get that look off your face right now. Make-up sex is not on my radar either."

Leaning back again, a petulant Summer crossed her arms once more and shook her head. Her gaze slanted out the window, and Kyanna could all but see the wheels turning. At length, Summer turned back to pin her with a probing stare.

"He asks about you," Summer prompted quietly.

“Drop it. I told you, Jack and I are through. It’s not happening.”

“Don’t think for a minute that this discussion is over.” Summer softened her admonishment with an affectionate smile before glancing at the big clock hanging above the café’s service window. She scrambled to gather her enormous, multi-colored gypsy bag. “Oh, shoot. I’m supposed to meet Duff over at the garage in ten minutes, so I better get a leg up.”

Kyanna snatched the green diner ticket, held it out of Summer’s reach with a smile. “Uh-huh. This one’s on me.” She shook her head as Summer opened her mouth to object. They stood and embraced. “I’ll get this, you go on. Don’t keep Duff waiting.”

After paying for supper, Kyanna stepped outside and drew a soul-deep breath of lake scented air, letting it sooth her raw nerves. She skirted a couple pushing a side-by-side stroller. The woman cooed at their drowsy young twins while the man, wearing a big camera with extended lenses around his neck, consulted a partially folded map. Kyanna edged around a large barrel planter filled with bright blossoms and climbed inside her battered gray sedan.

Mentally crossing her fingers, she prayed the ten-block drive back to Treasure Box would be uneventful. Summer’s impromptu invitation to supper had come as Kyanna had been on her way home from Minneapolis, where she’d finally procured a special order for a very picky client. That lamp and all the trouble she’d gone to in order to find it was going to earn her a pretty penny. She’d made it this far with no incidents. She’d been observant, just as her mother had trained her. She’d paid attention to her surroundings, to those people walking along the sidewalk, to those driving by, and to those looking out windows of stores she passed. So far so good. A slow, steady breath seeped out. Nearly home.

Thank goodness Isle wasn't overrun with demons, not like some of the other cities she'd lived in. This was a relatively small resort community, located on the southeast end of Mille Lacs Lake, only two hours north of Minneapolis. She'd lived in Isle for several years now, knew a good share of the town's 707 year-round residents in one way or another.

But Isle was also a tourist hot spot, swelling to nearly double its population in the summer, not to mention ice fishing season. Aside from flourishing shopping and business districts, thriving resorts, and gorgeous Isle Lakeview Park, Isle Bay possessed some of the best swimming beaches Mille Lacs had to offer, which meant a sea of unfamiliar faces many months of the year.

Her hand crept up to clasp the pendant hanging from the chain around her neck. She'd taken precautions. She always took precautions. Still, when it came to demons, one could never be too careful.

Slowing for a stoplight, Kyanna scanned the street. An elderly couple approached a nearby storefront, stopped a moment to gaze through the shop window at furniture. They stood side-by-side, holding hands, silver heads bent close together as they considered the accent-lit dining room set before tottering on. Mr. Bradley, owner of The Green Thumb next door to her own shop, ducked into the hardware store across the way, a skinny length of steel pipe with an on/off valve clutched in his hand.

A boy wearing a baseball jersey and cap rode by on a bike, his catcher's mitt dangling from the handlebars. His knees, one hip, and his shoulder were dusted with reddish brown sand. He hopped the curb, peddling madly beneath the glowing streetlights. A couple of kids stood outside the pet store, pointing at the fuzzy, gray and white kittens climbing through a carpeted kitty condo. The light changed. Stepping on the accelerator, Kyanna eased into the intersection and turned left at the next block.

Life went on all around her. Filled with everyday concerns. Everyday hopes and dreams. Normal. All of it so normal.

Why can't I *have normal?*

Chapter Two

Two of the demons took one look at Xander in all his demonic glory and vanished. A third—already palming a plasma ball—gaped at him. The plasma ball in the third demon's hand sputtered, then fizzled out completely.

Pansy.

The remaining nine rushed forward. Xander offered them a fang-filled grin, taunting them, challenging them to dance with death. No one who'd ever tangled with the Slayer lived to brag about it. Ever.

The oncoming horde of demons didn't pause in their forward rush, but several of them—he was pleased to note—had lost a bit of that burnt-orange color that marked them for what they were.

Only thing worse than a pansy?

A dumbass.

Chuckling gleefully, he let one of the plasma balls loose, aiming for the pansy. If that demon stood there shaking in his bloomers like that any longer he'd wet himself.

Only thing Xander hated worse than a dumbass? The smell of demon piss, which usually came right after some moron with delusions of grandeur finally realized he had about as much chance of surviving combat with the Slayer as Frosty had of surviving a five-minute vacation to the steamy eastern borderlands of Hell.

Pansy exploded in a screaming firestorm, taking three others with him.

Sweet Saint Christopher, this crap is so old!

Whipping his arm around, Xander let loose with another plasma ball and took two more down. That gave the remaining five pause. The plasma balls they held sputtered out. They lifted empty hands in surrender and began backing up.

Xander tsked, shaking his head. *Already poked the monster. Too late to throw the stick away and play nice now.*

His grin stretched wide. Malevolent. Lethal. Energy built, writhing, twisting, frothing through his veins. Crackling in the air around him. Darkness lurched up inside him, greedy to devour. It clawed and gnashed for release. A live, sentient thing.

Death. Destruction.

Good.

Raw, magnificent power.

So good.

Xander walked a fine line now. He let the beast within have more and more freedom as Hellfire boiled through his veins and raged forth, his grip on control hanging by stubborn threads. Deadly cravings held him in their talon sharp grip. Yet he managed to retain some semblance of sanity. Always, somewhere in the back of his mind, was the awareness of where he was. Awareness of the fact that this was a tourist town brimming with innocent human life.

He couldn't let go, not completely.

If he did, he'd be a far greater threat than an entire legion of the worst demons Hell had birthed. He'd already proven that, once upon a time.

With another unholy roar, he pushed the wave of Hellfire out from his core, using his palms to direct the flow. The demon front and center exploded from within, splattering his compatriots. The three that had spilled from the building a moment ago immediately beat a hasty retreat at the sight, tripping over each other in a mad dash to hide. No more demons were forthcoming.

Nifty little trick he'd stumbled upon several millennia back when he'd been far less judicial with his powers. Too bad it was an unreliable power that came and went with the tides.

The last of Xander's opponents skidded to a halt, glancing uncertainly at each other.

Like that, did ya? Well, you ain't seen nothin' yet, baby.

And just like that, it was on. Xander shimmered into their midst, literally standing upon the pulpy remains of his last victim. Spinning, he planted a solid roundhouse kick to the breadbasket of the demon to his right and knocked him down and out for the count. He reached around and grabbed the demon on his left by the base of his horns. Giving a brutal twist, he ripped the demon's head from his body.

The next demon went down just as easily. His companion finally—*finally!*—displayed the first shred of intelligence he'd seen out of these yahoos all night. Crossing his arms, thwapping clenched fists to his shoulders, the demon dropped to one knee and bowed his head in submission.

Slowly, Xander straightened. Without taking his gaze off the kneeling demon, he stretched out a palm, ignited a plasma ball, then tipped his hand over and dropped the blazing ball onto the chest of the unconscious demon. Within seconds, flames consumed the fallen demon's body. The corpse erupted in a shower of embers and ash.

Xander didn't so much as blink.

"M-mercy," the kneeling demon begged, his head tilted so far down Xander couldn't even see the tip of his burnt-orange nose.

"I am the Slayer," Xander snarled, aware that the harsh rasp of his voice struck fear just as his demonic appearance did. He dropped his chin to his chest and gave in to the darkness seething inside him. "I have no mercy."

Snapping his hands open at hip level, palms out, Xander let heat build and flow once more. He'd never tried to harness Hellfire again this quickly after using it. Could he control it? Or would he end up blowing himself up instead?

Giving a small mental shrug, he encouraged the power to sizzle through his veins.

"I-I have i-inform-m-mation," the demon squawked, visibly trembling.

Truth, the deep, demonic voice hissed in the back of his mind.

Though he continued to hold the threat of an excruciatingly painful death over the demon's head, Xander gritted his teeth and waited, the epitome of impatience, and growled, "Speak."

This better not be another dead end. Like the one indicating the Guardian of the Arc Stone was in Scotland. That lead had taken Sebastian, the Demon of Vengeance, on a pointless two-month jaunt. Or the information they'd uncovered on a possible Chosen

One that Mikhail had followed to Tibet. Another dead end.

Seemed as if one lead always led to another. And then that lead led to another. And another. He'd personally seen the inside of every craphole and demon-dive between Argentina and Zimbabwe. He wasn't ready to start the Grand Tour again.

But the thing that seriously sucked? Every one of his "informants" honestly thought they were telling the truth. And if anyone would know, he would. That had been his special little gift from Lucifer upon his fall, the ability to determine whether someone was lying.

Just call me Mr. Polygraph.

"I know you search for the Sacred Relics. For the Arc Stone," the demon whimpered.

And here we go. Again.

"I-I don't know where the stone is—but I know where th-the s-scrolls are," the Demon stuttered.

Heaving a sigh, Xander waited. The demon truly thought he knew. Much as he wanted to just end this, Xander owed it to his comrades-in-arms to listen.

'Cuz you just never knew.

"Where?" Xander rasped.

"H-here."

Xander let his scowl deepen. Even now, even in the demonic, he could feel his strength ebbing. His wounds must be worse than he'd thought. He didn't have time to toy with this miscreant. Asher, a demon mercenary with an impeccable reputation, had pointed them in this direction. Now this demon was confirming that a relic was here. The Scrolls of Prévnar.

Oh, for the love of—

Something better damned well be here this time.

"Where?" He let the increasing sizzle of a plasma ball finish his threat.

"Th-there." The demon tipped his head toward the back face of a two-story building not far away. The red brick façade was old, but well maintained.

"Treasure Box?" Xander read the black-and-white, stenciled sign indicating the rear entrance designated for deliveries.

"We've d-determined the scrolls are i-ins-side."

"Why have you not gone in after them?" The horrific sound of his own cursed voice grated on his ears, but he was too interested in getting answers to quibble over speaking more than he normally did.

"P-protected," the demon spit out. "Ward stones. Angelic e-enchantments. W-we couldn't breach them."

Angelic enchantments?

Only a Guardian would have knowledge of angelic enchantments. For the first time since he and the others had started this farce of a search, hope began to bubble in Xander's chest.

Until a wave of vertigo swept over him.

Then again, perhaps it was just the venom working its way deeper into his system.

Under the guise of an impatient sigh, Xander drew a careful breath. His vision had begun to waver, his hands to tremble. He needed to dispense with this conversation, and with this demon, before the demon figured out exactly how weak he really was and tried to take advantage of the situation.

"What of the employees?"

"Th-there is only one. The owner. Sïnsobar attempted possession, but he f-failed."

Xander's brow creased. Sïnsobar, otherwise known

as Sin, was Carpathï, a legendary shape-shifter that specialized in infiltration and possessions. If he'd failed in the attempted possession, there was definitely something going on here.

"I-it appears to b-be a hereditary line of Guardians."

Hereditary equaled human, then. But what about the angelic enchantments? How would a human obtain them? And the ward stones? Where would the owner have gotten ward stones, much less the knowledge of how to use them properly?

Was it possible the owner was under the protection of an angel? And then another thought occurred to him. One far more shocking.

Could there be a blood-tie?

Had some naughty little angel come down and done the dirty with a human?

It had happened before. Though unlikely since the Great Fall, it was still possible.

Following that startling line of thought, he pressed for a reaction. "Which line is the owner descended from? Seth? Marcus?" Apprehension balled like ice in his gut. The very idea was a stretch, but given what Xander knew of his angelic counterparts, it would have only been a matter of time. And so he queried, "Gabriel?"

"W-we don't know y-yet."

Truth.

"Who is your allegiance to? Who sent you to find the relic?" Another wave of dizziness nearly took his legs out from under him.

The demon took his time in replying. "Sïnsobar."

"Wrong answer," he snapped as the demon's lie

crawled over the back of Xander's neck like a thousand spiders.

He let the power in his hands grow again. A big risk, considering the way his insides quivered. Blood ran down his chest in streams, soaking the waistband of his camo pants.

"W-wait—"

The demon's gaze shifted. The only warning Xander had before the darkened alley exploded in a torrent of plasma balls once more. Damn, he must be weaker than he'd realized. He hadn't even sensed the arrival of three more demons.

Xander vaulted over his informant's head, taking said appendage with him as he went. He landed on his feet and staggered to the side under the loss of so much blood. Already focused on his next opponent, he chucked the dismembered head. Xander spun and dove for cover, as he randomly hurled plasma ball after plasma ball, praying he hit something vital. His vision had dimmed further, was blurring so badly he feared a total blackout was imminent.

The two demons fell in the blaze of a firestorm as the third demon ducked out of the way with the speed and skill of a weasel hopped up on steroids. Just as Xander began to summon the next plasma ball, the sound of an approaching car stilled his hand.

Xander swung around. The demon stood motionless as it scented the air. Fortunately, the last flames of firestorm had evaporated, gone in a burst of demon ash, taking all demon remains with it.

A battered, gray sedan pulled around the corner of the far building and idled down the now dark alley. Headlight beams slanted across the brick and wood rear faces of empty buildings. Xander blinked, peering hard as the car pulled up near the back entrance of Treasure Box and the engine cut out.

A minute later, a shapely, bare leg stretched out of the car, followed by its mate. He caught a glimpse of a long blonde ponytail being flipped over one bare shoulder and then a delicious, curvy bottom was thrust into the air as the owner of those gorgeous legs bent over and leaned back inside the sedan.

Xander cursed beneath his breath as a demon crept closer to the distracted woman. He needed to do something. Fast. She backed out from the car, a large, plain, brown box cradled in her arms. She eased around the door and elbowed it closed. The woman came to a dead stop and stared at the smoldering vehicle he'd took shelter beside earlier.

"What on earth?"

The demon crouched, ready to spring. Snarling, Xander lifted his hand, plasma ball palmed and ready to toss. He let it fly, but the demon was wily and dodged it, hissing at Xander like a scalded cat. The woman let out a strangled shriek and flattened herself against the car.

Sucking in a sharp breath, Xander summoned what little strength he had left and shimmered between the woman and the demon. Balls of fire erupted from his palms and shot out, deflecting an oncoming fiery projectile with one and catching the demon in the middle of his chest this time with the other. With a loud screech, the demon erupted into a ball of flames before he burst into ash.

Preparing himself to deal with a hysterical female, Xander swiftly changed back into human form so as not to frighten her further. Hell, it probably wouldn't matter. She'd already gotten an eyeful. He couldn't think straight. Pressing a fist to his throbbing temple, he shook his head, then staggered a bit as the world around him continued to shake and spin. *Gah!* Maybe his head would simply fall clean off and roll around on the ground. Wouldn't that be pleasant?

No, not so much. Though it couldn't possibly hurt worse than it did right now. Xander braced himself against the hood of her car, panting, knees shaking, head pounding, stomach rolling.

The woman gave another strangled screech. The package slipped from her hands and landed on the pavement at her feet with the unmistakable tinkle of broken glass. Clamping her hand around a small crystal dangling from the long, thin chain around her throat, she edged backward and peered up at him.

She had the most beautiful eyes he'd ever seen.

"Who are you?" She scooted one foot back, easing herself away from him. Slowly. As one would from a dangerous animal. "What do you want?"

He took a wobbly step toward her, stretched out a trembling hand. Her eyes. So blue. So. Big. So…

Pretty.

"Help…you." He fought, battled with all his might. But he'd lost too much blood. It'd been too long since he'd last fed. His injuries were too severe. Black swirled around him, narrowing the scope of his vision more and more. He couldn't catch his breath. Numbing cold settled all through him. Invasive. Suffocating.

Darkness slipped over him.

Chapter Three

Kyanna examined the demon lying at her feet in shock. And there was no doubt in her mind that's what he was. She'd gotten a good look at him, both before and after he'd done that morphing thing. A real live demon. In the flesh. Within poking distance.

He was a mess. Drenched in blood. Horrible burns covered his shoulders, neck, and arms. Huge gashes snaked across his chest. Deep, vicious wounds. And his face—

She bit her lip, wincing.

Oh, his face! How is he still alive?

Wait! Where was all this sympathy coming from? She gritted her teeth and firmed her resolve—or tried to.

Not human, Kyanna!

But he'd saved her? It made no sense. His kind didn't save humans. His kind hunted them. Tortured them. Killed them and gobbled up their souls like Summer scarfed down French silk pie.

Confusion held her immobile and indecisive.

A soft groan slipped from his lips, gearing her into action. She dragged her cell phone from her back pocket and thumbed it on. Only to turn it right back off and shove it back into her pocket.

Who was she going to call? It wasn't as if the local boys in blue had a special cell designed to detain—

contain—creatures like him. She'd have better luck with something like that inside her own store.

Growling in frustration, she dropped to her knees beside the injured…demon? Man? He sure looked like a whole lotta man right now.

Non-demon?

Regardless of what he was, he'd saved her from that monster-thing. Helping him in return was the least she could do. Right?

Danger, Will Robinson! Not human, Kyanna! Do not soften toward him.

A slim, silver chain glinted from around his throat. Her brow furrowing, she tentatively traced a finger over the smooth chain, did her best to ignore the warm flesh beneath it. Her fingertip paused as she reached the pendant. Power pulsed from the small crystals embedded in the silver and shimmered up her arm like a rush of warm liquid. Soothing. Blood smeared the stones, but she could still identify them. Brecciate jasper? Chrysoberyl?

What would a demon be doing with something like this?

According to the book, the recordings passed down from her mother and her mother's mother before her, this man/demon shouldn't even be able to come near these stones, let alone have them in constant contact with his flesh.

She scanned his face, his body. Soot smeared the golden patches of skin that weren't covered by blood and burns. One of his pant legs had been scorched from his ankle to his knee. And strapped to the other calf was the most vicious-looking, medieval dagger she'd ever seen. The blade alone was nearly as long as her forearm. Who was this guy?

A low groan gurgled in the back of his throat, dragging her from her musings. How could she help him? Did she dare? Or would she only be signing her own death warrant? She'd been raised to fear demons. Raised to avoid them at all cost. She'd also been raised to protect the innocent.

And to do no harm to those who did no harm to her.

Nowhere in the book had anyone ever written about a demon like this one. One who'd willingly put himself in harm's way to protect a human.

Dear Lord, she didn't even know where to touch him. His body had been so ravaged. Glancing up and down the alley, she chewed on the inside of her lower lip. Should she bring him inside? Could she trust him enough to breach the ward stones? Or the outer enchantments? She had a First Aid kit in the store. Not that the meager training she'd received back in Girl Scouts was going to cover something like this. But she had the book. Surely there must be something therein that would pertain to whatever he was.

Peering uncertainly at the wreckage of the small car, she cringed. If she left him here, vulnerable like this, she'd be no better than the evil Sheila Hughes had taught her to fight. But her mother wasn't here anymore to guide her. What was she to do? He was wounded, obviously in desperate need of help. Maybe that was what was confusing her. He confused her. He'd looked like a demon. For a little while there, at least. But he certainly hadn't acted like one.

And now here he was, completely at her mercy. Defenseless. And he looked so human now.

Kindness, Mom had always preached. Kindness had felled many a great foe. Though, somehow, she didn't think Mom might have had exactly this situation in mind.

Moaning softly, the man/demon turned his head. His brow puckered. Ever so carefully, she eased her hand along his cheek. The scrape of dark stubble against the sensitive skin on the inside of her wrist sent delicious shivers up her arm. Gently touching the unmarred side of his forehead, she worried her lower lip with her teeth. He was burning up. Had he been poisoned somehow? Was infection setting in? Could his kind get an infection? Gnawing on her lip again, she glanced around the alley.

A streetlight at the end of the alley popped, going out in a shower of sparks, startling her. Enough waffling. She had to decide. Now. What if more of those vile creatures came back?

What if he turns out to be just as evil as the rest?

No! She couldn't think like that. He'd stood before her, used his own body to shield her. She'd take him inside. Clean him up as payback for saving her. Once she'd seen to his injuries, healing him as best as she could, then she could decide what to do with him.

She could always surround him with ward stones for her own safety. And when he woke up, if his eyes were still glowing red and he went all *Village of the Damned* on her, then she'd douse him with holy water and use enough of the incantations in the book to bring down the wrath of Heaven on his head and make him wish he'd never stepped one of those Godzilla-sized combat boots outside the gates of Hell.

Kicking the box containing the now-shattered

Tiffany lamp aside—the lamp she'd spent far too long searching for—she scrabbled to reach beneath him. Kyanna hooked her hands under his arm pits and prayed his back wasn't in as rough shape as his chest was. Dear lord, he was a mess. *And hot!* And not in a sexy-hot way…well, okay, in all fairness, he was hot that way too. But he was hot in a burning fever-hot way. That couldn't be good.

"Buddy," she grunted, "you weigh a ton. Be a good fella and wake up. Help me get you inside, would ya?"

A groan. A muscle twitch.

"Hey," she panted, pushing him into a sitting position. His head lolled forward, his arms flopped onto the pavement at his hips. He was nearly twice her size and it took every ounce of her strength to get him up this far, let alone balance him against toppling over. She'd never get him on his feet and inside without help. "Hey, sexy demon-guy. Hey. Wake up."

His head lolled to the side and his eyes, rimmed by thick, long black lashes, slid open. Groggy. Unfocused. Turbulent gray. Compelling. Stealing her breath.

Woosa! Definitely not red.

Those were the most impressive bedroom eyes she'd ever seen.

"That's it," she croaked, clearing what she prayed was *not* a lump of lust from her throat. "Wake up, buddy. Can you stand?"

"Help…you," he croaked. It was all she could do not to cry in sympathy. His voice sounded as shredded as his chest looked.

"That's right. Help me out here. Help me get you on your feet," she coaxed. "That's my shop over there. I can help you, but I have to get you inside first. Can you get up?"

With a tortured groan, he began to move. All she could do was hang on, brace him so he didn't fall flat on his face, and push him in the right direction. The fact that he was still on his feet and moving under his own steam was beyond her comprehension, reminding her again that human he most definitely was not. Taking a deep breath, she offered up a little prayer.

Please, God, don't let this be the biggest—or the last—mistake I ever make.

Kyanna wedged his tall frame between the brick wall and her shoulder as she fumbled the keys from her pocket. She fitted the proper key into the lock and shoved the door open. Kyanna tucked herself beneath his arm. Obligingly, he shifted his weight, leaning heavily upon her. Kyanna staggered to the side before righting the both of them.

"Buddy," she grunted. "You weigh a ton."

Against her better judgment, Kyanna guided him up to the doorway, only to have his frame violently jerk back, as if flung from the entrance by invisible hands.

Having her suspicions confirmed so undeniably didn't ease her mind. Regardless of how he'd behaved, he was a demon. For sure. No question about it. The enchantments wouldn't let him pass.

With one last bit of reluctant hesitation—and plenty of second thoughts—she whispered the phrases needed to lower the enchantments, and swiftly tugged him inside. Just that quickly, she crossed herself and whispered the sacred words in a furious rush, restoring the enchantments.

Once the charms were back in place, she craned her neck and peered at her foundling. She'd broken the cardinal rule. She'd allowed the enemy inside her safe haven. Hard of head and soft of heart, that had always been Kyanna's problem, or so her mother had forever complained.

Mom must be rolling over in her grave right now.

With a wince of poorly stifled guilt, Kyanna maneuvered her semi-conscious companion through the storage room and into the small office. She'd like to believe she'd helped lower him gently to the plump sofa opposite her desk, but really, it had been more like a great oak crashing to the forest floor. She did her best to aim him in the right direction, and then just got the hell out of the way.

It was little wonder the sofa didn't simply collapse in a pile of stuffing and splintered wood. As it was, the antique claw-foot sofa had scraped a good six inches across the floor, only stopping once the back of the sofa slammed against the wall hard enough to rattle the framed business degrees she'd worked so hard for.

Struggling to lift his huge, booted feet, Kyanna huffed and puffed until she finally had his legs draped, more or less, over the arm of the sofa. Good Samaritan or not, she was no fool. Holding her breath, she performed a harried pat down. Her hands momentarily stilled, her eyes rounding as she searched his groin area. Forcibly tearing her mind away from the unbelievable size of the man, she made short work of removing the wicked looking dagger strapped to his ankle. Kyanna scurried out into the hallway and opened the door to her apartment.

With a swift glance over her shoulder, she tossed the heavy weapon—the *only* weapon she could find on his person—onto the steps. Centering her focus, calming her heart, she furtively whispered additional enchantments, reinforcing those secondary charms protecting her apartment. She grabbed a small stack of hand towels from the cleaning closet and stopped by the restroom long enough to wet them down. She then hurried back to her office and lifted his head to ease a small throw pillow under him.

He looked utterly ridiculous like this. Propped like a ragdoll—albeit an enormous, war-like, testosterone-injected ragdoll—on a pile of overstuffed chintz and filmy lace. As carefully as she could, Kyanna pressed a cloth to the wounds on his chest with one hand and began cleansing his face and neck with a damp cloth in the other. For a breath-stealing minute, her fingertips lingered on the lines of his face. High cheekbones, aristocratic nose. Soft, sculpted lips. And there, hidden in the shadows of stubble covering his jaw, a tiny cleft in his chin.

Dimple on the chin, devil within.

She'd always scoffed at antiquated, narrow-minded sayings like that. Old wives' tales. But something about this guy screamed danger. Maybe he was the one that had spawned the phrase.

Even with the livid burns on one side of his forehead and the upper edge of one cheek, he was a handsome specimen. As she moved the wet cloth over his arms, she caught her breath at what she'd unwittingly revealed. Tattoos wound themselves around both his arms, from his shoulders to his wrists.

Such odd writing...hmm.

She tilted her head, studying the graphic designs.

No, not all of it was writing. Strange runes she couldn't identify peppered his chest and ran down the length of his left arm. Graphic scenes of death and destruction. A likeness of the dagger she'd just, ah, relieved him of had been replicated along the inside of his forearm, the blade dripping with God only knew what. Strange wisps of curling, slithering smoke. Piles of bones—mountains of them—littered his flesh. Battle scenes from Hell, she imagined. All the more horrific for the real blood and soot she'd been wiping from him.

And on his right arm? Vine work and elaborately decorated crosses. High on one bicep, the Virgin Mother kneeling in prayer. On his forearm? The Crucifixion of Christ. Her hand stilled, washcloth dangling from her fingertips. All Christian religious symbols, she realized with a start. And what looked like Latin writing to her untrained eye.

On a demon?

How peculiar.

Shaking her head at her own curiosity, she dumped the stained towels in a pile near the doorway. She went to retrieve the First Aid kit and more towels. Kyanna dropped to her knees beside the sofa and popped the white, metal lid open. After pulling out fistfuls of gauze pads, she tore paper from cotton and pressed the unwieldy mass to what appeared to be the deepest of his wounds.

Dear Lord, even the shallow ones continued to trickle his lifeblood away. She picked at bits and pieces of what looked to be charred cotton stuck in his gashes. Should she try to clean the wounds? Could demons bleed out? He needed stitches.

She was in way over her head here. No question about that.

All she knew for certain was that this man—this

demon—had saved her, despite all her mother's most dire predictions to the contrary. She had to do something. She couldn't just let him die. If she brought the book down to the office, she might be able to find something in there that could help him.

Possibly.

Yes. There had to be an answer somewhere in there. Besides, she needed to gather more ward stones to form a protective circle around him like a mystical cage until she could figure out what to do with him. Bracing a hand on the sofa near his shoulder, she made to rise.

A harsh groan tore from deep in his throat, and he mumbled something.

Leaning closer, hoping for some bit of direction as far as his medical needs were concerned, Kyanna held her breath and searched his rugged face. Would he speak? Could he tell her what he needed? Those entrancing eyes opened slowly, blinked. Struggled to focus.

"Woman," the demon whispered. He squinted, blinked, and sucked in a sharp breath.

"Yes? I'm here." She smoothed a comforting hand over the short, silky hair at his temple. A buzz cut. A ripped body. Camo pants and combat boots. He looked military. Her own personal GI Joe. Appalled by her own sudden lack of mental control, she petted his hair with renewed vigor. "What can I do?"

"Forgive me," he panted.

He lifted a large, shaking hand and laid it flat upon her chest.

Before the fog of confusion fully had a chance to settle upon her, a searing burn ripped through her body.

She was being torn in two, splintered from the inside out. Helpless to resist, she hung loose-limbed and limp, suspended with her knees inches from the ground by nothing more than the contact of his bare palm where it touched her chest.

Oh Lord, it burns!

She couldn't catch her breath, couldn't scream for help, not that there was anyone else nearby at this hour. She couldn't see. Couldn't hear, but for the loud *thwap-thwap* of her heartbeat in her ears. How long the agony lasted, she couldn't say. But darkness eventually crowded around her. Cold. Lonely. A relief after the fierce burn, but yet so unfair.

How can you kill me? All I tried to do was save you?

Kyanna was losing her grip on her body. At first, she pushed through the pain. She couldn't let go. She had too much to live for. Too much to do.

The burn intensified, became unbearable.

Too much.

With a shuddering sigh, she let go and floated away.

Chapter Four

"We've found a Guardian, master." Dimiezlo's forked tongue slithered from his mouth. His furry arms crossed over his chest, fists pressed to his shoulders as he bowed his bald, horned head.

His goat-like legs prevented him from kneeling. Normally that alone would have been enough to earn him a long, slow, excruciating death. But, fortunately for this minion, he'd proven himself ingenious, as well as loyal.

Far too valuable a resource to waste frivolously.

Drumming his black claws on the obsidian table before him, Stolas considered his subject. The pungent scent of brimstone and Hellfire filled his nostrils, as always. In the distance, through the open door, tortured screams echoed from the valley below. How he loved that sound.

How he hated that smell.

Hmm. Found a Guardian, had they? Interesting.

With a subtle motion of one finger, he signaled the Charocté Demon hovering in the corner. The servant scurried to do as he was bid, head bowed, and gently closed the door behind him.

Assured of their privacy, Stolas examined this minion. He'd been searching the Earth over for centuries, or rather his minions had, in hopes of finding the Guardians. Holy warriors—or unholy, depending on your point of view—entrusted with the duty of hiding and protecting the four Sacred Relics. Relics that, according to the ancient Prophesy, would bring about Lucifer's fall.

The Arc Stone, said to make its bearer impervious to physical harm. The Scrolls of Prévnar, believed to contain incantations to make the speaker resistant to Lucifer's control. The Sword of Kathnesh, rumored to be the one sword capable of taking Lucifer's head.

And last, but certainly not least, the Chosen One. A child of human, angelic, and demonic bloodlines combined. The one and only being capable of harnessing the power of the other three relics simultaneously. The only being prophesied to defeat Lucifer and bring all of Hell under his complete control.

Thanks to the minion before him, Stolas was already in possession of one of those objects, the Sword of Kathnesh. Soon, it would seem, he would be in possession of another. He almost rubbed his hands together in anticipation. Almost.

Once he obtained the Arc Stone and the Scrolls of Prévnar, Stolas would have everything he needed to overthrow Lucifer. Well, nearly all of them. He'd yet to find a Halfling, a female of both human and angelic descent, strong enough to conceive and give birth to the Chosen One. He would personally supply—and therefore control—the demonic seed. So far, the few Halflings that had been found and brought to him had been unsuitable, their angelic bloodlines diluted over time by generations of mating with humans. Only three had conceived. None had been strong enough to carry demon spawn to term. All had failed him.

In short, he needed a first-generation Halfling.

And those were about as easy to come by as a snow in his own backyard.

"Rise," Stolas commanded. The minion dropped his arms to his side and lifted his head. His gaze, however, remained downcast. *Commendable*, Stolas thought with approval. So many minions nowadays overstepped their boundaries. Here, then, was one who knew his station. "Tell me about this Guardian."

"The Guardian is female, my lord," Dimiezlo replied.

He ground his teeth. Honestly, was it necessary to have to lead the minion through every step of this interview? Displeased power hummed and crackled through his veins. He fisted his hand, smothering the forming plasma ball.

Do not waste the resource.

"Does she exhibit any weaknesses? Any familial attachments?"

"No, my lord. From what we've learned, she is an only child of a single parent. The mother recently deceased." Dimiezlo continued, prattling on about some antique shop. Worthless information, all of it.

Do not waste the resource. Do not waste the resource.

"Do we know exactly which relic she has?"

"We believe she is in possession of the scrolls, my master."

"Have any of the Fallen found her yet?"

Stolas stilled. Had the minion just eased back?

"Yes, my lord."

"What?" With a twitch of Stolas's wrist, Dimiezlo flew backward and crashed into the wall. The fires in the sconces flared and crackled. Roaring his displeasure, Stolas slammed both fists onto the black, marble tabletop. The huge slab of granite broke in two and collapsed.

Dimiezlo scrabbled across the floor. Blood dripped from his nose and mouth. Chest heaving, he climbed to his cloven feet. Crossing his arms, he pressed his fists to his shoulders once more.

Rounding on the minion, he gnashed his teeth. "Which one?"

"The Slayer."

Stolas's fury knew no bounds. Chairs flew through the air, smashing against the walls. Dimiezlo ducked as golden chalices and silver platters hurled around the room. Stolas's ire turned toward the long table at the end of his hall, covered with the earthly offerings his minions brought to earn his favor. Somehow, he managed to pull back.

He was the mastermind behind what would be the greatest coup in history. Soon, with the success of his plans, he would be ruler of all Hell, and Earth as well. He must remain in control.

Calm, calm.

Clenching his fists, he struggled to contain his wrath. But it wasn't easy. The Fallen had been a thorn in his side. A constant plague upon his ambitions. Xander, the Slayer, and Niklas, the Seer, formerly the right and the left hands of Lucifer, had been heads of the Dark Prince's elite royal guard. They'd turned on the Dark Prince and broken their vows of loyalty, the ultimate betrayal by Lucifer's closest, most trusted generals. And to make matters worse, they'd managed to convince the Demons of Temptation, Vengeance, and War to revolt as well.

As a result, a jaded Lucifer now watched each and every one of his subjects with suspicion. In short, The Fallen had made Stolas's life and his plot to overthrow his own grandfather that much more difficult.

Garnoch feces.

But had they stopped there? Oh no. Escaping Hell and Lucifer's despotic rule hadn't been good enough. They'd banded together and ruthlessly hunted down and destroyed colonies of other earthbound demons. Foiling possessions, hindering rampant demonic invasions. Preventing summonings—his own in particular—had become their favorite pastime.

They'd more than earned the nickname, the Fallen. Shunned by Heaven, hunted by Hell. No longer beloved, righteous Archangels. No longer fearsome, revered princes of Hell. Now they were nothing more than mercenaries. The stuff of legends that gave grown demons nightmares.

But not him. He'd bring each and every last one of them to their knees. Right before he cut off their heads.

Drawing a deep breath, he worked to control his temper. "Why have you not yet taken the relic?"

"The Guardian has employed enchantments to safeguard herself and the relic."

That caught his attention. "Angelic enchantments?"

"Yes, my lord."

"*Powerful* angelic enchantments?"

"Yes, my lord. Very powerful." At last, as if sensing his master's impatience, Dimiezlo hurried to explain. "So far we've been unable to enter the dwelling. None can breach the perimeter, my lord."

"Have you tried Reapers?"

"No, my lord. If she is of angelic descent, as I

believe, then I thought you would want her taken alive, my master. It was my understanding that none of the other Halflings had…ah, survived captivity."

Another reminder that this wily, intelligent creature was worth keeping around. And worth keeping an eye on. He always seemed to know far more than he should.

"That doesn't concern you." Energy crackled and hissed in the palm of his hand. This time, he opened his fingers and let the ball of plasma hover threateningly. Just because Dimiezlo was a valued minion didn't mean he should forget his place.

Dimiezlo immediately ducked his head. "Apologies for overstepping, my liege."

Closing his fist and extinguishing the plasma ball, he brought his hand up and tapped a sharp claw against his chin. The female had to leave the dwelling at some point.

"Perhaps Sïnsobar would be of use?"

Dimiezlo looked as if he were searching for some nonexistent hole in the floor to crawl through. "The Carpathï was unsuccessful, master."

"So you mean to tell me that not only did the Slayer find her," Stolas snarled through gritted teeth, his breath sawing in and out, "but that the *legendary* Sïnsobar failed?"

Dimiezlo gulped as he stared at the floor. He nodded, remaining wisely silent and otherwise immobile.

Don't kill the resource. Don't kill the resource. Don't kill the resource!

Just now, the reminder wasn't helping much. The fury vibrating through him was too fresh and too powerful. Inflamed anew at each disappointing revelation. He could feel the scrolls slipping from his grasp. Unable to contain his energy, he began pacing the confines of his great hall, kicking aside the rubble that had once been ornate furniture. Obsidian. Gold. Wealth as befitting his royal station.

Stifling. Restricting. Frustrating.

This great hall was a prison. Hell was his prison. One he couldn't breach without those scrolls. One he couldn't breach without relying on lowly peasants on the Earth plane to summon him forth. How galling.

Raking a hand through his hair, he rounded on Dimiezlo. The minion cringed but remained steadfast.

"Bring Sïnsobar to me now."

"He was summoned by the Dark Prince, my lord."

Cold fear poured like rivers of the ice he'd heard about down his back as he skidded to a halt. Had Lucifer caught a hint of his plans? A merciless fist squeezed his chest.

"He will not speak, master," Dimiezlo rushed to reassure him. "Or I would have sent him to Oblivion myself."

Little good that assurance did to ease his worry. Desperation clawed at him. His very survival was on the line now. He fought to steady his breathing, still his hands. He could show no weakness.

"He has sworn a blood oath of silence. He will not break it. Of this I am certain. He hates the Dark Prince as much as you, my master."

No one hated Lucifer as much as Stolas did. But he didn't bother pointing that out. There was nothing he could do now. Sïnsobar had already been summoned. He could be, even now, in Lucifer's hall, kneeling before the Dark Prince. Would Lucifer delve into his mind, peer into his thoughts, his memories? Could Lucifer, even now, have a legion of Scathé—Lucifer's own elite guard—on the way to dispatch him, the favored grandson, to the unforgiving shores of Oblivion?

No. No, he could not panic. A mind full of fear was a weak mind. A mind full of fear made mistakes. He was better than that. Better than good old grandfather himself.

Squaring his shoulders, lifting his chin, he drew a deep breath. He clasped his trembling hands behind his back and paced for several moments, working to school his features. "The female took the Slayer inside the dwelling? Inside the enchantments? Willingly?"

"Yes, my liege."

He approached a raised dais at the end of the room. Claw-tipped fingers skimmed the offerings cluttering the top of the long table there. Seeking to calm his nerves, he picked up a small object. A gun, he'd been told it was called. A weapon used to fire deadly projectiles. It fit comfortably in his palm, but it was oddly light. Flimsy. In fact, he feared squeezing it too tightly, that it might shatter in his hand. Turning it this way and that, he examined it closely. The weapon was purple and yellow. Such an odd color for something supposedly lethal. Curious, he aimed the gun away from him and gently pulled the trigger.

Clear fluid erupted from the barrel of the gun. Blinking, frowning, he squeezed again. More fluid.

What manner of weapon is this?

If filled with holy water, he supposed, it might prove a valuable weapon. That thought had him gingerly replacing the gun on the table. Perhaps it was already filled with holy water. The only thing worse than Ralsha venom at leaving scars was holy water. Something he was not willing to risk.

Combing through the pile with more care, he encountered an odd shaped object. Lifting it, he held the piece up to the light. Organic. A long, green stalk. Slim, with broad, flat appendages. And at the tip, a cluster of roundish, flat velvety curls. Fragile. Soft. Of the deepest crimson. Though the longer he'd been in possession of the strange object, the more limp it became. Shriveling in the dry heat.

Lifting the tip to his nostrils, he inhaled the delicate scent. Very pleasant. Heady. Alluring. Rolling the stalk in his fingers, he drew the scent deeper, then let out a sharp hiss of pain. Opening his hand, he peered at the droplet of blood welling on the pad of his thumb. Sharp, pointed projections protruded from the stalk at sporadic spaces.

Clever.

Pleased, grinning approval over the lure and the unexpected viciousness of his new find, he set the piece aside for later examination and turned back to Dimiezlo, his temper under control now.

"We're just going to have to get her to lower the enchantments again." But how was the question. "Where is the woman located?"

"In a town called Isle. It's in Minnesota."

"And the Minnesota is near the Iowa?"

"Yes, my lord."

He growled, low and deep. Something very important was about to happen in the Iowa, something he wanted nothing to interfere with. Dare he risk a push of power so near there, at this crucial time? Would it tip his hand?

What was so damned appealing about this region of the North American continent anyway? He made a mental note that once he'd been liberated, he would have to visit this place, see it for himself.

Focus on the female.

One obstacle at a time. He couldn't lure her out. His minions had attempted that as well, it seemed. They couldn't get inside. The enchantments repelled his subjects like an invisible force field. He couldn't hold one of her loved ones as bait. She was an only child, and an orphan to boot.

Eliminating her was likely the best option. But, from the sounds of the situation, she could potentially be the Halfling he needed to obtain the fourth relic, the Chosen One.

Clenching his fists until he felt his claws sink into the flesh of his palm, he growled. Keeping her alive was becoming less and less appealing. Halfling or no, he'd already begun to visualize wrapping his hands around her throat and shaking the life from her—

That's it! Shake her.

He'd shake her from the dwelling. Shake her dwelling until it collapsed around her ears.

Rounding on Dimiezlo, he let a lethal smile unfurl.

"Bring Agares to me. Now."

Chapter Five

Groaning, Xander blinked himself awake in an unfamiliar place. A strange, completely baffling energy hummed through his veins, leaving him jittery. Timber beams crossed over his head. His vision blurred, then clarified. The walls were a muted tan. The room was small. He felt like Alice when she'd fallen down the rabbit hole, right after she'd drunk from the mysterious bottle labeled "drink me."

Or was it after she'd nibbled the cake?

Oh, who gave a damn? The fact that he was laying here, contemplating imaginary characters from one of Sebastian's precious books attested to the fact that he was in some seriously deep trouble.

Sweet heaven, speaking of books.

Shelves lined the wall at his feet, filled with oodles of books. No…no, not books. Binders. Ledgers. Tax Manuals. Magazines. Stacks of thick catalogues. Blinking, he turned his head and scanned the sturdy, matching, roll-top desk not five feet away. The cubbyholes were brimming with papers. Piles of invoices, clusters of pens and pencils, small receipt booklets, staplers, and office doodads filled every nook and cranny. A thick binder lay open on the surface. A closed laptop rested on the far edge of the desk. Lifting his head, he caught a glimpse of the words "accounts receivable" scrawled across the top of the page in neat, feminine script.

Lucifer's balls, where am I?

Then it slowly began to come back to him. The God-awful day he'd had. The ambush in the alley.

The woman!

Xander sat up too fast and the room swam like a bad mirage. Scrunching his eyes closed, he pressed his palm to his temple and shook his head, fighting through the pain and dizziness. And still his body felt energized. Electrified. So strange. He patted his chest. At least that didn't hurt anymore. The deepest lacerations were little more than scratches now, and those were healing quickly.

Gingerly probing his forehead and cheek, he was relieved to find his burns completely gone. Not that he worried much about his pretty face, but Ralsha venom was known to leave behind some nasty scars. That his face felt normal, not a bit of scar tissue evident, was a minor miracle.

No, not a miracle, he amended with a great deal of self-deprecation. *More like sheer, dumb luck.* God wouldn't waste miracles on the likes of him.

When he felt steady once more, he turned his head and carefully opened his eyes. And he started swearing all over again. There she lay, crumpled on the hardwood floor. Deathly pale. Unnaturally still. He shoved himself off the sofa and landed on his hands and knees beside her.

Sweet Saint Peter, what have I done?

His fingertips immediately went to her throat, probed, hesitated, probed harder. He held his breath as he scoured her face for some infinitesimal sign of life. Her skin was so pale, milk white against the deep brown of the wood beneath her. Her lips held a faint bluish tinge. Giving up on finding so much as a thready pulse at her throat, he lowered his head and pressed his ear to her chest, holding his breath once more.

He hadn't taken the life of an innocent in too long to remember. That he may have taken the life of this particular woman—however unintentionally—sat like a lead weight in the middle of his throat.

She could be their only connection to the scrolls. She'd given him a measure of her trust by bringing him inside. Never mind that she had the most gorgeous legs. Or the biggest, bluest eyes he'd ever seen this side of—

There! The faintest of heartbeats. But a heartbeat, nonetheless.

If he were the overzealous type, he would have jumped for joy, punched at the sky while shouting jubilant huzzahs. Instead, he began chafing warmth back into her hands and arms. Her skin was baby soft. She smelled like an armful of wild flowers. Fresh. Innocent. And so alive.

The muscles in her arms were toned. Her hands were delicate. He took a second to study her face, even as his fingers continued to move over her. Her features were rather plain. Except for those gorgeous eyes.

Involuntarily, he took in her ripe curves and the immodest expanse of creamy flesh that her snug, layered tank top and cutoff blue jean shorts revealed. And her hair. Lengths of spun gold swept up in a careless ponytail.

This looked like no businesswoman he'd ever seen. Perhaps this was the owner's daughter. Could he, in all fairness, consider using her as leverage? The Guardian must be made to see that the relics would be far safer with Xander and his lot than stashed away in a secret hiding place that wasn't a secret any longer.

Had he taken too much from her? He'd never taken only a partial essence before. Never stopped before he'd absorbed the entire soul. He had no clue if she could even survive something like this. Would she wake up at all?

And if she survived, what kind of repercussions had his actions wrought? Would she still be herself? Or some corrupted version?

And what of him? What was this violent energy bursting through his system? Was this some unexpected side effect of his feeding from her? He'd never fed from an angel before, or a Halfling, as rumor had it that she was. Was this strange energy coursing through him further proof of her angelic lineage?

He glowered at her, willing her to wake up. But she didn't stir.

This just proved the validity of his assessment that the scrolls would be far safer with him. Humans were a frail lot. Easily overcome. Easily broken. Unpredictable with their all-important free will.

His hands paused as guilt settled around him like a shroud. He'd done this to her. Not some other demon. He had. He'd been careless. And this little human/Halfling—whatever she was—was paying for his mistake.

Grim determination pushed aside the sudden and unexpected realization that he'd never worried over another human's condition, physical or emotional, before. There was nothing special about this one. He was only suffering guilt over endangering an innocent and possibly creating a huge obstacle to his mission.

That was all. Nothing more.

The Slayer forms no attachments.

Grinding his teeth, he renewed his efforts to revive her. His hands chafed her flesh, perhaps a bit more vigorously than necessary, but he couldn't get her to wake, damn it.

Should he call Mikhail? Mikhail could heal her with just a touch.

No, Mikhail won't be able to get past the enchantments.

And, without lowering the enchantments, Xander wouldn't be able to get out either.

Lucifer's balls! Talk about a royal f-u-b-a-r!

She'd lowered the enchantments briefly to let him inside. He'd been awake enough for that, sort of. But his ears had been ringing, and he hadn't quite been able to catch all the words.

His memory had a few black spots, and, by the time he'd caught lucidity again, she'd already recited the enchantments back in place. He could feel them. Surrounding him like a warm cocoon, dampening the world outside. No, Mikhail wouldn't be able to step past the threshold. And, provided he managed to lower the enchantments himself, if Xander took her outside, there was no guarantee she'd let him back in the door. Not after what he'd done to her. His hands moved along her torso, massaging, working to increase her circulation.

Some of the color had returned to her cheeks. A good sign. He hadn't meant to take so much of her essence from her. Hadn't wanted to take any at all, in fact. But he'd had no other choice—not really. He'd needed to feed. Desperately. And she'd been the only one around.

The problem was, he'd been so severely wounded that he'd had little control over his baser instincts. From the moment he'd broken with Lucy, he'd always fed from the criminal element, steering well clear of any and all innocent. Immoral lawbreakers that would otherwise escape punishment for their crimes had become his staple. Murders. Rapists. Drug dealers. Such offenders had not deserved leniency, and so he'd never attempted to stop himself before his victim's essence had been drained completely.

Lord, her ribcage was so fragile. He couldn't resist the urge to splay his hands over her hips and sweep them up her sides.

Sweet Jesus, her beautiful breasts! What I'd like to do with those—

Groaning, wrenching his gaze—and his hands—from the temptation of those alluring, lush mounds, Xander moved his attention lower. The gentle sweep of her waist and the womanly flare of her hips enticed his fingers to roam and explore rather than rub and heal.

The little human moaned. Her eyelids fluttered.

A weight lifted from his shoulders when she, at last, began to revive. She blinked woozily at him; her skin was still as pale as chalk.

He leaned over her, his face inches from hers. "Are you—"

Her small fist caught him unawares, landing dead center against the bridge of his nose. The resulting crunch and spurt of blood, the explosion of pain, assured him that not only had she hit her mark, but she'd damned well broken it as well. A kaleidoscope of stars burst before his eyes and blood gushed from his newest injury as he fell back and landed on his butt. His hand cupped protectively over his throbbing face.

Well, he supposed he had that one coming.

In a flurry of movement, she was off the floor and had backed herself into a corner. Her gaze darted to the doorway behind him, then flew around the room before landing on him once more. Without taking her unblinking stare from him, she reached over and snatched a large, cylindrical, dark reddish rock from her desk. The woman hefted it as an unlikely weapon.

"Stay back." Her voice was breathless, unsteady.

He could have shimmered to her in a blink, disarmed her, and forced her to do his bidding. He was easily twice her size. She wouldn't stand a chance. Nevertheless, he waited, quickly calculating. Perhaps he could reason with her. "Put the paper weight down."

All he got for his effort was an in-your-dreams snort and a disgusted glare. "Last I checked, the word 'stupid' wasn't tattooed to my forehead."

Her tone implied he should be looking in a mirror.

He eyed the rock in her hand. Small weapon, little threat. Though she held on to that thing like a lifeline. He could ignore it, and her. After all, he was inside the building. Right where he needed to be. He could tear the place apart, turn it inside out and pray the scrolls were here. But if they weren't, if she—or someone else—had hidden them elsewhere, he might never find them.

"Who owns this building?"

She peered at him suspiciously. "I do."

Truth. Okay.

"Are you the Guardian?"

She blinked. Her nostrils flared, and her chest lifted

slightly on a sharp inhalation. "I don't know what you're talking about."

He angled his head as creepy-crawlies skittered down the back of his neck. A thousand spiders oozing over his flesh.

Lie.

Why did he have to be the one stuck here? He wasn't the diplomat. Where the hell was Sebastian when you needed him? Hell, even Niklas would do.

Diplomat or not, he had to play his cards right. If he earned her trust, would she lead him to the scrolls? Would she give them over to him completely? Or would she laugh in his face and tell him to go screw himself.

Judging by her current expression, he'd bet on the latter. It was what he would do in her shoes.

Xander lifted his hand—the one not still protecting his bleeding nose—palm out to show her he meant no harm. Hells bells, he was still seeing stars. The woman had the right hook of a prize fighter on her.

"Put that away." She ducked sideways. "I know what you can do with those things."

Frowning, he blinked up at her. Had she lost her mind? What was she talking about? "Those things?"

And then it clicked. She'd seen him throw plasma balls with his hands. Slowly, he lowered his hand to the floor. Pinching the bridge of his nose to slow the bleeding, he tilted his head and regarded her solemnly.

The hand holding that big rock shook so badly he wondered that she didn't drop the thing on her own toes. She had to brace herself with one elbow on the wall beside her to hold herself up. Her face had lost what little color he'd managed to restore. But she was on her feet. And the light of battle was bright in her eyes. She looked like the fabled Valkyrie. Battle weary and beaten, but not defeated. Never defeated.

The edges of his lips curled up fully in a rare, admiring smile. She was magnificent.

But as his smile grew, the more upset she seemed to become. She gripped the rock even tighter. Aimed it at him as if he'd threatened her.

But he hadn't uttered a sound. Puzzling.

"I won't harm you," he coaxed.

She flinched at the sound of his voice, the raw rasp, like a fresh wound ground into the pavement, coated with gravel and rock salt. His own cross to bear. Long ago, when he'd been an Archangel, his voice had been one of the most magnificent in the heavens. So beautiful that other angels wept for the joy of hearing him speak. So powerful and persuasive, so utterly hypnotic others often found themselves doing his bidding without realizing it. Hence, upon his fall, along with his wings, his voice had been torn from him. And he'd been left with this offensive travesty.

She moved one hand to cup her own throat. Her beautiful eyes filled with concern and sympathy.

He scowled. Sympathy was the one thing he couldn't take. From anyone. Hatred. Sure. Disgust and loathing? No problem. Fear? Perfect. But sympathy was out of the question.

Then her hand slipped lower, settling on the same spot on her chest where he'd placed his palm upon her earlier. The spot where he'd fed from her. As quick as a flame extinguished beneath a deluge of icy water, the sympathy vanished and righteous indignation took hold.

"Yeah, sure ya won't." She shook the rock

menacingly at him once more. "What did you do to me?"

Oh, not much. Just drained part of your soul to heal myself.

He could only imagine how well that would go over. A change of subject seemed the best alternative.

He held out his blood-covered hand and arched an eyebrow.

She looked as if she were weighing her options.

She looked as if she were contemplating bloodying him some more.

"Floor's hardwood. It'll clean. Talk, demon. What did you do to me?"

Ah, so she knew what he was. That made things easier.

He took in her defensive stance. She adjusted her grip on that menacing rock the color of dried blood, looking for all the world like a Major League hitter winding up to knock one to the upper decks.

Well, maybe not quite so easy after all.

Once more, he considered shimmering to her. Again, he discarded the notion. He could change into his demonic form and scare the rest of her soul right out of her. Maybe she'd just faint dead-away. Or he could intimidate her into compliance.

He gave up on that notion as soon as it formed. Not only was he contending with the nagging edges of a headache, as often happened when he shifted between forms, but he also didn't trust himself in demonic form around her. His human body was reacting too strongly as it was. In demonic form, his control was tenuous in the best of circumstances. She might prove far too much temptation for the darkness seething inside him to resist. Besides, too long had he existed under the thumb of a tyrant. Too long had his own will been suppressed. Ignored. He would not willingly subjugate someone else—even if only for a short while—when there were other alternatives.

Even if it meant he'd be forced to use the harsh, offensive voice he'd been cursed with.

Trust. He had to gain her trust.

And trust meant telling the truth.

"I am Xander. I mean you no harm. I was forced to absorb some of your essence—but only in order to heal," he quickly asserted then frowned fiercely. "Had there been another human present, I would not have fed from you."

"So you'd have *fed* from some other innocent instead?" Her frown deepened into a fierce scowl.

Again, where the hell was Sebastian when you needed him? Even if his legendary patience deserted him, Sebastian could always rely on his boy-next-door good looks to seduce women to do anything he wanted. Anything at all.

Sweet Mary, he'd even take a chance on the surly Gideon just now.

"Look, I had no—" Xander began to lift his hand once more in a display of conciliation, but quickly lowered it when she tensed again. "I had no choice. I did not mean to cause you distress," he rasped. "You have my word. I will not harm you further."

"The word of a demon," she sneered.

Was it not enough that he'd already said more to her in the last few minutes than he had at one time to anyone else in decades? Her skepticism pricked his already sore pride. "I saved you from that demon out there," he reminded her through gritted teeth.

His throat was beginning to burn. And his meager supply of patience was fast depleting.

She said nothing, just watched him. Like a hawk. At last, grudgingly, she muttered, "There's a box of tissue in the bottom right drawer of the desk."

Progress.

Nodding, he scooted back a little and slowly opened the drawer. He plucked up a wad of tissue and blotted at his chin and nose, dabbed at his chest and fingers. The blood had begun to dry, however, and it only smeared in a sticky mess instead of wiping away. He could have conjured himself clean, but he was pretty sure that wouldn't further his case with her any more than shimmering to her and disarming her would.

Not that he really wanted to get close enough to touch her. Something about her presence had a strange, unwanted effect on him physically.

Long forgotten urges had begun to clamor inside him the minute she'd regained consciousness. Hell, even before then. When he'd had his hands on her. When that first scent of her had wrapped itself around him, taunting him, drawing him closer to that wicked, treacherous edge. And when she'd stood up to him, waving her little paper weight, defiance and courage all but radiating from her even though she had to know she stood no chance against him?

He wanted his hands on her again. Right now.

Those carnal urges blindsided him. And the hell of it was, they were growing stronger and stronger by the minute.

She looked like she could use a moment to regroup and calm down. Heaven knew he needed the time to get his body back under control.

“Not helping,” he pointed out the obvious, motioning to his blood-smeared chest. “Restroom?”

“Give an inch,” she growled, her lips pressed together in a tight, distrustful line.

Feisty. His cheek began to twitch, the edges of his lips began to lift. He bit the tip of his tongue and forced his face to smooth into his customary frown.

The Slayer does not smile.

But, damn!

She could really start to grow on him.

Wait. *What?*

He scowled ferociously. She pressed back against the wall, hard. The hand gripping the rock shook hard enough to rattle the thin strips of silver woven together around her wrist. Quickly, he schooled his features into his customary bland stare.

Lucifer’s balls, what was wrong with him? He was a master at keeping his emotions tucked away like a bad memory. But five minutes in this woman’s presence, and he was all but grinning like a loon. Even spitting mad and doing her level best to threaten him, she was just so damned cute.

It wasn’t like him to smile. It wasn’t even like him to let a grin slip out. And it sure as hell wasn’t his style to let anyone “grow on him.” Well, except maybe Gideon. The Demon of Temptation was like a wart. No matter how hard you tried to get rid of that wily, charming SOB—no matter how deep you dug—he just kept coming back.

At least, he had until recently. Before he’d become the poster child to promote anti-psychotic meds.

A central air conditioning unit kicked on. The vent,

just above her and to the left, blew down into the room, pushing cool air over her body and straight into his face. The scent of her filled his nostrils. Wildflowers and woman. Alluring. Intoxicating. His body reacted violently, catching him off guard. His gut clenched against the temptation, even as his nostrils flared, dragging more of her in. His gaze slid from her face to her bare shoulder, and he watched, spellbound, as tiny bumps rippled across her skin, over her arm and across the satiny expanse of her upper chest. And then, quite beyond his control he watched her nipples harden beneath the thin layers of cotton. To his utter chagrin, he went instantly—painfully—rock hard inside his pants.

Xander froze. Bewildered. Just a tiny bit horrified. More than a little excited. He'd never lost such complete control of his body like this before. Never, never had a woman affected him so powerfully. Suddenly the Sacred Relics, his demon compatriots, and the threat of Hell itself opening up and swallowing Earth whole slipped right out of his head.

Instead, explicit images of the two of them together began to infiltrate his mind. Erotic images. Her naked, welcoming body writhing beneath him, pulling him closer. Her breath panting in his ear. Her voice screaming his name. Her mouth on his. Her hands on his body. Her thighs parted, welcoming him in, urging him to plunder. His attention slowly lifted from the delectable swell of her generous breasts and greedily slid up to settle on the full curve of her lower lip. Like lush rose petals. Beckoning. Alluring. Begging to be ravished.

Lust curled insidiously through his veins. Primal

urges gripped him. He needed to fill his mouth with the taste of her, fill his hands with her decadent body, the way his nose was already overwhelmed by her scent. His hands ached to touch her, to explore and mold her curves. He had to lay claim to her. To dig his fingertips into the sweet flesh of her bottom and grip her tight as he plunged himself deep inside her. He wouldn't stop until he had her right where he wanted her.

Drawn to her like a magnet, his body began to move of its own accord.

Chapter Six

Kyanna caught her breath as the demon—*Xander*—as Xander's suddenly too-warm stare began to rove over her body. Assessing. Considering. Devouring. She wasn't an innocent. It wasn't as if she didn't know how to handle herself around alpha males. Heaven help her, she'd always had an unhealthy weakness for that whole bad-boy persona.

But no one had ever looked at her like that before. Like she was a decadent dessert he couldn't wait to gobble up. Like she was pure sunshine and he was a prisoner that had been locked in darkness for far too long. She'd pegged it right when she'd decided he had bedroom eyes. But those bedroom eyes were also a weapon.

All the more dangerous because he knew *exactly* how to use them.

Lord help her, he was using them now.

Without warning, he slowly pushed to his feet. Her stare followed him up. And up. She'd been so focused first on his injuries, then on holding him at bay, and finally on his enthralling eyes, that she'd forgotten how tall he was. She'd never considered herself tiny. If anything, she considered herself average. But as Xander gained his full height, he towered over her. The top of her head didn't even clear his shoulders. He wasn't exactly bulky, but his muscles were hard as tempered steel. She should know. She'd felt them when she'd helped him up and inside the building.

Sweet mama, she wanted to feel them again.

She looked at the angry red marks slashing their way across his smooth, muscled chest. Her mouth watered as she gawked at the well-defined six-pack she'd unveiled and the swath of golden skin dipping into the low-riding waistband of his pants.

Never before had she understood—or suffered from—the primitive urge to drop to her knees and worship someone's body with her mouth. And her tongue. But that was exactly what she wanted to do right now. Peel those pants from him. Touch him. And run her tongue all over those ridges, all over those indentations. All over that taut, golden skin.

He was delicious.

Lickable.

Wait. Wow. So not going there. Demon, remember?

Appalled, she mentally shook herself and backed up till her spine pressed hard against the wall. What was she thinking? He still had blood on him. Maybe not as much blood now that she'd cleaned him up some. But blood was blood, for pity sake.

Snap out of it, Kyanna!

Just because she hadn't been with a man in longer than she cared to consider did not mean it was acceptable to tumble into lust with a demon. So what if she hadn't let Jack get past second base…well, maybe he'd stolen into third. But she'd called him out soon thereafter. She was gaining a respectable reputation as a levelheaded, upstanding citizen. She had a business to run. One she was determined to make a go of.

And then there was her family legacy. She'd been

trained from the cradle to do everything in her power to avoid demons like him. To protect others from his kind.

She didn't have time for a man. Didn't have room in her life for collateral damage.

Much less for a demon.

All the same, she couldn't help but watch in abject fascination as all those muscles rippled and tightened with his every move. The lacerations on his chest had miraculously healed. The burns on his handsome face were gone completely.

She caught him staring at her lips, and unintentionally moistened them, the way you might brush at your nose after someone tells you that you have a bit of dirt, just there. He zeroed in on the motion and took a step closer, and then his eyes flickered. They turned completely flame red for a split second before reverting to that stormy, seductive gray. Her heart slammed into the back of her throat. She was trapped. Cornered. Enthralled. Drowning in his stare. The weight of the rock pulled her hand down until her arm hung limp at her side.

He closed the distance between them. Prowling. Stalking. Each purpose-laden step sent long, melting strokes deep in the most feminine part of her. She could barely catch her breath.

The rock began to slip from her fingers, and his eyes flickered again, snapping her attention back to the here and now. Here and now, she had a demon in her office. A sultry, testosterone-drenched demon that dominated the very air in the room.

Demon.

"The restroom is just out the door and to the right," she squawked, lifting her weapon once more, anxious to break the spell.

As if coming to his senses, he stopped and drew a deep breath. Without another word, he spun on his heel and strode for the door. Not a wobble in his gait. No signs of vertigo or weakness.

It was that exact moment that she got her first good look at his back. Her stomach dropped to her toes. Horrendous scars marred both of his shoulder blades. Pearly scar tissue, puckered and ridged and gruesome, attested to terrible wounds. The kind of wounds that left scars not only on the body, but on the soul as well.

How could anyone survive that kind of savage torture?

Staggered by the excruciating pain he must have suffered, she blindly dropped the stone into the top drawer of her desk and scurried after him.

"No! The restroom is the next door over."

As he swung the appropriate door open, she called out, "Hold on a minute." Kyanna rushed to the small utility closet across the hall and gathered an armful of towels and a tray of delicately scented, rose-shaped soaps.

"Here." She thrust the pile into his hands, doing her level best not to touch him. "Sorry about the soap, but it's the only thing I have down here."

He picked up one of the tiny, pink rosebud shaped soap offerings and sniffed, scowling. That expression seemed to be his default mode. He accepted her offering with little more than a grunt before disappearing inside the bathroom.

Kyanna stood in the hallway, staring at the closed door, willing her equilibrium to return to normal. She'd let a demon inside the enchantments. A real, live demon. A gorgeous, seductive, hunk of a demon. A demon that was no longer on death's door. Not anymore, thanks to whatever it was he'd done to her.

Wringing her hands, she paced away, paced back. Stared at the door, paced away.

What was she supposed to do with him now?

A few, not-so-G-rated ideas popped into her mind, filling her cheeks with bewildered heat. Just as quickly, she wanted to kick herself. She had no business even thinking those thoughts about someone like him. The only thing she should be doing was figuring out a way to get rid of him.

Unfortunately, she didn't think he'd meekly nod assent and go on his merry way with a handshake and an "It was so nice to meet you, so sorry you can't stay, don't let the door hit your gorgeous behind on the way out." Besides, she couldn't exactly unleash him back onto the world. He was a demon, for Jupiter's sake.

And he must sense the ward stones, to say nothing of the enchantments. Surely, he had to be wondering where she'd gotten them.

Or, more importantly, why she felt the need for them in the first place.

He knew that she knew what he was. Not many humans would. But he hadn't called her on that. Not yet, anyway. Why?

Question after question circled her brain like hungry vultures, waiting to pick the meat from any logical conclusion she managed to assemble, leaving her with nothing but the bare bones of insecurity. Biting her lip, she scurried upstairs to her apartment. As quickly as she could, she scrambled to gather ward stones, then hurried back down. With a quick glance at the closed restroom door, she stashed the stones in a nearby storage closet. By the time he emerged from the restroom, she was a ball of frazzled nerves.

Those nerves weren't helped any by his expression. Nor by the detailed tattoos adorning his clean body. She'd thought his ink was horrific before, splattered by blood and gore. Now that she could see the finer markings, they sent a fresh wave of chills through her. They were like a roadmap of his fall from grace, with every side street to destruction and pit stop to murder and mayhem clearly plotted out.

She had no idea why, but he was clearly furious about something now. His eyes blazed, his brow pinched tight. His jaw was clenched so tightly it was little wonder he hadn't shattered all his teeth. His body was rigid. Temper fairly crackled in the air.

What had happened in there to change his mood so drastically?

"We need to talk," he spat out.

"Really?" Kyanna snipped.

His slowly elevated eyebrow sent a wave of panic through her, and she cursed herself for letting her mouth run away with her.

That's right, Kyanna. Piss the demon off. She could have smacked herself upside the head for her stupidity.

Sooth the demon's ruffled feathers. That was what she needed to do. Reassure him that there is nothing—absolutely nothing—of interest here. Without being too obvious, of course. Then she needed to figure out what to do with him.

That was what her goal should be.

The pointed stare he sent her way pretty much told her that her goal was going to be easier said than done.

Heaving a sigh, she waved her hand, motioning him forward. “Fine. After you.”

His bearing was positively regal as he passed her, despite the faint scent of roses that now mingled with the earthy, spicy, masculine scent of him. And all that golden, tattooed skin was now clean. Lickable. Mentally giving herself a good swift kick in the butt, she followed him to the office and stood uncertainly in the doorway as he took a seat on the sofa.

“Sit,” he barked.

“I’m fine right where I am,” she denied, crossing her arms. But something about him pulled at her. Tempted her to take a little more time before she pushed him out the door.

Curiosity began to war with common sense. She should be trying to sooth him into compliance. Shouldn’t she? Probably, yes. Capturing him inside a ward stone cage. Absolutely.

But she had a real, live demon sitting in her office. One that wanted to talk.

Up until now, demons were something she’d only thought of in two-dimensional terms. They were creatures of legend. Monsters depicted in cautionary stories learned at her mother’s knee. Caricatures drawn on the pages of *the book* with brief descriptions and directions for incantations to temporarily paralyze them, crystals used to repel them.

She herself—present circumstances excluded—had only had one firsthand experience with a demon. At least, that she knew of. While she’d been in college, she’d gone with friends for a night out on the town. They’d visited a seedy little nightclub for drinks and dancing. She’d begun to get a headache from the smoke and noise, and so she'd stepped outside for some fresh air.

That was when she'd spotted him—the demon—slinking into a side alley. Curiosity had always been her Achilles heel. Against her better judgment, she'd followed at a distance. Hiding behind a dumpster, she'd caught sight of the demon in all his scaly, horned glory as he'd attacked a homeless bum. She'd been so frightened that she hadn't been able to do anything more than back silently from the alley, filled with horror.

Up until that point, she'd always—somewhere in the back of her mind—believed *the book* and the things her mother had so diligently taught her were nothing more than useless, obsolete legends. But after seeing that demon, Kyanna had devoted herself to learning all she could, practicing every bit of knowledge that was possible, so if she ever found herself in that position again, she would not only be able to defend herself, but also rescue the innocent victim as well.

But what had she done instead? She'd taken the demon inside her safe haven. Tried to heal him, for pity sake. And now they were going to sit down and have a civilized conversation?

She might have been stupid about letting him inside the enchantments. But that didn't mean she was out of the game yet. She could still protect others out there from him and others of his kind if need be. Still protect the innocent. Would he reveal information that might help in her endeavors?

The questions she could ask him. The information she could gather.

The things I could add to the book!

He didn't seem in any great rush to kill her. And he didn't seem inclined to leave either. What would he do when he realized she wasn't about to let him go on his blissful way?

"Where is my dagger?"

Okay, so they wouldn't be starting off on a positive note. Just as well get all the uncomfortable stuff out of the way. "It's safe."

"I want it back. Now."

She shook her head. "That's not gonna happen."

His scowl deepened.

"What's wrong with your voice?" Oh, yeah. That was pertinent. Great place to start. Especially considering the way his dark scowl turned positively black with menace. "Look, I'm sorry. I shouldn't have—"

"You know what I am," he countered, blatantly turning the conversation down a different path.

She nodded, nibbling on her lower lip while she waited for him to go on.

"How do you know what I am?"

He hadn't even tried to deny it. And suddenly, she was the one treading on dangerous ground. Lifting her chin, she feigned confidence. "I think I should be the one asking questions here."

"No."

"No? What do you mean, no?"

"I ask. You answer, little human."

She might be seriously in over her head here, but that didn't mean he had to be condescending. She succinctly countered, "No."

The muscle in his jaw began to tick. His head tilted ever so slightly. Thoughtfully. Kyanna pressed a fist to her trembling stomach. Had she pushed him too far?

No, it didn't matter. She refused to cower. Clenching her teeth, she stepped inside the room and pulled the chair from the desk, a safe distance from him. Easing onto the chair, Kyanna clasped her hands in her lap, ignoring the way they trembled as she leaned slightly forward. She had an opportunity here. The chance to gather valuable information, make a real contribution to her ancestors' work. She wouldn't lose out on that opportunity just because a demon had glared at her and turned her into a sniveling coward.

"You want information." She tightened her grip. "Well, so do I. The way I see it, we have two options. We can sit here glowering at each other and get nowhere. Or, we could share information."

Xander was silent for a long moment. Just as the urge to shift uncomfortably in her seat became nearly unbearable, one side of his mouth curled up in a frightening, and yet oddly seductive, grin. His stormy attention dropped to linger on her breasts with an intense consideration that was every bit as erotic as a physical caress.

His scorching gaze slowly lifted to pin her to the spot. "You forgot the third option."

"Third option?" Kyanna croaked, scooting back in her chair. *Oh crap. Oh crap.* She *had* pushed him too far. Now he was going to kill her.

"I could force you to tell me everything you know." He paused meaningfully. "And I won't have to tell you a damned thing."

She stuttered, "Y-you can't do that. Torturing me won't get you what you want."

His expression subtly changed. "There are other

ways."

"You can't kill me."

Without any warning whatsoever, he was kneeling before her. His hips wedged between her knees as he leaned over her. His warm, naked chest brushed hers, teasing her with his incredible body heat. His face inches from hers, his breath skimming her lips. His hands, large and impossibly warm, bracketed her forearms, anchoring them to the office chair, effectively caging her in place.

"Why can't I?" His words whispered across the corner of her mouth.

"The enchantments," she murmured, breathless. "If you kill me, you'll be trapped inside the enchantments. You'll never get out."

His smoldering gray stare dipped, tracing the curve of her lips. The trembling in the pit of her stomach intensified. But this trembling burned with a new kind of fire. Something she refused to acknowledge. He was a demon. An evil being from Hell. She had no business having that kind of reaction to him.

"I could make you lower them, make you tell me the spells."

She shook her head slowly; her stare never leaving his. "No. You can't. Dark influence has no hold on me. I won't tell you anything. You can't make me." Lord, she sounded like a petulant six-year-old. Damn it, this wasn't her fault. She couldn't think straight with him like this. So close. So tempting.

"You wouldn't be able to resist."

"I would," she denied. The crystal pendant on her necklace insured that. Yet even as she argued with him, she was forced to bite back a groan. Why was her body responding like this? The trembling had moved lower. Her thighs all but quivered with the need to wrap around his lean waist. Her breasts aching to rub against him. She pressed her spine firmly against the back of the chair in a desperate bid not to arch against him and purr like a love-starved kitten. "I won't let you back out on the streets to prey on some poor unsuspecting innocent."

Surprise, and something darker, something more sinister, flamed in his expression. "You think to keep me trapped here? You would sacrifice yourself to protect people you might not even know?"

She jutted her chin, defiant. Resolved. "If I have to."

"Why?"

"That's my business."

"That's no answer, little human."

"My name is Kyanna."

He assessed her in silence, though he didn't back off, didn't allow her even an inch of breathing room.

"You believe I would end your life. You think I would be a threat to other humans, so you think to trap me here inside this building. But ask yourself this, Kyanna—"

His heated stare dropped to her lips. The backs of his fingers skimmed up her arm, his touch feather-light. Gently, soft as the flutter of a butterfly's wings, Xander caressed her lower lip with the pad of his thumb. Mesmerizing her.

"What if I don't"—his scorching gaze captured hers, and held—"*kill* you?"

Chapter Seven

He should never have gotten this close to her, but he hadn't seemed to be able to stop himself. He should have learned his lesson earlier when he'd almost kissed her. When he'd almost lost control. The scent of her moved through him like lightning even now. Setting his body—dead to emotion, dead to hungers such as these for so long—aflame with need. Her lips were so close. So, enticing. Just a few, slim inches from his own. Her sweet breath fanned his skin. Fanned the flames of need higher. Her breasts—so plump, so ripe—rose and fell, faster and faster. Beckoning him.

The darkness inside him swirled closer and closer to the surface. His mouth watered for a taste of her. Forbidden fruit.

The slap of her hand against his bare chest brought reason crashing down.

Sweet lord. He'd been that close to seducing her. That close to taking her whether she wanted to be taken or not. What had gotten into him? He couldn't afford to be distracted, not like this.

Yet even with that knowledge sending icy waves of unease through him, he hungered for her still. She'd stirred desire in him. Appetites he'd long suppressed. No, appetites the likes of which he'd never experienced. Something deeper and greedier. Something with a life force all its own. No other woman had ever affected him like this. Not since before he'd come under Lucifer's rule, and not after. Never like this.

"No," she insisted, but her hand trembled against him. She wanted him too. He could see it all over her face. It wouldn't take much to turn that "no" into a "yes, Xander, oh God, yes."

But he wasn't here for sex. He was here for the scrolls. He jerked back, shoved to his feet, and returned to the sofa. Xander dropped his elbows to his knees, and he eased forward, regarding her solemnly. He pressed his clenched fists to his lips for a long, tenuous moment.

"You want to exchange information?"

"I do," she agreed. "An answer for an answer?"

Weighing his options, he dropped his laced fingers over his stomach. He despised bargaining. But he couldn't see any other way around it. She was a stubborn little thing. And brave. Often a lethal combination.

But she'd singlehandedly done the one thing no one else ever had.

She'd effectively trapped him.

She'd captured the Slayer.

He'd tried to *shimmer* from the restroom. But he couldn't leave. Something about the enchantments she'd cast over the building was blocking him, effectively locking his powers up tighter than a drum. All his powers. All but his gift to discern lies from truth. He couldn't even conjure clean clothing for himself. And then he'd noticed she'd relieved him of his favorite blade. Insult to injury. Fury still battled with admiration over her daring. No one else could lay claim to that feat. This one little human had disarmed the Slayer.

But she was right on one point. He couldn't bring himself to harm her. Why? He wasn't altogether certain. He only knew that the very idea left him cold and hollow.

She intrigued him in a way no other had before. Her mind was quick, her spirit fearless. And her body was made for pleasure. He wouldn't be averse to seducing the answers he wanted from her. Granted, that was more in keeping with Sebastian's modus operandi, or Gideon's, before he'd been cursed. But Xander could, theoretically, give it a try.

Kyanna had already proven susceptible to him. The pace of her heartbeat and her accelerated breathing were strong indicators. The dilated pupils and the way her hungry stare kept roving over him were all the confirmation he needed.

She was definitely attracted to him.

Stifling a groan, he leaned forward again, trying unobtrusively to readjust his painfully hard erection.

Seduction was not an option. The way she affected him might leave *him* at *her* mercy instead. But he was already too far into that trap as it was. And she was entirely too desirable. Good intentions and honorable quests might well fall by the wayside if he slipped past her defenses and got inside those delectable shorts. Dragging his ravenous gaze from the smooth flesh of her still parted thighs, he focused on her face.

Then again, the way his body was reacting to her, if he didn't get out of here soon, he might not have any choice at all. The urge to strip her bare, to sink himself deep inside her could possibly be more than he could resist.

Seeming to snap herself from her daze, she sat up straighter in her seat and pressed her knees together. Cleared her throat.

Disappointing. But probably more conducive to conversation that way.

"You are a demon, yes?"

"Yes."

"Did you—"

He shook his head. "One answer for one answer."

A thwarted breath seethed from her and a muscle clenched in her jaw, but she nodded grudgingly.

"How did you know I was a demon?"

"Normal men don't shape-shift into what you did. Huge. Red skin. Horns. Red eyes. Jagged teeth. And they aren't capable of forming balls of…of…of flaming yellow…*stuff*…in the palms of their hands either."

Again, he felt the strange tick. The unbidden urge to smile at her temerity—to let the emotionless mask he habitually wore crack—took him by surprise. She'd answered his question with the obvious answer, and answered truthfully, thereby avoiding giving a direct, revealing answer. And then there were the enchantments, which she'd completely avoided talking about. Smart cookie. He couldn't say whether it was her courage, or his desire for her, but he found himself speaking without thought.

"Plasma," he informed her. She blinked, then nodded, silently acknowledging him.

So she had seen him. Fully demonic. And she hadn't run screaming into the night. Amazing.

Intriguing. There was that word again.

"Did you really fall from the heavens? Were you an angel?"

His amusement died at the remembered pain of his wings being ripped from his body, at the memory of Gabriel's and the others cruel laughter while they completed the task. And when they'd torn into his throat… He shut that thought down quickly. He still couldn't recall that act without the fury boiling over. "Yes."

She was smart. She'd slipped two questions in there without really answering any of her own. Well, he'd just be smarter. "Who taught you about us?"

"The Bible."

Creepy-crawlies on his neck made him want to shiver. He rolled his shoulders and made to rise. This was a waste of time. He'd tried the diplomatic way. Now he'd do things his way. He'd tear the place down and find the damned scrolls for himself.

"Okay, wait," she exclaimed, throwing her hands up in the air. "My mother. My mother taught me about your kind."

Truth.

Temporarily mollified, he settled back, letting his scowl warn her that he would no longer tolerate word games.

"Why did you save me from that…"

"Demon," he supplied.

"Demon."

"I have renounced Lucifer. I protect the innocent from others of my kind."

"That's not really an answer," she complained. "*Why* you renounced Lucifer is implied in my previous—"

He held up a hand to interrupt. She might be more willing to impart information, but she wasn't going to let him off the hook for one minute. And he remembered his early conclusion. Truth earned trust.

"After the Great Fall, for time untold, we followed Lucifer. Reveling in the most depraved of sins. Pillaging and destruction. Murder and—"

"I get the point," she hurried to impart.

"I was Lucifer's most elite Assassin. The Slayer." There was no pride in him over this. Only cold fact. His past was what it was and he could no more change it than he could save every innocent. "When he wanted a demon brought down, when no one else could do the job, Lucifer sent me. No one survives the Slayer."

He fell silent for a while. Schooling his thoughts. She must have sensed he wasn't finished yet, because she too remained quiet. Waiting.

"A time came when Niklas, the Collector of Souls, could no longer stomach the debauchery of Lucifer's court. He broke his vow of allegiance and escaped to Earth. Niklas was like a brother to me. Before Lucifer could command me to hunt him down, to end him, I left too." He leaned back in his seat, readjusting his long legs. "We now guard the innocent in hopes of..." He stopped, licked his lips.

"Of what?" Kyanna finally pressed when he'd been silent for too long.

"We long to one day return to Heaven." He fought the urge to cringe. Even he couldn't miss the bleak despair in his voice.

Kyanna's expression softened as she tilted her head. Had he gained a measure of her trust with his admission?

"Where are the scrolls?"

Her head snapped back as if he'd slapped her. She

pressed her lips together. Nope. No trust there.

"I don't know anything about any scrolls."

Truth? a layered voice whispered in the back of his head. Just as puzzled as he was.

So she wasn't protecting the scrolls. Or maybe she truly didn't realize she was protecting them. But she was definitely hiding something. The way the darkness prowled around inside him, edgy, wary, only confirmed that.

"What's up with your tattoos? Why do you have Christian religious symbols in some places, and all those…those gruesome images everywhere else?"

"They are called Cryptoglyphs. Only Lucifer's most elite generals are allowed to chronicle their achievements thusly. The more glyphs, the greater the accomplishments. As to the religious symbols, they're a reminder of…of what I strive for."

She studied his extensive collection, and her eyes slowly widened in comprehension. Good. Then she would have a better understanding of the lengths to which he would go to achieve his objectives.

"Who taught you the enchantments?"

"My mother," she replied absently, still staring at his ink. "So if your Cryptoglyphs are to denote your…success as a general in the ultimate army of evil, why the holy images?"

"To remind me of my goals. Who taught your mother the enchantments?"

"Her mother. Why did you come here?"

He chewed that one over for a moment. How would she react when she found out that all of Hell would soon be gunning for her? If they weren't already. Given who she now had as neighbors, it appeared only a matter of time.

How would she respond when she found out that he was her only hope of protection?

"Long ago, a Prophesy was recorded. It states that four Sacred Relics would be combined to overthrow Lucifer. The Sword of Kathnesh. The Arc Stone. The Scrolls of Prévnar. And the Chosen One—a child born of human, angelic, and demonic blood."

"Why would a child be called a relic?"

"The child's bloodlines would be ancient. Undiluted. And with those bloodlines would come the inherent knowledge and power of the ages."

"I see." She paused, a deep frown marring her brow. "Actually, no, I don't. But go on."

"Someone in Hell is staging a coup. If he succeeds, he will bring about the Apocalypse. The boundaries between Earth and Hell are dependent upon Lucifer himself. If he falls, the boundaries come crashing down."

"You mean Armageddon?"

He simply nodded.

"Who is it that's trying to overthrow Lucifer?"

He gritted his teeth. That was the million-dollar question. "We do not know yet."

She arched a brow, as if she didn't believe that for one minute, but she didn't press. "What I don't understand is why have I been involved? Why did you come to my shop?"

Unable to ignore the confusion in her beautiful blue eyes, he let her out-of-order question pass.

"Because we believe you are a Guardian. A sacred warrior charged with keeping one of the relics safe."

She fell silent, her brow wrinkled. Then, without

warning, she gave a small snort, shaking her head.

"You find this amusing?"

"Oh, only the part about me being a warrior. I was picturing me dressed up like Xena for a minute there. Sorry, a leather bustier just doesn't work for me."

Xander's attention dipped to parts south of her chin as his imagination shook off its leash. Oh, he could imagine her in leather. He could imagine her in lace. He could also imagine her in a whole hell of a lot of nothing. That was the problem. His groin pulsed painfully, jolting back to the here and now.

"Where did you get the angelic enchantments and the ward stones?"

"They've been passed down in my family for generations," she replied absently.

Generations. Then she wasn't a first-generation Halfling. *Okay. Good. Right?*

But that still begged the question, was she of angelic descent at all? And if she was, would she even know? He couldn't sense angelic blood, but would he if it were diluted enough? Too many unknown factors. The Slayer didn't like dealing with uncertainties.

She had to be, though. That strange electrical sizzle still hummed through his veins.

And what did *that* mean?

"So you're here looking for the relic, or whatever it is that you think I have." She peered at him suspiciously. "Are you the one that wants to overthrow Lucifer?"

Ah, they'd circled back around to the disbelief. To the doubt.

"No. I have come for the relic, but not to use it. We only want to protect them. Keep them away from the one who wants them."

"And who is that?"

"As I told you already, we don't know yet."

"I can't give you what I don't have."

Truth.

Maybe.

His demonic lie detector wasn't so sure. She was hiding something. Or were the enchantments messing with him? He wanted to get up, wanted to pace, wanted some of this unusual energy humming in his body to dissipate. Instead, he stayed where he was, stayed focused on the task at hand.

"Look," she stated quietly. "I believe you don't mean to harm any innocents. I believe you didn't come here to harm me. Actions speak louder than words, and you've already protected me from that demon. I believe what you've told me. But—"

He should have seen that *but* coming a mile away. She'd accepted all this too quickly, given in much too easily.

"I'm sorry, I can't lower the enchantments. I can't let you go."

This was unbelievable. "Why not?"

"Because I can't take the chance you won't relapse. That you won't decide being a demon is far more fun than trying to clean up your act. I can't live with the knowledge that you might eventually take a human life again and I would be directly responsible for that."

"So you're going to keep me a prisoner here?"

Lips compressed, she nodded.

Floored, he simply stared at her for the longest time. "For how long?"

Panic flashed across her features. Her gaze darted

to the door and back. She licked her lips and shifted in her seat.

Ah, so she apparently hadn't thought that far ahead.

"So you, what? Plan to keep me here indefinitely? I'm a demon, Kyanna, not a tame house pet. And I'm millennia old. I will outlive you."

She crossed her arms. Her jaw set mutinously.

All right. Time to lay all the cards out there. "You're hiding something. And I'm not the only one that believes so. In the building next to this one, there is a nest—a gathering of Earthbound demons. They also believe you possess a relic. And they will take it by any means, fair or foul. Most assuredly foul. They've already tried." He waited for that to sink in before adding, "They brought in a Carpathï. Carpathï are demons capable of shape-shifting and possessions. Have you had anyone—a customer, a stranger or even someone you know—come right up to the door, and then suddenly change their mind and turn away? Anyone approach you on the street? Speak in a strange language to you while they tried to touch you?"

She lost a good bit of color at those direct hits, but, trooper that she was, she lifted her chin and pointed out, "Obviously they didn't succeed, or you wouldn't be here now."

"Neither would you," he countered softly with an arched eyebrow.

She forced a swallow. "As long as the enchantments remain in place, I'll be safe."

"Not good enough," Xander maintained. "You can't hide here forever. Sooner or later, they will get to you. They will force your hand."

Her mouth fell open as she sought in vain for a valid argument.

"So here's how this is going to work," he informed her, growing angrier by the moment. He was trapped. By her precious enchantments. By her evasiveness concerning the relic. By his decision to seek redemption. By the mission he'd given himself to protect the innocent.

By his lust for her.

"You are a Guardian," he ground out. His throat felt so raw by now from all the talking it was little wonder it wasn't bleeding. "Your job is to protect the relic. It has now become my job to protect you, until such time that you give the relic over to me to protect directly. In short? You stay, I stay. Wherever you go, I go. So you might as well turn it over now. Because if you won't relinquish it to me for safekeeping"—he let his deliberate, suggestive gaze skim down her body—"you're not getting rid of me. Regardless of whether you choose to lower the enchantments or not."

There, give her an intimidating, in-your-face stare and frighten her into submission.

Lie, taunted that inner demonic voice. Those damned creepy-crawlies skated over the back of his neck even with his own lies.

Okay, okay, he caved immediately.

It was more of a lingering, intimate caress, he conceded. The creepy-crawlies continued to swarm him.

All right! It was a blatant, strip-her-naked-with-my-eyes ravishment. Happy now?

Creepy-crawlies? Gone.

"If I'm trapped here, then so are you. You aren't

going anywhere without me." Stone-faced, he crossed his arms as he leaned back and propped his booted ankle on his knee. "Consider me your own"—he intentionally, provokingly, let his stare wander—"*personal* bodyguard."

Chapter Eight

"I don't want a bodyguard."

"Too bad." Apparently finished with the conversation, Xander rose and prowled from the office.

How dare he be so…so…highhanded?

She stared after him, slack-jawed, until she realized he was headed toward her storefront. Scrambling up, she chased after him.

"I don't need you," she protested. "I can take care of myself."

Just like that he was gone. She stumbled to a halt, blinking. He'd moved so quickly, she'd barely been able to track him. Before she could spin around in defense, he was behind her. One steely arm caging hers to her side. One calloused hand gripping her chin, tilting it to the side, angling her head. His breath skated up the side of her throat.

"I could have snapped your neck," he whispered in her ear.

"I-I wasn't ready." Breathless. And not because his arms were so strong, his body so hard and hot against her. No, he simply held her too tightly. Not tight enough to hurt her, but firmly enough that she couldn't escape. Her breasts rested upon his forearm.

"Do you think *they* would give you warning?" His husky rumble sent gooseflesh dancing over her body. His warm breath slid over the side of her neck again, the rough stubble on his chin abraded her skin. His heat surrounded her. His solid chest pressed against her back.

And lower—*dear lord!* Were all demons so well endowed? Did they all walk around constantly at *attention*?

The hand gripping her chin slid down her neck. Feather soft now. His thumb came to rest on the frantic pulse hammering at the base of her throat.

Xander's lips—moist and oh so soft—branded her neck, right at that most tender, most sensitive spot, just below her ear. Her knees were turning to jelly, fast. And he was barely nibbling.

Check that. His teeth scraped flesh, erotic as hell, and she gasped aloud. Shuddered. She couldn't help it. He groaned, and the sound of his torment tugged something inside her loose. Warm pleasure. Hungry need. Her hands, still caged at her sides, slid back seemingly of their own accord until she gripped his thighs.

Rock. Hard. Thighs.

More heat. So much heat surrounded her. He cupped her breast. His thumb stroked her nipple. His lips cruised her jaw, angling for the corner of her mouth. A fraction of a heartbeat from connecting—a slight sound, so soft, she almost missed it—broke her concentration. The sound originated from behind them and just down the hall.

"Let me go," she panted.

It was as if he hadn't heard her. Or he flat out refused to heed her order. That warm, hard hand of his continued to knead her breast. That startling, hard ridge pressed more insistently against her backside. Rubbed.

And his wonderfully gifted lips parted. His tongue swirled along the soft flesh beneath the edge of her jaw.

Kyanna shivered.

That *scritch-scritch* sounded again.

"Xander," she groaned.

"Yes," he whispered, passion slurred his voice.

"Stop," she panted.

He froze.

"Wait…what?"

Xander jerked away from her. He stared at his hands, incredulous, as if they were some insidious, foreign objects that had sprouted on their own.

Scritch-scritch.

Finally, he looked up. His gaze lingered on her for a moment, swept over her. Took in the rapid rise and fall of her chest. Blinking, he stepped back, raked a splayed hand over his short hair. Xander glanced at the back door, where the scratching emanated. "If I open the door will the enchantment hold?"

"Yes, but you won't be able to step through." She hurried to follow as he strode purposefully toward the door. "Wait. If you do that plasma ball thing, I don't know if it will pass through or if it will ricochet back inside." She shook her head. "You can't do the plasma ball thing."

He stopped, cursed, and she nearly crashed into his broad back.

He strode forth. She scrambled to keep up.

He was going to give her whiplash at this rate.

Once he reached the door, he flung it open without warning. There, just on the stoop, stood a hideous creature. It sprang back at the sight of Xander. Xander held his hand out to the side, palm up. Threatening.

Thankfully, for her peace of mind at least, he didn't ignite one of those frightening plasma balls.

But the threat remained as he stared the beast down. She scurried ahead and grasped his waist, frantic to get his attention. Peering around his arm, she opened her mouth to remind him of the enchantments, but the words died in her throat.

His eyes were red again. Eerie. Demonic. And the smile on his face was—

Completely. Curdle-your-blood. Terrifying.

"Give your master a message," he snarled. His voice was deep and layered, as if many voices spoke at once.

The creature blinked, but he lingered. Waiting. Worried Xander might forget her admonition about the plasma balls, Kyanna dug her fingers into his hips.

"This woman belongs to the Slayer," Xander snarled.

Kyanna frowned. She didn't belong to him. She didn't belong to anyone but herself. Why was he saying such a thing? But then it clicked. He was warning the other demons away. It had nothing to do with her personally. Only with what he hoped to gain from her.

Nodding, the creature crossed his arms and slapped fists to shoulders. And then he vanished.

She thought that would be the end of it and began to relax. But then Xander spoke in that deeply layered voice again, addressing the darkened alley, though no one—as far as she could tell—remained. *"Gie tuski mulchoi, cami ghia."*

Her breath catching in her throat, she strained to see into the darkness of the alley. But Xander closed the door before she could make anything specific out of the wavering shadows.

Her fingertips began to tingle. Suddenly realizing she was still clutching him, she released him and jumped back. Xander slowly turned on his heel. His expression was set, grim. Shaking his head, he stalked around her without so much as a glance in her direction. At least his eyes were no longer red.

"Wait," she called, chasing after him.

He stopped. She nearly crashed into him. Again.

"Will you stop doing that?" Her head was spinning as it was. All the things she'd seen and heard tonight. All the revelations. And he wasn't helping with all these abrupt stops and starts.

He gave a small grunt and stalked off again.

"What was that last bit? What did you say after that…that thing left?"

"I informed the others hiding in the shadows that you are under my protection."

That gave her a moment's pause. But then she plowed on. "What was that thing anyway?"

"Charocté," he called over his shoulder. "A servant class of demon. They're normally docile and obedient. It had to have been scratching around here, looking for another way in on its master's orders. They won't scratch their own asses without permission."

Well that's certainly a pleasant bit of imagery.

"Then why can't you identify it, figure out who it belongs to?"

"Charocté all pretty much look alike. It's nearly impossible to tell them apart. And it would be virtually impossible to tell exactly who it belongs to."

"Why couldn't you capture it, make it talk?"

He stopped once more, only this time she managed

to pull up as well so she didn't bounce off his broad back. Slowly he turned to stare down at her, just as slowly he elevated an eyebrow.

"Oh, right." *Duh, Ky.* The enchantments had prevented him from stepping foot past the threshold.

"Where do you sleep?"

"What?" she squeaked.

"Sleep, woman. Where do you sleep?"

"Upstairs."

He turned toward the door she'd shooed him away from earlier.

"Wait! You can't go—"

Her words strangled off with a gasp as he jerked the door open and took the first step up, an army general claiming new territory. His momentum sent him ricocheting off the secondary enchantments like a basketball off the backboard. He landed on his butt. At her feet. With a very angry grunt.

"Up there," she finished, wincing.

Glaring up at her, he gingerly climbed to his feet.

"There are secondary enchantments on the apartment. And before you ask, no, I'm not lowering that one either."

The grim set of his mouth expressed his displeasure eloquently.

"No," she reiterated, edging backward with a great deal of caution as he took an intimidating step toward her. "And that wasn't meant as a challenge. You stay. But you sleep down here, in the office."

He looked back to the steps, to the dagger on the fifth step up. So close, yet impossible for him to reach.

"I want my dagger."

"No."

"Woman—"

"Kyanna."

"Kyanna," he conceded less than graciously. "If I wanted to kill you, you'd be dead already. By my bare hands."

She weighed his words. Biting her lip, she conceded the point. A measure of trust for a measure of trust? "Do I have your word you won't use that thing on me?"

"The word of a demon." He tossed her earlier mistrust back at her with an eloquently arched brow.

Cute. But she wasn't about to let him off so easily. He might intimidate others into doing his bidding with those menacing looks—okay, he might intimidate her more than a little as well—but this was her life she was putting on the line. She at least wanted the illusion of a sworn promise. Crossing her arms, she stared him down. Mutiny etched in every tense muscle.

At length, he lifted his gaze to the ceiling, muttering something beneath his breath. The words sounded remarkably similar to the language she used while casting enchantments. Finally, he turned his attention to her. His expression was placid, though she could see the effort it cost him.

"I swear I will do you no harm."

"With the dagger," she prompted.

"With the dagger."

"Nor with your bare hands," she added.

The muscle in his jaw leapt.

"Nor with my bare hands."

"Nor with plasma balls," she wheedled.

His nostrils flared and he drew a deep, deep breath. "Nor with plasma balls."

"Ever."

"Woman!"

"Ever," she insisted, planting her fists to her hips.

"Ever," Xander snarled.

With a healthy dose of unease, she stepped unimpeded past the secondary enchantments and picked up the weapon. Drawing a deep breath, praying she wasn't about to make a huge mistake, she returned to the hallway and handed him the dagger.

Grim, his gaze never leaving hers, he reclaimed his property and slapped it back in its sheath.

He straightened, glowering. "I cannot protect you with enchantments between us."

"If you can't get through them, then they can't get through them either, correct?"

Put like that, either he'd be forced to acknowledge her point, or admit that someone else was better than he was, thereby rendering himself useless. She could have patted herself on the back for her quick thinking. A guy like him—a *demon*, she corrected—wouldn't willingly admit to a personal flaw if there was any possible way around it.

Why is it so hard to remember that crucial fact? He's a demon. Not a man. Not some guy. A demon!

Probably because right now he looks very, very human. And too damned sexy for my own piece of mind.

His eyes flickered red, and she quickly stifled the urge to run for cover. In the end, he nodded, surprising her.

"Good. I'll be right back," she announced, then escaped upstairs before he could change his mind, or make some crazy pronouncement that she sleep down here instead.

A few moments later, she pounded down the stairs, a pillow and a stack of blankets filling her arms. Sweeping by a scowling Xander, she hurried to the office and began making up the sofa. Just as she was plumping the pillow, a thought occurred to her.

"I didn't think," she admitted, nibbling her lower lip as she assessed him. "You do sleep, right?"

He'd come to stand in the doorway. Filled it. Muscled arms crossed over his bare chest, feet spread. His expression impassive.

At length, once he'd caused her to begin fidgeting nervously, he finally deigned to reply. "Yes, I sleep."

"All righty then." Rubbing her damp palms up and down her hips, glancing anxiously around the room, she cleared her throat. "I'll, ah, I'll just be upstairs. If you need anything just, um, just give a shout, I guess."

She'd said the last as she'd crossed the small room, expecting him to step aside. But he didn't. Xander's steady gaze had followed every move she'd made, fidgets and all. But he'd not twitched a muscle otherwise.

She came to stand before him, chin held high. Never mind the panicky way her insides quivered.

"Excuse me." She kept a polite smile pasted to her mouth.

He stared at her, inscrutable. Frustratingly silent.

Did he think to force her to stay with him here in the office? Because if he did, he had another—

Without warning, he leaned forward and captured her lips with his own, though he didn't touch her anywhere else. Shocked, she stared up in to turbulent gray. The moment her eyes slid shut, the tip of his tongue swept the seam of her lips, prodding, demanding entrance.

To her mortification, her body responded, yielding to his without the slightest resistance.

This was no brush. No flutter. No gentle flirtation.

This was firm. Possessive. A succinct exertion of will.

And damned effective.

The moment her hands drifted to his chest and she leaned into him in surrender, Xander drew back, leaving her weaving on her feet. Kyanna blinked up at him, utterly speechless.

"Sweet dreams, Kyanna," he murmured in that raw, husky rasp of his. A rasp that now sent thrilling shudders skating down her spine.

His expression hadn't changed. Not one bristly whisker moved. And yet his eyes held depths she couldn't fathom. Irritation swirled therein. And desire. Unmistakable and hungry.

"Goodnight, Xander," she replied firmly, squeezing around him.

Disappointment. Resignation. Relief. Was she really reading all these emotions in his steady gaze? Or was it wishful thinking on her part? A reflection of her own emotions?

She hesitated there in the hallway, just outside the door, the taste of him fresh upon her lips. He'd kissed her. Shaken her to the depths of her soul. Firming her resolve, she glanced over her shoulder to make certain he'd remained in the office. He had. He stood with his back to the door, staring at the sofa. Fisted hands clenched at his sides. His shoulders rising and falling on slow, measured breaths. Trying to keep her steps slow and casual, she crossed to the storage closet and drew out the ward stones, tucking them furtively against her stomach.

As she returned to the office, Kyanna kept wary watch on Xander's broad back. She caught the way he suddenly stiffened. Kyanna kicked her speed up a notch as he whirled toward the door, and she scrambled to drop the stones in place across the threshold, her lips moving silently as she rushed to whisper more enchantments into place.

Fury lit his features. His eyes glowed red. His muscles seemed to swell before her eyes.

"Damn it, woman," he snarled, his rough voice deep and oddly layered. He stormed right up to the doorway, and no farther. Xander reached his hand out, only to hiss and jerk it back.

"I'm sorry," she whispered, leaping back despite the barrier between them. "I can't allow you to wander around out here all night."

He said not a word. He didn't need to. His red eyes spoke volumes. As did his clenched, bulging muscles. Kyanna licked her lower lip nervously, then caught it between her teeth. He stilled, his unswerving attention suddenly riveted to her mouth. A furrow dug deep between his brows. Heat of a new kind boiled through the doorway. Kyanna spun on her heel, and she fled.

A single, enraged roar followed her. She escaped upstairs and closed the door behind her. Once safely behind additional enchantments and ward stones and locked doors, she leaned back, trying in vain to catch her breath.

He kissed me.

Holy hell, she'd just been kissed by a demon. And she'd liked it.

This was insane. This was a disaster in the making. *What am I going to do now?*

Chapter Nine

Xander prowled the confines of the minuscule office. He sent a vicious glare toward the ceiling—whether directed at that unpredictable female or higher yet, he couldn't say—as he laced his fingers and propped his hands on the top of his head. Only centuries of exercising rigid self-control prevented him from kicking holes in the walls and pulverizing her desk into toothpick sized splinters.

What the hell did I just do?

He'd meant the kiss to be a manipulation. Sneak inside her defenses, use her weak human hormones against her, snag the relic, and jet. He'd sorely miscalculated. Instead of her being completely at his mercy, he'd been the one caught in her silken web. Just as he'd feared. The taste of her lingered on his lips, making him crave more of her.

Talk about seduction gone awry. Might as well label this one an epic failure.

And then she'd done it again. Caught him by surprise. She'd been doing it all night, every time she'd stood her ground with him, refusing to budge an inch. He sure as hell hadn't expected her to cage him inside the office. He'd been so busy worrying over that ill advised kiss and contemplating the tiny bed she'd made up for him—what did she think he was, a freakin' dwarf?—that he hadn't realized what she'd been up to until it was too late.

Hell, who was he trying to fool? He'd been so wrapped up in thinking about her lips, about how they'd been so soft and yielding, so delicious, that Lucy himself could probably have walked up and shaken his hand and he wouldn't have realized it. Sweet Christ, if a simple kiss could render him senseless, imagine what having her beneath him, writhing and moaning as he buried himself between her sweet thighs would do to him. Her arms holding him close. Her legs wrapped around his waist—

Dragging both hands over his face, he battled the urge to roar once more. This time not in frustration, but in thwarted torment. He had to get a grip on his control or he'd be a wild, slathering, lust-driven beast by the time she returned tomorrow morning. Xander paced to the doorway. He squatted down and peered at the crystals she'd strewn in front of the door. Anglesite, quartz, ruby and—

Halite, maybe?

It was difficult to tell with the hallway dark now. And every time he tried to reach out to nudge them aside he got an unpleasant jolt. Like a damned dog with a bark collar. Or invisible fencing. The analogy didn't sit well. Pissed off all over again, he reached out once more. The tips of his fingers began to blacken, his flesh began to smoke. Swearing, he jerked his hand back and pushed to his feet.

He concentrated hard, tried to conjure a fresh shirt. A bottle of pain killer. A freakin' soda.

Nada.

He pulled his fist back. It would serve her right to wake up to holes in her walls. But it wouldn't help him one bit to bring the damned ceiling down on his own head. Closing his eyes, he centered his focus and relaxed his fist. He imagined Sebastian's farmhouse. The rustic, outdoorsy furnishings. The fresh, clean air.

He opened his eyes—to Kyanna's office.

Scowling, he closed them once more, dug deeper for the darkness within, called to mind Niklas's flat in Paris. Or Gideon's sprawling plantation house in Tennessee.

Opened to business ledgers.

Closed, brow furrowed deep in concentration, he thought of his own log cabin in the Rockies. The scent of pine, the chirping of birds. The babbling brook out back.

Open. That friggin' doll-sized sofa.

Closed, he imagined war ravaged village streets. Screams and exploding bombs. Rampant gunfire. Smoke and death.

Open. Kyanna's businesslike desk. Tidy and professional. And dead silence all but for some clock ticking away in the far recesses of Kyanna's store. *Tick. Tock.* Like the *drip-drip* of cunning water torture designed to slowly drive prisoners insane.

Again he desperately tried to conjure that can of soda one more time. An exercise in futility, he knew. But damn, he could use a drink right now.

Nothing.

The sound of footsteps crossed above him. Back and forth. Back and forth. A twisted sort of grim satisfaction niggled. If he wasn't going to get an easy night's rest, then why should she?

But then another thought occurred.

Would she be all right up there without him?

Something like that would never have occurred to him before. What was the matter with him?

Cursing, he reached into his back pocket, pulled his cell phone out. Xander thumbed in a quick sequence of numbers, then settled onto the seat at the desk and glowered at the dinky bed as he waited for the call to connect.

"Dude," Sebastian answered.

"It's me."

"That's what the ringtone said."

Smartass.

"I have a Guardian," Xander said.

Something loud thunked in the background. A pop and a fizz. "No kidding? Where?"

"Isle, Minnesota."

"You gonna bring the relic in or do we need to come to you?" Sebastian asked.

"Not yet."

"Which?"

"Either. Both."

"You don't have the relic yet?"

"No." For the love of Saint Gabriel, he hated phones. It never failed. Every damned time he called somebody, it was twenty questions.

"Well for Christ's sake, Slayer. You're a damned tease. Get a guy's hopes up when you ain't got any intention of puttin' out." Plastic rattled in the background. "Guardian ain't talkin', huh? Well, bring him in." Crunching crackled through the line. Sebastian and his damned chips. The way the guy constantly stuffed his face it was a wonder he wasn't as big as his farmhouse. "We'll get the location out of him."

"Female," Xander corrected. "And for heaven's

sake, quit talking with your mouth full."

"Yes, Mom," Sebastian responded automatically. Then, with decidedly more interest he added, "A woman, huh? Is she hot? Bring her in and I'll—"

"No," he snarled.

The crunching immediately stopped. He could have kicked himself. Why had he had to react like that? So quick. So possessive.

"Ah," Sebastian drawled. "It's like that, is it?"

"No," he denied, though he knew it would do no good. "Just complicated."

That earned him an enigmatic grunt. And again with the chip crunching.

"Um-hmm." Another particularly loud crunch echoed over the line.

Does he never stop eating?

"Not like that," Xander snapped. Hell's bells, he wasn't going to hear the end of this. "Angelic enchantments surround the building we're in. It's a long story. But she won't lower them." He ground his teeth. Oh, this was galling. The great Slayer trapped by a mere human woman. "While they are in place…I can't leave."

Ten seconds of dead silence. Not even the sound of chewing could be heard. And then Xander ripped the phone from his ear as uproarious laughter exploded though the line. He settled back, drummed his fingertips on the arm of the chair, and waited for Sebastian to wind down.

It took much longer than necessary.

"So, let me get this straight," Sebastian wheezed. "*She* caught *you*."

Another seemingly unending round of whooping

laughs. Xander drew a deep breath, praying for patience. He'd almost made up his mind to simply hang up and call Gideon. Brooding asshole sounded more appealing right now than being the butt of Sebastian's misplaced humor.

"Okay. Okay." Sebastian snorted one last time. "Angelic enchantments? Obviously, she has the scrolls then."

Silence was the only appropriate response to that lame remark.

"Sooooo," Sebastian drawled. Xander gritted his teeth—judging by the tone and length of that *so*, he was in for more ribbing. "Do you need the cavalry to come rescue you from this big bad human female?"

Again, silence was the only appropriate response.

"Screw you," slipped out of nowhere.

"Aw now, baby, don't be like that," Sebastian crooned, his voice filled with amusement.

Silence. Patience. *Ten. Nine. Eight. Seven—*

"Okay, I'm done. For now," Sebastian promised. "Fill me in. Has the other team found her yet?"

"Definite yeah. Bottom of the third. Bases loaded and Sïnsobar struck out."

"Sïnsobar? No crap." Finally some sobriety.

In twenty words or less, Xander brought Sebastian up to speed.

"You sure you don't want backup?"

"Positive."

"I'll fill the others in." Sebastian would be point man on this one, and he knew the drill. "Oh, and Slayer? How about some pics for Facebook? I can see the caption already. Big bad demon pu—"

Xander disconnected the call before Sebastian

could finish.

The pacing overhead had ceased. What was she doing up there? Undressing? Slipping into bed?

Forcefully yanking his thoughts from that track before his control was completely derailed, Xander stared at the makeshift bed and he grimaced. No way was he sleeping on that with his legs dangling off the end. Ugh, he was filthy. He needed a shower in the worst way. And a change of clothes. Just as the urge to conjure himself clean and a fresh set of clothing occurred to him, he swore again. His calculating gaze tracking up to the ceiling once more. One corner of his mouth edged upward. Ten to one, she kept the scrolls up there with her, somewhere. He'd get into that apartment, one way or another. He stood, stripped down to his skin, and tossed his filthy pants and boots on the floor in the corner.

With a resigned groan, he pulled the blankets and the pillow from the sofa and snapped them out on the floor. Naked, he lay down and shifted around until he got comfortable. Sort of.

Hardwood sucks.

Rolling to his side, he settled in for a long, uncomfortable night. Just that quickly, images filled his mind. Soft, lush breasts. Long, shapely, bare legs. A slim waist. Toned arms. Creamy skin. Long, golden hair. Lips so soft, so delectable—

Groaning, doing his level best to ignore the needful ache in his swollen erection, he rolled to the other side and tried to clear his head. Pounded the pillow with his fist. Twice. Temptation. She was temptation. Pure and simple.

Pray, just pray.

Maybe—just this once—God would see fit to grant him a little peace.

Our Father who art in Heaven, hallowed be Thy name—

****

It was no use. She tossed the tangled sheets back, kicked them to the side with a disgusted sigh. She wasn't going to get any sleep. Not like this. With all this stuff running circles in her head. With all these images of him tormenting her. With the memory of his mouth on hers, his hands on her body, his unyielding strength pressed against hers. She was making herself crazy.

Pushing to her feet, Kyanna tugged her long, flannel robe on over the plain white T-shirt and cotton boxer shorts she'd pulled on after her shower. After grabbing a scrunchie from the nightstand, she wrapped her still damp, tangled hair up in a quick, sloppy bun. Kyanna jerked woolen socks on her cold feet and padded from her bedroom.

A glass of milk is supposed to help when you can't sleep, right? Warm milk? Yeah.

But then she wondered if chocolate milk did the same thing. She couldn't stand plain white milk. But warm chocolate milk?

Shrugging, she pulled a canister of hot chocolate from the cupboard.

Same thing, right?

A short while later, armed with a hot cup of cocoa, Kyanna entered the second bedroom and flipped on the overhead light. Maybe if she wrote down some of the information swimming in her head, she might be able to clear her mind. Get some sleep.

Relegating her untouched cup to the edge of the desk, she pulled the slim volume—no bigger really than a notebook—to her and picked up a pen. The sum of her family's heritage rested inside this aged leather cover. Kyanna switched on the antique reading lamp. Kyanna gingerly opened the cracking leather, and she skimmed the first few pages. Blotchy chicken-scratches. Every stroke, every bit of information as familiar as the lines of her own face.

First and foremost, the enchantments and incantations given to her ancient ancestor centuries ago by an angelic benefactor. Next came a complete list of guard and ward stones designated to thwart and repel demons. Somewhere along the line, one of her predecessors had added an index of herbs and potions with healing properties. Others, over the course of time, had included an abbreviated list of demon species. Though information on that front was sparse at best, and questionable in its reliability.

But the most important section in the book—the information her family had been charged to protect with their lives—was a list of angelic offspring. Otherwise known as Halflings. She'd glanced through that section once, long ago. But she hadn't recognized any of the names. Of course, that section hadn't been updated in over twenty years. Those Halflings could potentially have had offspring of their own by now. Generations had passed since the first name had been inscribed. And she'd never been instructed to add to this portion of the book, so she could only assume that no other Halflings had been conceived.

Then again, maybe she wasn't the only one charged with this kind of task? Was this book just one of many? Was her family not so unique? What if this book only held a portion of information? And somewhere out there, there were others, with different sets of information? Different sets of names. Like a big puzzle. Or torn pieces of some biblical treasure map. Each only effective in a limited capacity, but when paired with the whole, the information therein could be…unfathomable.

Rubbing some of the sudden tension from the back of her neck, she centered her focus on the here and now.

She located the last thin strip of aged silk at the bottom of the book and pulled it slightly to the side to open the fragile tome. Picking up a pen, she stared at the stiff, yellowed, blank page and took a deep breath. Writing anything in this journal was serious business. No one had done so in nearly a quarter of a century.

She started with the date. Her name. There was so much she could write. So much she'd gathered from her one, brief conversation with Xander. But the only things that came immediately to mind were things like sexy bedroom eyes. Kisses so enthralling they made a girl forget where she was. *Who* she was.

A male that defined sin incarnate.

No. She had to get serious. Provided there might be—some far, far off day—a new generation to pass the book on to, she wanted them prepared for whatever Hell tossed their way. What had Xander told her about?

The Sacred Relics. The Prophesy. The demon species she'd seen tonight. Charocté, he'd called them. Xander himself.

But where to start?

Quickly, methodically, she penned in her notations

and what definitions she could, going into as much detail as possible. Recording her impressions. When she was finished, she sat back and read what she'd written.

Not bad. At least it was coherent.

Then she remembered something. "*The Slayer.*" Xander had called himself that a couple of times. Curiosity pricked her. She began cautiously thumbing back through the delicate book, searching for any entries regarding the Slayer.

All too soon she found what she was looking for. And what she found had her eyes all but bugging out of her head.

"'Recorded in the year of our Lord, Eighteen-Fifteen by Sarah Thompson. The Slayer,'" she whispered aloud. Was she afraid he could hear her? Maybe a little, considering the shocking page she was staring at. He'd rated an entire page. All to himself.

On paper he was completely and utterly horrifying.

Holy crap on a cracker!

"'Lucifer's deadliest assassin,'" she murmured. "'A top general in Lucifer's army. Origins: Believed to be one of the original Archangels. Age: Unknown. Weakness: Unknown. This dangerous demon is unpredictable and greatly feared by others of his kind. Do not engage. Avoid at all cost.'" Setting the book aside, she leaned back, tipped her head against the back of the chair, and covered her face with both hands.

Do not engage?

Avoid at all cost?

Oh, dear Lord. What have I done?

For a long moment, she was beyond words, beyond thought. And then it all came crashing in on her. Not only had she brought possibly one of the deadliest beings on Earth—as well as in Hell apparently—into her sanctuary. But she'd just told him she intended to hold him captive for an indeterminate amount of time.

Kyanna placed a shaking hand flat on the page and leaned closer. Her however-many-greats grandmother had even added a crude drawing of him in demon form. Amazingly accurate, if memory served.

Oh Lord. Oh Lord.

Peering at the spider-scrawl, she held her breath and prayed she'd misread.

Nope. No such luck. The words remained the same. In addition, smaller script toward the bottom of the page accused him of all manner of evil, up to and including withering the crops in the fields, breathing fire, making livestock fall over dead for no apparent reason, causing solar eclipses, and sacrificing virgins.

Okay, so some of this obviously had to have been wild, superstitious paranoia. Solar eclipses? Breathing fire? Withering crops? Really? She couldn't buy into any of that.

The virginal sacrifices?

Considering the smoldering stares he was capable of, not to mention his mad talent at kissing?

She'd be willing to bet ten to one every virgin within a fifty mile radius had willingly thrown herself upon his alter and begged to be his sacrifice.

Kyanna gently closed the book and pushed it back into place before rising. She took a long gulp of tepid chocolate, her mind racing. What on earth was she going to do with him? She couldn't very well have him wandering through her store while innocent customers shopped. She couldn't let him up here while she wasn't around. Couldn't risk him finding *the book*. And she couldn't very well lock him in the basement.

Or could I?

No!

She wasn't that cruel. And something told her he wouldn't exactly go quietly either.

Back to square one.

Unsettled, she returned the cup to the kitchen, washed it, and set it in the rack to dry. She should go to bed. Get some rest. But she was too revved up to sleep. Or too spooked, considering what she'd just read. Chewing a thumbnail—something she never did anymore except in times of extreme stress—Kyanna began pacing the confines of her living room.

Again.

Now what am I going to do?

Chapter Ten

Xander reclined on the sofa, his fingers laced over his stomach, pillow and blankets folded neatly beside him. He cracked his jaw and glowered at the door, at the crystals caging him in. Kyanna's footsteps descended the stairs. *Finally.* He checked the wall clock before returning his attention to the crystals. Seven a.m.

About damned time.

He'd been up for longer than he cared to think about. He was tired and bruised from her double-damned hardwood floor. His clothing was filthy. He had a headache, and he was hungry.

And he hadn't had a soda in over twenty-four hours.

The very idea was more than any demon should have to tolerate.

As Kyanna cautiously stepped up to the door of the office, he caught his breath, his physical discomfort all but forgotten. Hunger of another kind punched through his system, catching him off guard. Her hair, damp and fragrant, was caught up in a messy top-knot, taunting a male to pull it down and wrap it around his fist. She wore layered tanks in both bright and dark shades of purple and a jagged edged skirt that reminded him of an overlarge handkerchief. Barely-there, strappy sandals emphasized her narrow feet. Her dainty toes were festive with bright purple nail polish.

Dark, spiky lashes framed gorgeous, luminous blue. But other than a slim bit of mascara, her face was unadorned by makeup. Even if he hadn't heard her pacing overhead until the wee hours of the morning, he'd easily have been able to tell she'd spent a sleepless night. Dark shadows smudged beneath her eyes. Even now, she smothered a yawn.

Her skin was flawless. Strawberries and cream. He greedily took in her flushed, freshly-scrubbed cheeks, the ivory column of her throat, and the smooth bare expanse of her shoulder. The swell of her breasts was more temptation than he could take. His mouth began to water. His shaft began to harden. Making a conscious effort, he uncurled his fingers from the cushions and dragged his focus back up to her face.

Xander deliberately blanked his features, arched an eyebrow, and he waited for her to speak. Keeping his expression impassive took far more effort than he was accustomed to expending.

"Good morning." Her voice was husky, dragging at something deep in the pit of his stomach.

He grunted. That was a matter of opinion. Curious about how she intended to proceed, he crossed his arms and let out a long, seething breath.

"Um, are you hungry? Can I get you some breakfast?"

He remained silent. As long as she had those damned crystals in place, caging him in this tiny cell, she wasn't getting even the sorriest excuse for cooperation. She blatantly stared at his naked chest. Lingered on the bloodstained waistband of his pants. He watched as she caught the edge of her lower lip between small white teeth. A crease formed between her brows.

If she stared much longer there, he'd be sporting wood the likes of which she'd probably never witnessed before.

"Shower," he barked. A command, not a request.

"A shower. Right. A shirt. Clothes," she murmured. "Clean clothes. Definitely a shirt." She seemed in a daze, her gaze loitering overlong on his abdomen. As predicted, his shaft continued to harden.

Her gaze dropped a few inches. She dragged in a shuddering breath and color flooded her cheeks. Her eyes grew round as saucers, and all movement arrested. He cleared his throat, whether for her benefit or his, he didn't know. Kyanna jolted, blinking guiltily at him as color swamped her cheeks. That unfamiliar tick in his cheek came back, despite his pissy mood. He bit down on the inside of his lower lip.

The Slayer did not grin.

At least, not unless it was a wickedly evil grin.

And he wasn't feeling particularly evil just now. Wicked, yes. But not evil.

He leaned forward, clasped his hands between his knees. She stared, and the color in her cheeks heightened. Kyanna cleared her throat and snapped steel into her spine. "You can come upstairs, take a shower. I've lowered the secondary enchantments on the apartment, but it's only temporary. You'll sleep down here again tonight," she warned. "And I'll get you new clothing."

He stiffened. "You do not leave the building without me."

Her lips pursed thoughtfully. "I'll call a friend."

With a terse nod, Xander shoved to his feet and

prowled toward the doorway. Kyanna hastily removed the crystals and hurried to tuck them back into the storage closet. The minute she turned back around, he was in her face.

Big. Bad. And supremely pissed off.

"Do not think to trap me in that office again with your ward stones. If you try it, I will bring this building down in pieces. I have given you my word I will not harm you." He paused, letting his eyes flash red for a moment. "But that doesn't mean I will tolerate being treated like a caged dog."

He watched as she forced a swallow and stared up at him. She slowly nodded. He stood there a moment longer, just to make sure his warning had properly sunk in before he stepped back. Xander trudged sullenly up the stairs, Kyanna scurrying along at his heels.

The room he stepped inside was large, open, and airy. A living area that flowed smoothly into a dining area which, in turn, flowed into the kitchen. Three, evenly spaced doors lined the wall on the north side of the apartment. One closed. Two open. There wasn't much in the way of clutter. A few well-chosen, antique pieces of furniture. A bright red vase filled with flowers here. A cluster of decorative candles there. Gilt-framed landscapes hung on the walls. A huge, thick, pile rug covered hardwood in the center of the living area. Aesthetically pleasing. The room smelled of Kyanna. Enticing. Vibrant.

His skin prickled, warning him that there were ward stones here. And more enchantments.

"The bathroom is over here," she said, pointing to an open doorway. "I left a fresh towel and washcloth on the hook for you. I'll work on getting some new clothes while you shower."

Inclining his head, he strode past her on his way toward the bathroom. A few feet from the bathroom door—though his step did not falter—his gaze cut to the closed door on his right. The itch in his skin intensified. She'd employed both incantations as well as ward stones in that room.

Is that where she's keeping the scrolls?

Filing that bit of speculation away for later, Xander entered the bathroom and closed the door behind him. Tidy. Spotless, like the rest of the apartment. A thick, pink bath sheet hung from a brass hook on the wall. A neatly folded, matching washcloth rested atop the hook.

He began to strip off his pants, but the sound of her voice filtered through the door and he paused, one leg all the way in, one leg half out.

"Hey, it's me." A long silence ensued.

He wrestled with his conscience for one very brief moment, then did a hobble step closer to the door. Xander cursed when he tripped on the edge of the rug and nearly landed on his face. *Damned clothing.* So much easier when you could just conjure and vanish them at will. But even up here in the apartment, he was thwarted. No matter how badly he wanted it, that blessed can of soda never appeared in his hand.

"No, that's not why I'm calling. I didn't change my mind. I told you before, I don't want to talk about Jack." Xander's brows snapped together. His attention focused solely on her voice now, his pants pooled, forgotten, around his ankle.

Jack? Jack who?

He leaned closer to the door, bracing his hand on the doorframe, hoping to catch a bit more information.

Like a last name.

Or where this Jack lived.

Again, silence thwarted him for a moment.

"Look, Summer, I need a favor." Who was this *Summer*? Kyanna's footsteps shuffled across the dining area. Shuffled back. Her voice clear one moment, muffled the next, frustrating him to no end. "I know. And please, no questions, just—"

Another long silence, followed by a deep, beleaguered sigh on Kyanna's end of the conversation. "Yes, just not now, all right?"

The clink of ice in a glass rattled, water rushed from a faucet, drowning out her words for a moment. He pressed his ear closer to the door and concentrated.

"Yes, that's what I said. Clothing. Jeans and a T-shirt. On second thought, you better make it three of each. I'm not sure how long he'll be here. I'll pay you back. No! He's not—geez, Summer." She groaned. "Why does everything with you have to be about sex? Just bring the clothes over, sooner rather than later. Yes, I'm sure about that. No," she hissed furiously, "I won't be needing any of those!"

She'd stopped pacing just on the other side of the door, but the steady *thump-thump* indicated she was tapping something. Her foot perhaps.

"I'm always careful too, Summer Ann." Now she was pissed off. He could tell by her tone. And even that was turning him on.

Silence reigned for what felt like an eternity.

"I'm sorry. You're right," she replied contritely. "No, it's just been a long night. No! Not *that* kind of long night. Ugh! I just need the clothes, okay? Size?

Um, the shirts, I guess an extra large. Jeans? No—bigger than Jack, I think. Taller. More Duff's size. I don't know, he's like 6' 4" or so. Maybe a little taller."

Again silence, but she'd resumed pacing.

"No, he has boots, but I suppose you probably better get socks." A brief pause. "No, I'm not sure of his boot size." A short beat of silence. "They're huge, why?" A scandalized gasp filled his ears. "I would not know what size his—I am so not having this discussion with you right now!" She paused, then let out a long, put-upon sigh. "I don't know if he wears boxers or briefs. I didn't ask. Just. Get. Some. Clothes."

Another moment of silence, and then, "Fine. Come in the back way—wait. You better make that the front door. You still have your key, right? No there's, ah, there's something wrong with the back door. It's, um, sticking." A short pause. "No, I already have someone scheduled to fix it. Just come to the front. Give me a call when you get here and I'll run down and meet you. Thanks. See you in a few."

The phone clattered on to the hook, and Xander hurried to turn the water on. He finished wrestling off his pants and stepped under the spray. Bracing his hands on the wall, Xander dropped his head forward, and let the hot water pound on the back of his stiff neck and his tight shoulders before reaching for the washcloth. He looked around for another bar of soap—heaven forbid, even one of those rose scented, flower shaped ones like in the bathroom downstairs—but could only find a bottle of floral-scented body wash. He groaned aloud but began lathering the cloth.

As irritating as this situation was, he could use it in his favor. Inconvenience her. Make her bear the full weight of confining him. Deal with his needs—

His body reacted instantly with those leading thoughts.

No, she wouldn't be dealing with those needs, he sternly reminded himself. He didn't have those needs anymore. He'd learned to deny those needs. He trusted in his faith to overcome those sinful urges.

With a frustrated growl, he squeezed a generous amount of gel into the cloth once more and worked up more lather. More lather, more fragrance. Soon the steamy shower was saturated with the enticing scent of Kyanna. Glancing down, he grimaced at the painful, rock hard erection he now sported.

Not good, Xander. Get your head in the game.

He tried to clear away the lustful thoughts, offered prayer after prayer for self-control and patience. As with last night, his prayers weren't helping much. Not when all he had to do was close his eyes and imagine the slick of rich, fragrant lather sliding down his body was the caress of Kyanna's small, competent hands.

****

Kyanna checked the heat on the skillet, turned the knob down two settings, and then glanced over at the coffee pot. She couldn't think on an empty stomach. He might not want or need breakfast. But she did. So what if she made a little extra. He had to eat too, didn't he?

Or does he?

Gah, she'd drive herself crazy at this rate.

She could have used more time to herself. More time to think, to come up with a feasible plan. She'd bought some time with his shower, but she knew that wouldn't last much longer. Why hadn't she thought to call Summer earlier? Then she would have had clothing waiting for him already.

As if on cue, a muffled curse echoed through the thin walls. The water in the shower cut off quickly after that. She had a water heater the size of a goldfish tank. She should have warned him.

A small, mischievous smile quirked her lips.

Oops.

Kyanna dropped thick slices of bacon into the skillet and watched them sizzle for a moment before she set to work cracking eggs into a mixing bowl. It was Saturday. Treasure Box didn't open until ten. Closed at two. Then she had the rest of the weekend off. Alone. With the demon.

No, she wasn't going there. She'd deal with it when the time came.

She glanced at the clock. Two hours to go. Plenty of time for a decent, relaxed breakfast.

Plenty of time for Summer to buy clothes for Xander.

Then what was she going to do with him?

In short order, she had coffee brewing, bacon sizzling, and a second pan ready for eggs. Just as she picked up the bowl of whipped eggs, a solid wall of heat curled around her from behind.

Xander's inhalation was soul deep, and far too close to the side of her neck for her comfort. Sweet hollyhocks in a hamper, how had he snuck up on her without her noticing? A rough, unmistakably approving growl gurgled deep in his throat. She bobbled the bowl and swiftly set it on the counter before spinning around. Her mouth came so close to brushing up against his that she felt the heat of his breath skate her bottom lip. Her heart slammed, stuttered, slammed.

His hair was still damp. Except for that towel, he was so…*naked*. And his eyes—

His compelling, smoldering gray eyes all but devoured her.

For a split second, they flickered flaming red before returning to that turbulent gray.

Kyanna jolted. The edge of the countertop dug into the small of her spine as she pressed herself back. And still, scant inches separated them. Droplets of water glinted in his damp, spiky hair. Glistened on his golden skin. Lots and lots…and lots…of golden, very-naked skin. Crystalline beads rippled along his freshly shaved cheeks, slid down his neck, and tracked along the ridges of his defined abdomen to finally be absorbed by the thick pink towel wrapped around his lean waist. Low on his waist. Low enough to showcase an intriguing dusting of dark, coarse hair below his navel that thickened the farther south it went.

Her gaze dropped lower, drawn to—snagging on—the thick bulge that the terrycloth couldn't conceal. A thick bulge that seemed to be growing larger the longer she stared. The palms of her hands began to itch. Need fluttered low in the pit of her stomach. How she longed to peel aside the towel and stroke what it concealed. The harsh grate of his voice brought her out of her hormone induced daze.

"Huh?" Kyanna squeaked, dragging her focus up the delectable expanse of male chest.

The edge of his mouth twitched, then his lower lip flattened. "You're burning the bacon."

"Oh." She blinked, started. Jolted. "Oh!"

Turning, she snatched up the tongs and began flipping bacon. *Not too bad,* she breathed. *Crispy but still edible.*

Edible…hmm…

No! Do not go there, Ky.

Extending every possible effort not to even glance in his direction, Kyanna finished preparing breakfast. But she was fighting a losing battle. No matter how hard she tried, she just couldn't ignore the heaping helping of eye candy in the room. It took every last ounce of her willpower not to stare and drool as he bent forward to assess the contents of her refrigerator. He muttered beneath his breath, pushing salad components aside, rummaging through drawers.

"Sweet blessed Mary!"

Curious, bracing herself against the eye-candy on display, she peeked over her shoulder. Xander stood with the fridge door wide open, a can of cola clutched in his hand, his expression that of a man who'd just discovered the Holy Grail. In a rush, he popped the top and set the can to his lips. Tilting his head back, he guzzled, never once coming up for air. She watched, mesmerized, as his Adam's apple bobbed with each swallow.

When the can was at last empty, he lowered it, his eyes closed, and he shuddered. Any other man, any other time, and she'd have sworn he's just achieved a soul stroking climax. That look on his face did funny things to her insides.

After snagging another can of cola from the fridge, Xander crossed the room and drew a chair from the table. Settling on the seat, he cracked the can open and sipped slowly this time, clearly savoring every drop.

"You will get more soda," he commanded.

Blinking, eyebrows lifted at his imperious order,

she turned away long enough to scoop the last of the eggs from the skillet and then confronted him. "What's the magic word?"

His scowl came, swift and dark.

"You want soda? You ask nicely."

His eyes narrowed, but then his gaze dropped to the can in his hand. Dear heavens, it wasn't as if she'd asked him to chew broken glass. And yet that was exactly how he was acting.

"Please."

Yep. Broken glass. In every letter.

Clutching a fist to her chest, she gasped and grabbed the back of a chair, pretending to stagger. "Would you look at that? The demon used good manners. And he didn't explode gooey green stuff all over my kitchen."

He did not look amused.

Grinning, Kyanna began carrying everything to the table. "Would you like any of this?"

He stared for a long, dubious moment at the platter of eggs. Finally, Xander nudged his plate toward her with the backs of his knuckles. She scrapped a large helping onto the plate, added a few slices of bacon, and some toast. And then she stood there, staring at him. Waiting.

He stared right back.

She arched an eyebrow, pursing her lips. When he didn't respond, she prompted, "Thank you?"

"You're welcome." His bland expression couldn't mask the sarcasm in his tone. He forked up a mouthful of eggs, offering a short grunt of what she could, at best, assume was approval.

Amused despite herself, she took a seat and dished

up her own plate. She could have been eating cardboard, however, for all the good it was doing her. Her attention kept drifting to his naked chest.

Conversation. Make conversation.

But what did one talk about with one's prisoner?

"So, tell me about Heaven."

His expression went completely blank, all but for the raw longing swirling in the deep gray depths.

"You miss it, huh?"

"Obviously."

Good morning, ladies and gentlemen. For your breakfast entertainment, allow me to present Captain Sarcasm.

"What's it like there?"

"Quiet," he instantly shot back. Then he drew a deep breath, and it seemed his attention turned inward. "Soothing. Solitary."

Now it was Kyanna's turn to frown. *Solitary?*

"And what's Hell like?"

"Hot."

Encore, Captain Sarcasm. Please hold your applause, folks. He'll be here…indefinitely.

Before she could press for more details, however, he surprised her, offering, "Crowded. Loud. The smell of brimstone sears your nose."

Hmm. So Xander preferred peace and quiet. She was slowly learning more and more about him. She just had to read between the lines.

"How long have you been—?"

He shoveled in another huge forkful of eggs and waited.

"Penitent? Is that the correct word?"

A terse nod of his head was her only answer.

"Well?" *Why won't he look at me?*

"Almost two hundred years." Bacon followed the eggs. She stared as he inhaled the food on his plate. Demon had a healthy appetite. Which begged the question, were all his appetites so healthy?

Focus, Ky!

"Two hundred years," she echoed. "And you've fought other demons the whole time, put yourself in harm's way like last night to save humans? Done all this in hopes of being forgiven and returned to Heaven?"

Again with the terse nod. "I have sworn to uphold good and battle evil wherever I find it. I renounce sins of the flesh and sins of the soul."

Renounce sins of the flesh and sins of the soul?

That sounded so…monkish.

Wait. Was that what he had decided a portion of his penance should be? Living the life of a monk? A celibate monk?

She watched him devour his food and scoop more from the pan onto his plate, recalling her earlier musings about *all* his appetites.

Two hundred years' worth of suppressed appetites?

Had the central air in here broken down? She barely stifled the urge to fan herself.

No. Surely, she had to be wrong. A beyond-attractive guy like him? Celibate? The idea was too far-fetched to even lend credence.

Kyanna cleared her throat. "So what else do you do, you know, in between demon battles?"

He glanced up and frowned, clearly puzzled.

"Come on, you gotta have some down time, right?" She took a sip of coffee. Black with three teaspoons of sugar. Sweet perfection on her tongue. "What do you do? Watch TV? Read?" She couldn't possibly be right about the whole celibate thing. And then an unsettling thought occurred to her. Would there be an angry demoness banging on her door soon? That possibility bothered her far more than it should, for all the wrong reasons. "Should I be on the lookout for one of your demon buddies to come looking for you? Or a girlfriend? Demoness or otherwise?"

A long moment passed, in which he began stirring the food around on his plate. A troubled frown darkened his brow. "I read."

Such a font of information! Do I really need to resort to thumbscrews?

"Okay, what do you read?"

"Scripture."

"And…"

"That is all."

"No TV?"

He shook his head.

"And no girlfriend?" So, she was being nosy. And maybe a bit obvious, considering the way he looked at her just then. She was just too surprised to care. At least that was the story she was going to go with.

Again, the shake of his head. This time, he pushed his nearly empty plate away and downed the rest of his cola in one long gulp. "I am penitent."

Okay, she couldn't stand the suspense a moment longer. "Are you saying you've been celibate all this time? As in like a monk celibate?"

Oh, why couldn't she get past that?

A muscle leaped in his jaw, but he nodded. Once.

"Two hundred years celibate?" She couldn't help

it. She stared, her mouth hanging open. He stared right back. Grim.

Just as she finally managed to gather her scattered wits, began to ask him…well, she wasn't sure what her next question would be, the door to her apartment burst open.

Summer's voice filled the air, contorted in a poor imitation of one of her favorite old black and white TV shows. "Lucy, I'm home!"

Chapter Eleven

Xander's instincts went into battle mode, every ounce of his focus on the woman who'd just entered Kyanna's apartment as if she owned the place. Vivid red hair was tugged up in short pigtails. Bright freckles dusted her alabaster skin. He hadn't seen clothing like that since hippies had roamed the streets flying peace signs and preaching brotherly love.

Instinctively, he pushed to his feet. Tense. Alert. Ready to attack. Kyanna sprang up between them. Hands held out, palms facing him. At the same moment, the woman dropped the bags she'd been holding on the end of the sofa and pivoted to stare.

"Holy sex-on-a-stick!" Summer leered at Xander, making him want to climb right back into the shower, cold water or not.

"What are you doing, Summer? I told you I'd meet you down stairs. Why didn't you call?"

"Had to see what you were hiding away up here, Ky." Summer stepped farther into the apartment, her gaze never leaving Xander. Not even to blink. "Va-va-voom! Gotta say, if this is what's been keeping you holed up in here all this time, you have my whole-hearted approval!"

"Did you bring the clothes?" Kyanna frowned at him warily. She hurried across the room to dig in the shopping bags.

"Yeah, yeah." Summer waved an idle hand over her shoulder. Extending her free hand to Xander, she beamed a sunny smile. "I'm Kyanna's oh-so-envious friend, Summer Thomas. It's a pleasure to meet you. And you are?"

Xander ignored her offered hand. He made it a habit of not interacting with humans any more than strictly necessary. Which was to say, not at all. He had no interest in touching this woman's hand. Or any other part of her.

Now if Kyanna were the one offering a body part—

Kyanna had begun to sort through the packages. But she realized how close Summer was standing to him, and she froze. Xander could all but read her mind. She may as well have posted a neon sign.

Imminent hostage situation.

Before Kyanna could come racing to the rescue, Xander folded his arms and scowled at the intruder. "I am Xander."

She blinked. One hand lifting to cup her throat.

Kyanna bolted across the room anyway, carting all the bags in her fists. "Here." She shoved them against his chest. "You can get dressed in my room. Just pick out whatever you like."

Kyanna latched on to his wrist and tugged, only to be drawn up short when he refused to budge. She turned a beseeching gaze on him. His lips compressed. Two could play at that game.

"Please," she whispered.

Satisfied he'd made his point, he allowed her to lead him away. She all but dragged him across the room and shoved him inside the first open doorway. But before she could slip away, he grabbed her elbow and hauled her into the room and up against him. Well out of sight of the human in Kyanna's kitchen.

"I told you, I protect the innocent," he grated. "I don't use them as hostages."

Her eyes widened, lips parted. "I didn't—"

"Yes, you did. It was written all over your face." Her reaction had offended him. And that he was offended by her reaction baffled him.

The Slayer didn't give a flying rat's rear end what anyone thought of him.

A long, pregnant moment passed. Slowly, he became aware of several things. The darker, sapphire ring around the paler inner circle of blue in her eyes. The thickness of her eyelashes. The curve of her cheek. The silken texture of her skin beneath his fingertips. The lush attraction of her lips. Lips so very close to his own. And the decadence of her body fitted against his.

The air around them grew heavy. The warmth of her drew him closer.

She was the one lure he couldn't seem to resist.

Snapping his head back, he released her with a low growl. Kyanna stared up at him for a long moment. Blinking rapidly, she finally stepped away. Without a word, she pivoted and left the room. The door slammed behind her. Heaving a sigh, Xander clenched his fist and gritted his teeth. He studied the room, plastic bags crushed under his arm. The scent of Kyanna was strongest here. It settled in the pit of his stomach, a hot aching pool of need.

This wasn't going to work. He needed to get out of here before he did something really stupid. Like throw two hundred years of penance out the window.

Desperate for something to distract him, he peered around the room. Although the curtains and the comforter matched, they were not overly fussy. Tranquil garden scenes had been matted and framed and hung on the sage colored walls at strategic points. The dressers, heavy dark oak, were clearly antiques and free of clutter. The bed was large, with a massive, intricately carved matching headboard. And, as with the rest of her apartment, everything was neat as a pin.

Dumping the bags on the bed, he drew a deep breath, closed his eyes as a strange longing filled him. Images battered at him. The long lengths of Kyanna's spun gold hair spread out upon her pillow as she slept, curled against his flesh. Pale moonlight streaming across her glowing flesh. Her warm limbs entangled with his. Her deep, even breathing—the only sound in the room—soft upon his skin.

A gentle oasis in the middle of a brutal, bloody war. Contentment as he'd never known. Not even as an angel in Heaven.

Shaking himself free of those useless, detrimental thoughts, he upended the bags and began picking through the offerings. He needed to convince Kyanna—the human—he needed to convince *the human* to hand over the relic and then get the hell out of here.

Head in the game, Slayer.

****

Summer propped her fists on her hips. "You've been holding out on me."

"It's not what you think." Kyanna pushed a stray lock of hair behind her ear and set to work gathering the remnants of breakfast. She carted it all to the kitchen counter.

“Sure it isn’t.” Summer dropped onto the chair Kyanna had vacated earlier and picked up Kyanna’s coffee cup. She took a sip and grimaced before setting the cup back down. “Tell that to the bags under your eyes, Ky. You look like he kept you up all night long.” Summer’s eyebrows did a limber tango.

She refused to rise to the bait. Kyanna balanced plates and glasses in her hands, then dumped the works in the sink before returning to the table with a warm, soapy washcloth. “Thank you for bringing the clothing. How much do I owe you?”

“Big. Huge. You can start with answers.” Propping her elbows on the freshly scrubbed table, Summer turned a rapt gaze on Kyanna as she loaded the dish washer. “Where did you meet tall, dark, and hunkalicious? What does he do for a living? I bet he’s a firefighter. He has to be, ’cause that boy is smokin’ hot.” Again with the eyebrow wiggle.

“How about I give you a call later?”

“Uh-uh.” Summer leaned back in her seat. A gamine smile easing on to her lips. “I want deets, girl. Dish!”

Man, she was tired all of a sudden. “Listen, Summer—”

“He’s good in bed, right? Tell me he’s good. Don’t crush the fantasy.”

“Summer.” She dropped the towel she’d been using to dry her hands onto the counter.

“Oh, man.” Summer snapped her fingers. A fleeting look of disappointment crossed over her features. “I should have bought that vintage ‘*Got Beef*?’ T-shirt. I don’t even care where you found him, ’cuz that is one grade A, prime piece of—”

"Summer!"

"What a great way to break the old dry spell, Ky. Talk about getting back in the saddle. Ride 'em, cowgirl. And here I've been so worried about you closeting yourself away like a nun. I mean, Jack was never one to kiss and tell, and you can tell when a guy isn't getting any, which obviously he wasn't. But he wanted it. Bad. Still does, from what I can tell."

A loud thump sounded from the bedroom. A muffled curse. Oh, lord, he was probably listening to every word.

"Summer!" Shooting a horrified glance at the closed bedroom door, Kyanna tugged her friend up from the chair and all but stiff-armed her toward the exit.

"Oh, I get it," Summer stage-whispered. She stopped at the couch to snatch up her purse before patting Kyanna on the shoulder. "I'll lock up on my way out. Have fun! And don't worry. I took care of everything."

With those enigmatic words, and a sassy wink, Summer slipped from the apartment.

Frowning, Kyanna closed the door behind her. She turned and leaned back, her palms pressed to the door behind her. Sometimes dealing with Summer was exhausting. Shaking her head, she drew a deep breath and straightened. Then she caught sight of Xander, and froze. The bottom of her stomach fell away.

Xander stood in the doorway of her bedroom. A plain white V-necked T-shirt stretched taut across sculpted muscles, his golden skin glowing against the stark white. Dark jeans fit him in all the right places, as if tailor made for him. His hair had dried. Auburn highlights glinted in the already forming stubble on his jaw. A small, blue cellophane covered box rested on his open palm.

His questioning gaze lifted to her as she approached him. And, as she crossed the room, she got a good look at the box. Printed across the front in bold white lettering was the brand name of a well-known condom manufacturer. She nearly tripped, almost swallowed her tongue.

"Oh God!" Kyanna bolted forward and snatched the box of condoms from his hands before thrusting it behind her back. Fire raced from her neck upward, engulfing her face.

Filterless Summer, score one million and two.

"Why did your friend bring—"

"Just forget them, okay?" Kyanna hurried across the room and blindly shoved them into the first cupboard she came to.

"I do not believe those belong in the—"

"Please, just don't go there!" Spinning around, she caught the faintest twitch at the corner of his mouth, right before his bottom lip flattened.

Solemn, he inclined his head. "As you wish."

Flustered, Kyanna surveyed the kitchen. Everything had been put away, cleaned up, wiped down. Satisfied, she turned on the dishwasher and marched toward the stairs. At the doorway, however, she turned to him. He'd remained in the entrance to her bedroom. Unmoving. Wrestling with her choices, she considered him. He could have used Summer as leverage, demanding his release. Could have tortured her friend to force her hand, killed her even. But he hadn't, insisting once again that he was a protector, not a predator.

She considered the closed, protected second bedroom. Trust him up here? Alone? Unsupervised? Or take him downstairs with her? Into the shop?

With customers?

He hadn't hurt Summer.

Actions speak louder than words, Ky.

She licked her lower lip and caught it between her teeth as she made up her mind. "It's nearly time to open the store. Will you come downstairs with me, please?"

His expression grew frosty and he stiffened. "I will not be locked in the office."

"No, I won't lock you up again." Folding her hands before her, she waited. And she watched him. As he watched her.

Xander finally crossed the room, regal and uncompromising. She let out the breath she hadn't realized she'd been holding. Feeling as if they'd come to some tentative truce, she led him down the steps.

He followed her to the front of the store, where she flipped the closed sign over, turned the big florescent overhead lights on, and snicked the deadbolt open. Xander glanced around, taking in her store for the first time. Though his expression was as meticulously inscrutable as always, tiny tells gave away his puzzlement. Microscopic lines etched the creases of his eyes. His lips had compressed, and his right eyebrow dipped so slightly it was barely noticeable. She tried to see the store from his perspective.

Her business. Every bit of space was taken, filled with knickknacks and doodads. Treasured plate sets. Lovingly polished silver services. Aged pieces of furniture and more. All of it precisely arranged to the most advantageous display. Orderly and neat. At first, watching him wander around the store, studying this, skimming over that, had been nerve wracking. But when he kept his hands safely at his sides, looking but not touching, she relaxed a bit.

Kyanna seated herself behind the long counter, turned on the adding machine, and pulled out her bookwork. But no matter how hard she tried to concentrate, she couldn't force her attention far from Xander. Suddenly he reached out for something—she couldn't tell what—and he picked up the object of his interest. She tensed, ready to caution him, but then thought better of it. Instead, she got up, skirted the counter, and quietly approached him. What could compel Xander, the king of emotionally distant demons, to be so curious about something that he had to have a closer look at it?

Stepping close, she peered at the object cradled so carefully in the palm of his hand.

"Ah, the Jesus and Mary porcelain figurine. Circa 1900. It's inspiring, isn't it?"

"It's chipped," he noted.

"Yes, but still inspiring."

He harrumphed but set the figurine down with all due respect before moving on. She trailed in his wake, absently noting a bit of dust. A smudge of tarnish. Things she mentally filed away, things that would need to be seen to, even as she made note of the objects that drew his regard. At length he stopped once more, lifting a fragile bone china teacup adorned with pink flowers, holding it up in the light.

"Why are you scowling?"

"Why do you choose to sell this old junk?"

Now she was the one scowling. Sternly but gently, she claimed the teacup from him and returned it to its display. "It isn't junk."

Stiffly, she turned on her heel, intent on ignoring him. But his voice stopped her. "What good is it? All old. All worn. In this day and age, why would someone want this stuff when they could simply buy new? After all, isn't that the saying? New and improved?"

Turning back to face him, she regarded him warily. He was so cynical. "New doesn't always mean improved."

By his finely arched brow, he begged to differ. His expression was just shy of a sneer. Suddenly, he turned to peer down at her. As if he'd had one of those *ah-ha!* moments. As if she were a puzzle and he'd just found a missing piece. "You're sentimental."

"Perhaps." She picked up another small figurine. This one crystal. A dancing bear. Kyanna traced her thumb fondly over the soft etching, the quaint lines. "Each object here was once someone's treasure. Someone held this once. Treasured it. Took care of it and passed it on to the next generation." Suddenly it was important to her that he understand. Vital that he do so.

Xander was obviously unconvinced. He crossed his arms. His face remained impassive. But his eyes…they were locked on her face as he drank in her words. Absorbed them. Weighed them.

"Holding this, touching it? It's like holding a piece of someone's life, a piece of their memories," she pressed. "Was this a Christmas gift once? A token of someone's love? A family heirloom? These were all important to someone once upon a time. They meant something, to someone."

Still he remained quiet. Unmoved.

Frustrated, she set the bear aside. Nudged it back into place with a crooked knuckle. "Each innocent you save, each soul you spare? They are important to someone as well. Cherished. Beloved. Right?"

He rolled one shoulder in an unconcerned shrug. "It's not my problem. I prevent their death at another demon's hands. They live another day. End of story."

"But don't you see? That's not the end of the story. Did you just save a father? A sister? A son? Someone's friend? What will he or she do when they wake up in the morning? Don't you ever wonder?"

"No."

She blinked at him, uncomprehending. "Don't you ever think about the lives you save? What that person is doing? If they've changed somehow, altered their priorities because they got a second chance at life? Did they go out and do something nice for someone else? A kind of pay-it-forward thing?"

"Their life was saved. What they do with it isn't my problem."

"And yet you save these souls in hopes of what? Forgiveness? The chance to return to Heaven?"

He nodded.

"I would say that I don't understand," she said quietly, her bleak gaze searching his features. "But maybe it would be more accurate to say that you don't."

With a disappointed shake of her head, Kyanna returned to her accounting books, refusing to glance his way again. How could someone as old, as worldly as Xander be so dense? So closed off? So pessimistic?

Her mind raced as she stared blindly at balances

and figures. Why was Xander so content with feeling nothing for those he saved? Where was his compassion? As with any challenge, Kyanna set to picking the conundrum apart. Pecking away at it until she found the threads of understanding.

No, her question wasn't correct. He felt. She was certain of that. She'd caught fleeting glimpses of emotion lurking in the sullen, stormy depths of his gray eyes, though he was ever diligent at masking those emotions. Pretending they didn't exist.

Perhaps the better question would be, why he was so bent on keeping such distance between himself and everyone else? What was his motive? Obviously he wanted to return to Heaven, or he wouldn't have fought his nature, wouldn't have turned his back on what was surely *the easy way*. Lucifer's way. What had he to gain?

She'd seen, first hand, the shape he'd been in after that demon battle in the alley. She could only assume that was a regular occurrence for him. How could he choose that way of life, how could he sacrifice so much of himself to save the human race, and yet go out of his way to never know those he'd spared. This made no sense to her.

She idly twirled a pen between her fingers, clicked it in, out, in, chewed on the end. Kyanna had always believed everything happened for a reason. Why would fate—or God—drop this demon in her lap, so to speak? He was prickly. Sullen. Domineering. Insensitive and withdrawn. What could she possibly learn from him?

The pen stilled in her hand, and she sought him out. Assessed him as he bent over, peering at a crystal vase.

Am I meant to be the teacher?

All these years, her family had been keeper of the book. Raised to be aware of this other world. Perhaps there had been a reason. Maybe it had all led up to this moment. Maybe this was the reason her family was so different.

Has he been sent to learn from me?

The small bell over the door tinkled. Glancing up, mildly irritated at her thoughts being interrupted, she pasted on a welcoming smile. Kyanna froze. Talk about bad timing. Inwardly groaning, she slid from her chair and hurried to intercept the tall blond.

Catching sight of her, Jack pulled a massive spray of flowers from behind his back and grinned. Surprised, embarrassed, she winced. What was he doing here? She'd made it abundantly, painfully clear that they were through. That there would never be another chance for them. She refused to put him at risk any longer. How hard did he have to make this on himself?

How hard did he have to make it on her?

"I know you said I shouldn't come back, honey." He laid the flowers on the counter at her side. "But I just can't stop thinking about you."

"Jack—"

"Hear me out now." He held his hands up. "We could be good together. I know it. Hell, we were good together. I don't know what happened. I don't understand why you called it quits, baby." He stepped closer, reaching out to slip his arm around her waist, his obvious intent to haul her into his arms, and into his kiss. A classic Jack move if ever there was one. "Give us one more chance and—"

"Touch her, and you'll pray for death."

Jack stilled. Kyanna swung her head around to stare at Xander. She hadn't heard him approach. And she'd never heard Xander speak in such chilling, menacing tones. Not even when he'd addressed the demon on her doorstep last night. Gulping, she sidled around the counter, placing herself squarely between the two bristling males.

"Xander, don't." She held a hand up behind her to warn him off.

"Who the hell are you?" Jack's angry gaze drilled into Xander, who in turn appeared completely unaffected.

"It doesn't matter who he is," Kyanna quickly inserted before Xander could speak again, no doubt to make some hideous threat. "What matters is that we're over, Jack. Nothing is going to change that. You need to accept that and move on."

"It isn't over." He glowered at her now and closed the distance between them once more, reached for her wrist. "Tell him to get lost so we can talk—"

Before Jack could reach her, however, a forge-hot band of steel wrapped possessively around her waist. Without warning, Xander hauled her unceremoniously back against his granite frame. Feeling suddenly like the tug rope in a grossly unbalanced game of keep-away, Kyanna stiffened. A second band of steel came around her. The hoarse rasp of Xander's voice near her ear cut off any explanation she was likely to give.

"She belongs to me now."

Kyanna's mouth fell open. A delicious shiver went down her spine at his words. She couldn't see his face, but she could feel the steely strength, the raw tension in his body. And then Xander did something so unexpected. He smoothed his cheek over the hair at her temple before pressing a kiss there. His large hands splayed, one over her ribcage, the other on her hip, and he gave her an unmistakable, affectionate squeeze. Effectively locking her in what would appear to anyone as an intimate lover's embrace.

Jack glowered at the two of them. The pain of betrayal upon his face shredded her heart. She may not have truly loved him, but she did care about him. Very much. She didn't want him hurt, not like this. But the bottom line here was that nothing she could say, nothing she could do would make this situation better for either of them. Not without giving him false hope. Jack's mutinous stare locked on Xander's face. Something he saw there made his eyes widen, his face pale. His Adam's apple bobbed, and he nodded his head slightly, just once.

"Leave," Xander grated. "And do not return."

Jack spun on his heel and all but sprinted from the store. As the door closed behind him, Xander released her.

Whirling around, Kyanna clenched her fists at her sides to keep from smacking him. Her body vibrated with indignation. "What the hell was that all about? '*She belongs to me*,'" she mimicked his deep growl. "Why would you say something like that? Why would you humiliate him? Make him believe that you and I— That we've— Now he's going to—"

Gah, she was so mad she was actually sputtering.

"Stay the hell away from you," he barked. "Isn't that what you wanted?"

Seething, she crossed her arms. "Not like that."

"What difference does it make? The result is the

same."

"It makes a lot of difference. But you wouldn't understand that either, would you?" Drawing both hands down the sides of her face, she emitted a low groan of frustration. Then she shook her finger at him. "Just stay out of my business."

He stepped right up to her, towered over her, his face inches from hers. "You are the one keeping me here. Give me the damned relic, and I'm gone."

Chapter Twelve

Two o'clock had never come so slowly. After Xander's blunt demand to hand over the relic, Kyanna had frozen him out with stony silence, retreating to her bookwork in simmering fury. Xander had stomped off to her study and slammed the door behind him. There he had remained. For three hours. Immersed in silence. To make matters worse, it had been a slow day at the store. Aside from Jack, only two other people had ventured inside. Of those two, only one had actually made a purchase, leaving her to stew over the confrontation with Jack, as well as the conclusions she'd drawn prior.

Teacher to a demon? She snorted. How could she have been so egotistical? So narcissistic?

What could I possibly teach him?

Kyanna closed the store down and dragged her feet all the way to the office. A brief internal debate ensued in which her knuckles hovered at the door. With a disgusted grunt that sounded a little too much like something Xander might make—*crap, he's starting to rub off on me*—Kyanna squared her shoulders and opened the door without knocking. It was her office, why should she be the one knocking?

Expecting to find him snoring on the sofa, she blinked in surprise. Xander was in the middle of the room, on the floor, on his knees. His head was bent. His eyes were closed. His lips moved silently and his hands were loosely clasped in his lap.

He's praying. Brought up short, she stared. Has he been here like this, praying the whole time?

Oddly touched, she cleared her throat. "I'm going upstairs now."

His slate gray eyes opened, and he slowly turned to look at her. His expression was as closed off as she'd ever seen it. So distant. A hollow ache unfurled deep in her chest. An ache far more unsettling than the one she'd experienced when Jack had looked at her as if she'd stabbed him in the back.

"Come up if you like." Without further comment, she turned and made her way upstairs, leaving the doors open behind her. That was the only concession she was willing to make. She was still sore at him over the way he'd behaved with Jack.

Barbaric, high-handed jerk.

And yet the sight of him kneeling in prayer had moved her, despite her anger.

Kyanna nibbled her thumbnail as she crossed the apartment, went to the fridge, and opened the door. In a way, he had been right. She was the one holding him here. Against his will. She'd brought him down to the store. She'd inadvertently made him privy to her conversation—disaster that it had been—with Jack.

That Xander had reacted the way he had certainly hadn't soothed the situation. He'd humiliated Jack. On purpose. So that was a mark against him. But considering Xander's social skills, or lack thereof, she was lucky he'd chosen humiliation over some other tact. Like, say, evisceration. Or frying.

Damn it, she was just as much to blame for what

had happened as he was. And she hated being wrong.

What's more, he could have come charging out of the office at any time, could have made one of her customers a prisoner, used them to force her hand. But he hadn't.

Actions speak louder than words.

Bottom line? Despite his poor social skills, he'd continued to behave nobly. Time and time again.

Dropping her forehead against the freezer door, she groaned. Xander had done nothing to support any of the accusations in the book. Nothing to merit the extreme caution levied against him.

Oh sure. She was certain that at one point or other, probably for millennia untold, he'd been a scourge upon the Earth. Even he hadn't denied it. But he'd also stated that he'd changed, was working toward redeeming himself. She'd seen it with her own eyes, though she could hardly lend credence to it. And, to the best of her knowledge, he hadn't lied to her.

Granted his methods might be a little...misguided at times. But he was trying.

So who was the real villain here?

In short order, she organized on the counter an array of fresh fruit and the makings for sandwiches. Feeling off balance, she prepped a sandwich for herself, hesitated, and then made one for her unwilling—*undeserving?*—houseguest. She'd just begun to run water over the grapes when the heavy thunk of his boots echoed up the steps. Hypersensitive to the tension in the room, she kept her focus on her work as she added the grapes to the strawberries, sliced bananas, and chunks of fresh pineapple that already filled two bowls.

A chair at the table scraped back as she was cleaning the counter off. Without looking at him, she gently placed the sandwich plate and the bowl of fruit before him. Silent, she carried her own to the table, set them down. She returned to the fridge one last time and poured herself a glass of iced tea. And all the while, she mentally castigated herself for procrastinating. As she returned the tea jar to the fridge, she spied the last can of soda.

Kyanna's pursed lips slid to the side.

"I'm sorry for snapping at you." She put the can on the table at his elbow. Kyanna paused, drew a deep breath, and took the chair across from him. Still, she couldn't look him in the eye. "It was a difficult situation all the way around."

"Your boyfriend has been dealt with."

"Why do you say it like that?" Her gaze snapped to his. She could literally feel her temper beginning to simmer anew. Kyanna gritted her teeth and ruthlessly tamped it down. "*Boy*friend. He isn't a child." She took a sip of tea, more to have something to do with her hands than because she was thirsty. "And he isn't my boyfriend."

"Not anymore," came the snide remark.

"It's over. Just let it go, all right?"

Xander grunted as he picked up his sandwich. Took a healthy bite. Washed it down with a big gulp of soda. Lifting a dubious brow, he used his fork to poke at the fruit. "Why would you choose to be with someone like that anyway?"

Kyanna nearly choked on a half-chewed chunk of pineapple. Eyes watering, she hastily took a drink. Clearing her throat, she reminded herself to have patience. "Like what?"

"Such a…" Xander paused, as if searching for the appropriate word, and then settled for, "Wuss." He tossed a shoulder, his expression markedly bored.

Yet he'd asked the question.

She was slowly beginning to pick up on his little tells. Like the way the corners of his eyes crinkled, just the tiniest bit when he was curious about something. Or the way his lower lip flattened, as if he were chewing on the inside of it, whenever he found something humorous but was behaving all "me-big-bad-demon-too-mean-to-smile."

"Jack is not a wuss."

Xander stared at her. Deadpan.

How could he argue without saying a blasted word?

"Jack is compassionate. Caring and intelligent and…why am I bothering to defend him?"

"Indeed." Xander forked up a strawberry.

Setting her fork aside, she regarded him with a frown. "Why do you equate compassion with weakness?"

"Compassion has nothing to do with it. The male obviously wants you for his mate. And yet he put up no fight for you. He did not challenge me when I laid claim to you. He ran from the fight with his tail between his legs. He is a coward. He is unworthy of you."

Kyanna leaned back in her chair, nonplussed. Had that been a backhanded compliment? Or just one more jab at Jack?

"Maybe he was respecting my wishes. Respecting the fact that the relationship truly is over."

“Wuss,” Xander growled around a mouth full of ham and provolone.

Straining for patience, Kyanna folded her hands in her lap. Okay, so maybe it was more like fisting them, but at least she wasn’t yelling.

Woohoo. Points for her.

“Why do you keep saying that? He was respecting my wishes.”

After taking another long draw of soda, he cleared his throat. Was that a fleeting grimace of pain? And something finally occurred to her. The longer he spoke, the more strained his voice became. She should have picked up on that before. He also hadn’t answered her before when she’d asked why his voice was like that. Did his throat actually physically hurt him?

“It obviously wasn’t over for him. Yet he let you dictate to him, let you decide the relationship was over.”

“That’s the way things are done here in my world,” she replied, exasperated. “It’s the civilized thing to do when one partner decides a relationship is no longer viable.”

“Civilized.” He sneered. “More like convenient. Temporary relationships.” Pushing his empty plate away as if the conversation had caused him to lose his appetite, he regarded her in a way that made her want to squirm. Want to get up and pace. Anything to alleviate the tightness in her chest. “God meant for relationships to be permanent. Enduring. In *my* world, males pursue what they want. And once they won their mates affection, they work to keep it. They protect what belongs to them, they’d fight to the death for it. They don’t meekly let their females walk away if she grows weary or bored. He finds a way to keep her happy. He works harder to keep her interested."

"So you're saying, in your world, if you pursued a female and claimed her, that you would hold on to her? Would refuse to let her go, regardless of her wishes?"

He gave a terse nod, his gaze fever bright. "She would have no *cause* to want to leave."

"In your opinion."

His response was a very male grunt.

"Do demons even have mates?"

"Yes." He eyed her suspiciously. "Some do."

"And do they share your views?"

"Any demon, no matter the species, would sooner die than be parted from his female."

How utterly archaic!

And yet, oddly enough, something about his opinion excited her. She'd been raised in a single parent household; her own father having disappeared before she'd been old enough to have formed any lasting impressions of him. Whenever she'd asked about him, her mom had always gotten this sad, far-away look and changed the subject. Over the years, Sheila Hughes had had a cursory date here or there. Shadowy figures with no name, no face in Kyanna's memory. But she'd never, ever brought anyone home to meet Kyanna.

Maybe, subconsciously, Kyanna had modeled her own life after her mother's. Shallow dating. Temporary, just as Xander had accused. Convenient.

Never long lasting.

Maybe she wasn't any better than Xander. Socially stunted. Crossing her arms, she frowned at her plate. That wasn't right. She had lots of—

Acquaintances.

She had lots of acquaintances. Even a few close acquaintances. But none who truly knew all there was to know about her. If it weren't for a very select few, Kyanna would have relatively no real, meaningful relationships in her life at all now.

She studied him. And she made up her mind. If her eyes were to be opened to the sad state of her existence, well, then, so were his. It was high time he met some of the humans he put his life on the line every day to save. Time he learned that every soul he rescued had a face and a name. A personality and life. That the good he did had long reaching consequences. And she was just the one to show him. Perhaps this was what she'd always been meant to do, to show Xander—a demon—the personal side of humanity. But to do that, she must take him out into the community. A long-ingrained part of her revolted at the idea. Taking a demon into an innocent population.

But this was no ordinary demon. This was Xander.

How best to proceed, when he obviously went well out of his way to avoid interacting with humans?

Clearing the table, she silently mulled this latest predicament over. Xander had left the room and was, even now, wandering her apartment. Prowling it like the caged predator he was. When she finished with the kitchen, without saying anything, she picked her purse up from the counter, took her car keys down from the peg.

In a flash, he stood before her, blocking the apartment's doorway. "Where do you think you're going?"

"I have errands."

"You do not leave this building without me," he

commanded imperiously. Direfully.

She offered him a loaded smile. “I was hoping you’d say that.”

****

Stolas brushed ash from his chair, calmly took a seat, and waved a hand toward the chair at the other end of his table. Agares, hands clasped behind his back, his expression wary, nodded and crossed the hall. He flipped his long, red dreadlocks over his shoulder and sat.

“To what do I owe the pleasure of your unexpected invitation?” Agares nodded to the Charocté hovering nearby, granting the servant permission to fill his goblet. As soon as the servant was finished, he bowed, backed away, and then vanished.

Instead of addressing Agares, Stolas turned his deadened stare to Dimiezlo. “You are excused.”

Head bowed, the minion thwapped his fists to his shoulders and he, too, disappeared.

One of Agares’s finely arched brows rose. “Doesn’t he belong to Ronové?”

Pointedly ignoring the question, drumming his claws upon the table, Stolas leaned back to survey his guest. Agares displayed a good bit of discretion, staring blandly back, showing none of the burning questions that must be bouncing around inside his head.

“As to your earlier question, you are a duke. Nobility. A distant cousin, if you will. Why should I not invite you into my hall?”

“You have not done so in all these millennia. What has changed?”

He stared long and hard at the demon before him. He’d followed Agares’s work from afar, kept tabs on him as he did with many others. Gauging his loyalty to Lucifer, and his discontent. Noted his successes. Analyzed his failures, and those were few and far between.

Stolas spun a slim metallic device on the table before him. Attached to the contraption were long cords that ended in little spongy bumps. Bumps that, when the metallic device was activated, emitted the most interesting sounds. This—and others just like it—numbered among his favorite offerings. Unfortunately, device, he'd sadly discovered, only worked for a certain length of time. And then it would simply stop making the sounds. Music, he belatedly remembered it was called. It would stop creating the music. So far, he'd not been able to figure out why they'd stopped working. He'd torn one apart once, but the inner workings baffled him, one tiny component looking too much like all the rest. He'd been forced to rely on luck that one of his minions would stumble upon another of it's kind and bring it back to him.

His attention lingered on the small pile on the table on the dais. So far, his luck was holding. Soon, he hoped, he'd be able to obtain music-makers for himself someday, rather than being forced to rely on his minions for the luxury.

"What is that thing? I'd heard rumors you amuse yourself with earthen objects." Agares's expression finished the rest of his thoughts for him. Clearly, he hadn't believed the rumor. Clearly, he could not fathom the attraction, found it distasteful.

"I did not—" He'd been about to say *summon*, until he recalled with whom he spoke. This was no lowly servant, not some uncivilized mercenary. Agares was nobility. Nearly—but not quite—his equal, and so he politely amended. "*Request* your presence to discuss my collection."

"Why then?"

"I, too, have heard rumors, Agares."

Agares tensed in his seat.

"Rumors of unrest." He watched Agares shift in his seat, savored the other demon's discomfort. Fed off his poorly concealed panic. "Rumors of rebellion."

"Your grandfather—"

"Is not privy to my sources." He paused for a long, meaningful moment. "Or my information."

Agares frowned.

Good. Keep him guessing.

"What if I told you there were others interested in a new regime?" He tested the waters, deliberately stirring the pot.

"Lucifer is invincible. His reign unchallenged since the Great Battle."

"What if I told you Lucifer can, in fact, be defeated?"

"You speak of sedition." Interest had definitely sparked to life in Agares's eyes, but he accused, "Is this some kind of trick? Some trap set up by the Dark Prince to ferret out dissidence?"

"You will not find Scathé lurking in my hall," he snapped, referring to Lucifer's personal guard. "I speak of the Prophesy."

"Myth," his guest jeered, leaning back in his seat. And yet he remained alert. Watchful.

"Fact," he countered, pleased when Agares's nostrils flared and the muscle along his jaw began to tick.

“There is no proof to those old rumors—”

“The Guardian of the scrolls has been located.” He leaned back in his seat, steepling his fingers before him. “Whomsoever controls the relics will defeat the Dark Prince.”

“Located.” Agares settled more comfortably in his chair, crossing his arms. “But not recovered.”

“Simply a matter of time.”

Agares scoffed, toying with the stem of his chalice.

And then he dropped the bomb. “The Sword of Kathnesh is already in my possession.”

Agares’s gaze shot to Stolas’s face, his expression cold, calculating. His head tilted to the side. “Tell me of these relics.”

Chapter Thirteen

Ducking her head to hide her smile, Kyanna tossed the plastic sack into the trunk of the sedan beside the four cases of soda Xander had insisted on buying. She really hadn't needed to make quite so many stops. But the look on Xander's face throughout the afternoon at each new person she'd introduced him to, had been too comical to forgo. Though, admittedly, this last stop may have pushed him a bit too far. By the time they'd hit the checkouts, there was no doubt he was more than a little overwhelmed. Perspiration had beaded his forehead, and his darting gaze had gone glassy. Even leaving his supposed "relic" behind, unprotected by anything other than her paltry angelic enchantments, hadn't elicited this level of anxiety.

He stood beside her now, stalwart and alert, as she unloaded the shopping cart. As if every vehicle in the parking lot that roared to life intended to mow her down. As if every customer that poured from the store's sliding glass doors might be a demon in disguise, come to slaughter her and steal away his precious relic if he should have even one moment of inattentiveness.

She'd been so sure that Gina Taylor's six-year-old twins would have chipped away at a little of the ice around Xander's emotions. Gina was the local librarian, and while she swore those two little boys could drive a preacher to take up drinking, Kyanna had always had a soft spot for them. She could never resist dropping down to sit "pretzel-legged"—as they called it—on the floor to read with them.

Today's reading selection had been *If You Give A Pig A Pancake*, with Matt nestled in her lap and Mark taking up post hanging from one of her arms. Xander had stood near the window, angled slightly toward her, his legs braced apart, his arms crossed over his chest. She'd caught him watching her and the boys. He'd turned away quickly, but not before she'd seen the way the muscle in his jaw had clenched, or the way his eyes had flickered red for a moment.

Even old Mr. Dobbs at the gas station, with his loose dentures and his knobby cane, couldn't coax a full out smile from Xander. He'd garnered nothing more than that flattened lip. And that man knew more dirty jokes than a cable comedy channel.

"Have you finished yet?" had become Xander's repetitive refrain.

As if on cue, he heaved a gut deep sigh. "Are you finished yet?"

His plaintive question as he glared around the parking lot sounded so put-upon, so tortured, that she very nearly conceded defeat. And that was what it would have been. Defeat, pure and simple. Not once had he shaken a single hand. Not once had he cracked a real smile. Getting him to talk to anyone had been all but impossible. At best, he'd uttered monosyllabic responses, at worst, he'd grunted his answers. He flat out refused to hold a baby. And when eighty-three-year-old Kitty Davis needed help crossing the street and Kyanna had offered the use of Xander's arm?

Well, if looks could actually kill, she'd be pushing

up daisies right about now.

She was forced to stifle a chuckle as she remembered the way Xander had assisted the elderly woman. He was going to have to keep working on that Boy Scout badge. He'd hoisted the old lady up by her armpits, careful to hold her well away from his body. Then he'd stomped across the street and plopped her down on the sidewalk. As soon as her orthopedic soles hit pavement, he spun about and stalked back to Kyanna's side without so much as a by-your-leave, glaring every step of the way.

"One more stop to go." After slamming the trunk closed, she pushed the shopping cart into the corral beside her car.

He didn't groan aloud, and his bland expression never faltered. She had to give him points for that. But then she did a double take. Had his left eyelid just twitched?

No, it couldn't be.

Wait, there it is again.

She'd given him a *nervous tick.* Smothering a nearly uncontrollable jolt of laughter, she motioned for him to get into the car. The twitch in his eyelid seemed to grow stronger. There was something else she had to fight laughing over. His aversion to motor vehicles. He was an immortal. A demon. Fearless and dangerous. And yet he treated her car like a deathtrap. Granted, it wasn't exactly showroom floor new. But it wasn't the instrument of torture he was acting like.

Taking the seat behind the wheel, she glanced over at him. His seatbelt was cinched tight. It had to be cutting off circulation to portions of his body that she had no business contemplating in the first place. He'd braced one hand on the dash, while the other white-knuckled the seat. He bowed his head, and his lips were silently moving.

Praying again. She stifled a disgusted snort.

Really?

Un-freakin'-believable. What a baby!

She might have taken offense about her driving abilities if he hadn't ground out a terse, "Demons do not travel this way, Kyanna. This just isn't natural," when she'd asked him earlier what his problem was.

"How do you travel then?"

He'd simply given her one of his enigmatic stares and remained silent.

Kyanna clicked her own seatbelt into place. Checking her mirrors, she started the car and eased them from the parking stall. Taking pity on him, she laid her hand on his and gently squeezed. He flipped his hand over and caught hers, locking his fingers around her hand like a lifeline. He'd caught her so by surprise, she nearly ran the stop sign. She twisted her hand a bit until she could lace her fingers more comfortably between his. His hand immediately engulfed hers. And he didn't let go. Not until they pulled up in front of the Pizza Parlor.

"We're here." Awkwardly turning off the engine with her left hand, she glanced over at him.

Xander stared at the building in front of them as if shocked they'd made it there in one piece.

"You have to let go of me now," she prompted with a small smile. "But you can hold my hand again once we're out of the car, if you like."

"It is no longer necessary. The automobile had come to a halt."

She blinked, frowning. Had he just insulted her driving after all?

"Why would holding my hand be necessary?"

"If your body had become placed in the way of imminent physical harm, I would have shimmered you from the vehicle."

"Shimmered?"

He stared at her again, silent. She sat back and crossed her arms, determined not to move an inch until he finally answered at least one stinking question.

Popping his jaw, he glared out the window. Lord, he acted as if he were revealing some devastating national secret. "A demon's primary form of travel is shimmering. We focus on a destination—it must be someplace we can either see clearly or have already been—and, using the dark powers within, we can literally will ourselves there."

"Why must it be someplace you've already been, or someplace you can clearly see?"

"Would you want to miscalculate and solidify halfway through a wall? Inside a mountain rather than atop it? Two feet beyond the edge of a cliff?"

Good point.

But really, did he have to make his lack of faith in her driving so obvious? And here she'd been willing to give him the benefit of the doubt.

Without another word—or one of the grunts she was fast becoming familiar with—he climbed from the car. It was almost surprising he didn't turn around and kick the door, for as much loathing as he'd expressed in his own way for the thing. The sidewalk they traversed was lined with small flowering shrubs, each bud a deep purple. Huge windows gleamed in the setting sun. The front of the restaurant was stucco and designed like an Italian villa. A marble cherub pouring water from a bucket in the middle of a rock bed was the centerpiece of the small eating area to the side of the flat-roofed building. Wrought iron bistro sets peppered the mosaic-tiled patio at the side of the building. Nearly every seat was filled.

As Xander opened the door for her, a cacophony of sound flooded over them. Dozens of voices all talking at once, and music playing softly in the background. Something classical and elegant. A symphony of smells hung heavy in the air—garlic and rich tomato sauces and yeasty breads—making her stomach clutch and growl in anticipation.

"Hi, Gerald," Kyanna greeted the tall, thin man behind the counter.

"There ye be, lassie." His heavy Irish brogue was thick tonight, as was often the case when the restaurant was hopping busy. "The missus and I'd begun to worry over the likes o' you. Young Murphy's been asking after you."

Xander took one look around the crowded, noisy, pizza joint, and began backing from the restaurant. She grabbed hold of his arm before he could clear the doorway. His muscles were like tempered steel beneath her fingertips. His entire body tense.

"Sorry," she told Gerald as she tugged him closer to the counter. "We had a few extra stops to make this afternoon."

"You're here now, then. You go on back and I'll have Murphy bake up the usual."

"Better make it a jumbo this time. And toss in an order of breadsticks and two large sodas."

"You got it." He winked, then turned to the long serving window. "Hey, Murphy. Kyanna's here. And she brings with her a date."

Several heads popped up from the surrounding booths. Necks craned to see the man Kyanna had replaced Jack with. Heat rushed to her cheeks, but she brazened it out, smiling as she passed familiar faces as well as a few she didn't recognize. At the back of the restaurant, Kyanna slipped into a darkened booth, one that was shielded for the most part from prying eyes. Xander folded himself into the opposite seat. Setting her purse down on the seat beside her, she pushed the laminated advertiser toward the back of the table.

"So, what do you think of Isle?"

Xander grunted, noncommittal, as he warily scanned the crowd.

"Will you relax and just let yourself have a little fun for a change?"

"To what end?"

"How about fun for the sake of fun?"

Heaving a sigh, determined not to let him ruin her Saturday night tradition, she leaned back when the waitress, a local high schooler, came over to place their drinks and the breadsticks on the table. He sniffed the glass suspiciously as the waitress sashayed away. Took a tentative sip. The miniscule lines around his eyes eased a bit as he gulped down the soda. Funny. She'd done everything she could think of to show him the world he'd worked so hard to save. Exerted every bit of hospitality she'd ever been taught. And had he relaxed? No. Had he loosened up even the slightest?

Not one iota.

Put a soda in front of the guy and watch him

become Mr. Chill.

Well, almost.

Snorting with self-deprecation, she pulled her own glass to her and sipped. When the pizza arrived, Murphy himself was carrying it. Tall, slim, and Irish to the tips of his toes, he was the spitting image of his father. Only with more hair and less paunch.

"So, who's the bounder that's beat me out of a night of fine conversation with the fair Kyanna?" Murphy braced his forearm on the back of Kyanna's booth, crossed his ankles.

His grin was good-natured. His tone joking. But he was unmistakably curious, and more than a bit protective. Next to Summer, Murphy was the only true friend she had. Actually, he'd been like a big brother to her since her first week in town when her old truck had finally given up the good fight three miles from town. He'd been passing by, given her a lift to town, and put her in touch with a friend of a friend who happened to be selling a reliable sedan.

"Murphy, this is my…ah, friend, Xander. Xander, this handsome young devil is Murphy O'Shea." Smiling up at the young man beside her, she offered a fair mimic of his lilting brogue. "'Tis Murphy's fine dream to one day be takin' o'r the family business. Teach these poor Italians the proper way to be makin' a pizza pie."

Murphy chuckled. Xander stared at her, a blank slate. She seriously considered kicking him beneath the table just to see if he'd react.

"How's the car, wee Kyanna?"

"Still running like a top. How's the wife?"

"Still running me ragged." His eyes twinkled.

Kyanna knew for a fact that he loved every moment of it.

"So where be ye from, Xander?"

Xander's cold gaze lifted to Murphy. "Hell."

"Hel—ena," Kyanna rushed to speak over him, shooting him a warning look. "Xander's from Helena."

Murphy gave her a puzzled frown before turning back to Xander. "And what is it that you do in Helena?"

"I kill things," Xander replied solemnly.

"Ah, he's, ah, an exterminator," Kyanna inserted, giving in to the urge to kick him under the table after all.

He didn't jolt. Didn't even snap "ow," like a normal person would. Instead, his stare locked on her. And stayed there.

"Thanks so much for the pizza, Murphy. It smells delicious. I can't wait to dig in." She was babbling now as she began loading plates up for herself and Xander, but she couldn't seem to help it. The way Xander was staring at her, as if he'd like nothing better than to turn her over his knee—or simply incinerate her with one of his plasma balls—was starting to get to her.

"Well, then, I'd best be leavin' ye to it." Dusting his hands on the hips of his apron, he nodded to Xander. "Nice to be meetin' ye, Xander from Helena."

Xander grunted.

"Really?" Kyanna whispered furiously as soon as Murphy was out of earshot. "Could you at least pretend to make an effort? Murphy happens to be a good friend."

"Give me the scrolls and my lack of effort will no longer be your problem," he countered.

Grinding her teeth, she dropped her attention to the

plate in front of her. Somehow, she managed to get two pieces down. But the normally decadent pizza tasted like greasy cardboard in her mouth. Xander, however, didn't seem to be experiencing any difficulties with his appetite. He'd already consumed four of the six breadsticks, just polished off slice number five, and was reaching for number six. Where was he putting it all?

She stared, mesmerized, as he licked sauce from his thumb.

Finally satisfied, Xander pushed his empty plate away. Exasperated, Kyanna motioned to the waitress for the check and a small to-go box. She paid the bill and ushered Xander from the restaurant. As she stowed the leftover pizza in the trunk of the car, she made the mistake of mentioning the ice cream parlor. He had to be full to bursting, but the mere mention of the confection had him craning his neck to scan the street. And yet he didn't utter a sound. God, she was such a sucker. That, or a glutton for punishment.

Fifteen minutes later, armed with a triple-scoop cone, Xander followed her to the end of a vacant dock just off the park. Kyanna sat on the bench, scooted over a bit as Xander joined her. She dipped her spoon into her sundae. Warm, sweet fudge melted across her palate, contrasting perfectly with the cold, vanilla, soft-serve ice cream, and she marveled at how *normal* this felt.

Sitting with Xander by the lake eating ice cream.

Who'd'a thunk it?

Night had begun to close in all around them, but for once it didn't bother her. She didn't let herself dwell too long on that unsettling fact. Moonlight flickered and danced upon the glittering surface of the lake, stirred by the whispering breeze. Waves lapped gently at the shoreline behind them, lulling the senses. Every now and then, a stronger push of wind would shush through the trees a few yards down the shore. But then silence would fall again. No one walked along the beach to disturb the soothing quiet.

For the first time since he'd exploded into her life, Kyanna could actually see the tension melt from Xander's shoulders. Even the silence between them seemed mellow. Comfortable. She finished her sundae, tossed the cup in a nearby receptacle, and then settled back to wait for Xander to finish his cone. As she waited, her eyelids grew heavy.

She woke with a start sometime later, nestled in the warm cocoon of Xander's arms. Her head tucked into the crook of his shoulder, her arm draped across his belly. His chest rose and fell in a smooth rhythm. Xander's strong, steady heartbeat throbbed against her ear. Dear heavens, she was all but sprawled across him. Mortified, she pushed up into a sitting position and shoved the hair from her face.

Oh God. Please don't let me have drooled on him.

Xander's arms fell away from her slowly, as if reluctant to give up their treasure. She blinked up at him, completely at a loss for words. Struggling to school her drowsy thought, Kyanna started when Xander lifted a hand and traced a finger over a lock of hair at her temple. He eased the wayward tendrils behind her ear, but continued to trace the line of her jaw, eventually hooking his curled finger beneath her chin.

Silent, his stare holding her captive, he slowly tilted his head. His warm breath came first, brushing over her lips, teasing her with the scent of strawberry ice cream. And then came the heat. The press of his lips. Smooth and firm. He nipped her lower lip between his. Suckled. Laved his tongue over the inside of her lip. So excruciatingly slow. And then, at last, the long, languid glide of his tongue slipping past her teeth, stroking against hers. Exploring. It was as if he was trying to learn the taste and textures of her mouth, and he had all the time in the universe to do so. She gave herself up to the kiss, to him, and her body melted into his.

His hand drifted down to settle on her hip as his other arm came around her once more, cradling her, drawing her closer as he continued the easy rhythm he'd set in motion. A steady, irresistible seduction of her senses.

She didn't know how long they sat there like that, mouths perfectly mated. It could have been minutes, or an eternity. All she knew was that when he finally drew away, she would have happily sacrificed an appendage, any appendage to continue on kissing him till the sun rose in the east and set once more in the west. Could have, would have kissed him until the Earth stopped spinning.

Because when he kissed her, he was no longer a demon fighting a brutal war. And she was no longer a desperate woman scrambling to protect herself and her family's secrets.

They were just a man and a woman kissing in the moonlight.

Kyanna blinked at him, sucking in a sharp breath. Snapping back to her senses, she blurted, "We should go back now."

But go back to what? Back to her store, her apartment? Or back to the way things were before they'd shared that soul-shaping kissed?

She was adrift. Lost in a sea of confusion.

Xander was no help. He rose, stiff and silent, and followed her along the dock, up the sandy shore, and into the car. The drive to Treasure Box was long and tense. Kyanna guided the sedan down the darkened ally, parked behind her store, and turned the engine off. Xander glanced warily around as they climbed from her battered vehicle. He paused, studying the adjoining building with an odd intensity. Kyanna called his name. Frowning, he joined her at the trunk and loaded himself down with her shopping bags, leaving her only one small sack and the pizza box. He hurried her across the alley.

Quickly dropping the enchantments on the back door, she crossed the threshold, waited until Xander had done the same, and then she whispered the incantations in a rush, experiencing an even greater unease than normal. Something was different now. Was she still dazed over his kiss? Had the dynamics between them altered somehow?

Or was she picking up on some outside factor? Tuning in to the unease radiating from Xander?

He carried her purchases up the apartment steps in silence and deposited them on the table in the kitchen, sat down and watched as she began putting things away. Unable to bear the silence a moment longer, she stopped, a bag of dried pasta in her hand, and stared at him. "You kissed me. Again."

He didn't respond. Didn't blink. But a muscle in his jaw leaped. And the tiny lines at the corners of his eyes crinkled.

So he was just as confused as she was, and he was angry about it. Well, that was just great.

"So, what now? We're not supposed to talk about it? Not supposed to discuss it at all?"

He looked to the package in her hand, then glanced away. He stared at the wine wrack on the top of her fridge. She set the package aside, laid her palms flat on the table, leaned forward and pinned him with an indignant stare.

"Fine. You want to pretend it didn't happen. Go for it. But the least you could have done was acknowledge the people I introduced you to today. I know those people. And while they may not mean anything to you, they mean something to me."

His gaze cut back to her, and this time it was hot. Anger swirled in the turbulent gray depths. His pupils dilated. Throwing her hands up, she shook her head. "And now you're mad. No, now you're furious. I don't get you. For the love of God, say something. Anything!"

"What did you hope to accomplish?" He pushed back from the table, rose to prowl the kitchen.

"I wanted to help you put faces to the lives you save every day. Put names with them. Let you see that you are doing something good, every time you save a soul." Lowering her voice, she approached him, but he drew back. Stiff. Unyielding. "Why are you so afraid to let anybody in, afraid to get to know anyone?"

The look he shot her should have scorched her to her toes. Incinerated her to ash. Probably would have, if she'd cared. But right now, she was just too reckless, too focused on ferreting out his secret.

Saying nothing, he pivoted and began stomping toward the door.

"Xander!"

He came to an abrupt halt, and spun about, scowling. His fists were clenched at his sides. Ridged tension gripped his body. She'd never seen him express any kind of emotion to this extent. Honestly, it was a little bit frightening.

"Where will they all be fifty years from now, Kyanna? A hundred years?"

She blinked, taken aback by the bleak fury in his voice.

"Dust," he finally blurted. "Maybe, if somebody gets really lucky, they'll end up a well-preserved corpse in some museum. The Egyptians did a damned fine job with that art form." He grew hoarser by the moment. Xander stomped back across the room, stopping a few short feet from her. It could just as well have been miles for the chasm she felt opening up between them. "They'll all be dead. You'll be dead. And where will I be? Still alive. Cursed with a bunch of damned memories I don't want. Probably still fighting for something that's never going to damned well happen."

On those fateful words, he whirled about and stormed from the apartment. The door slammed behind him, making her start. His boots pounded down the stairs. A few moments later, the office door downstairs slammed, and she jumped once more. Kyanna slowly lowered herself onto one of the chairs at the table.

She'd been so sure of herself. So confident. Convinced that she could make him a better person, if only she could show him the world he saved. Force him to interact with the souls he protected and conquer his fear of emotional attachment. His fear of emotion, period.

How arrogant could I have been?

His lack of attachment hadn't been that he just didn't care. Hadn't been that he didn't know any better. His emotional distance was a defense mechanism. A way for him to cope with millennia upon millennia of death.

Millennia upon millennia of surviving.

God, she was a sorry fool.

Crossing her arms on the table, she dropped her head to her forearms. Kyanna tried desperately to block the raw anguish in his eyes as he'd spoke of fighting for something that he obviously believed would never happen. She knew in her heart of hearts that he'd been talking about his redemption. That he truly believed he'd never receive forgiveness. Perhaps he thought himself unworthy of it.

And yet, every day he got up and went out and fought to save humankind, asking for nothing in return from the humans he saved.

What have I done?

****

Xander jolted awake. Blinked at the darkness around him. The haunting memory of Kyanna asleep in his arms followed him up from the depths of slumber. A dream. He'd been dreaming about their kiss on the dock.

The floor beneath him shook again, violently. He braced himself on his hands and knees and shook his head to clear his thoughts. A framed document fell from the wall and shattered nearby. A hunk of plaster soon followed. Something loud and heavy crashed overhead.

Plaster dust began to fill the air.

No, that wasn't dust. At least, not all of it. Whiffs of smoke began to burn his eyes, clog his lungs, making breathing a chore. Xander grabbed his jeans and jerked them on, not bothering to button them. Another violent tremor knocked him off his feet. Crawling out into the hallway, he threw an arm up to shield his face from the sparks dancing across the floor. A live wire had ripped loose from some electrical box, showering the area in sparks that were quickly igniting cardboard boxes in the storage area.

The floor stopped shaking, and one goal solidified in his mind. Kyanna. He didn't know what the hell was going on. Didn't know why they were having a damned earthquake in Minnesota. But he had to get to Kyanna. Had to get her to safety.

When he was halfway up the stairs, the ground began to shake once more. A loosened brick crashed to the step behind him. Another hit him on the shoulder. Unfazed, he charged on. Bursting through the door, he scoured the apartment for signs of her. He squinted through the thickening smoke.

"Kyanna," he roared, racing toward her bedroom. "Ky—"

Without warning, he slammed into an invisible wall, was thrown back on his ass. His breath exploded from his lungs in a startled rush.

Damn it! Not another one.

This was the last damned time she'd be putting enchantments and ward stones between them.

The building stopped shaking, and he crawled forward, deciding it might be better for him to remain lower to the floor—beneath the rapidly growing cloud of smoke.

"Kyanna!"

Why isn't she answering?

Her bedroom door was cracked open. Through it, he could see her lying on the floor, her face turned away from the door. Unmoving. A large chunk of plaster rested half on her shoulder, half on the floor. Smaller chunks of plaster littered the floor all around her. Plaster dust covered her hair and back.

His heart skipped a beat, lodging in his throat. No, she wasn't dead. Couldn't be dead. He'd know it if she were. Wouldn't he? He could still feel that odd hum in his veins. Uncertainty, fear as he'd never before experienced, rushed up to choke him.

"Kyanna!" he bellowed. His throat was raw. From yelling? From speaking too much earlier? From the smoke? It didn't matter. He'd bellow until his vocal cords bled, if only she'd answer.

Had her hand moved? Praying, acrid tears streaming from his burning eyes, he scrabbled forward. And was met with resistance once more. She hadn't used the enchantments, thank heaven. He'd never be able to get through those. But she had used ward stones. Powerful ones.

The building began to shake once more. Harder this time. Something in the living room crashed. The microwave fell from the counter in the kitchen. Plates and glasses danced from the cupboards to shatter on the counters, shards rained down on the floor. Massive chunks of ceiling were beginning to fall in every room. Walls were cracking. He had to get to her. Now.

Sweat poured down his spine. Gritting his teeth, he reached one hand into the barrier, forcing himself to stretch for the biggest stone. Shaking from the sheer agony, he bore down on the pain, strained to channel the darkness within him. Darkness that was, even now, dampened by the enchantments surrounding the building. Skin began to bubble on his fingertips. His nails blackened. And then flesh began peeling from bone. And still he reached, roaring now. His whole body shook from the pain. Sweat beaded on his skin. So close. His claws had somehow come out. They scratched across the surface of the stone, barely edging it a fraction of a centimeter.

Just. A. Little. More.

Chapter Fourteen

Giving a gut-deep roar, Xander thrust his hand farther into the barrier. Muscle, tendon, nerves disintegrated. With one last great push, harnessing the evil inside him for added strength, he batted the stone aside, breaking the connection. Chest heaving, he crawled inside the bedroom, straight to her side. His injured hand hung limp near his waist. Useless. Pain ripped through his body, worse than from any other injury he'd ever sustained.

"Kyanna?" His voice was little more than a strained whisper now. He shoved the heavy chunk of ceiling from her and gently turned her over. Xander smoothed the hair from her face with his good hand. "Sweetheart, wake up."

Her eyelids fluttered, and he swore his heart did the same. She roused briefly, blinked, but her pupils were huge, unfocused. And then she lost consciousness once more.

Swearing, he cupped her cheek. "Kyanna, no! You must not go back to sleep. You have to lower the enchantments. Listen to—"

A massive length of crown molding came crashing down near the door. Instinctively, Xander covered her with his body. Pain erupted anew in his hand. Glancing down, he grimaced. His hand had begun to regenerate. He was about to be in for a boatload of agony.

"Kyanna, wake up." Desperate, he shook her. Her head lolled to the side, but did little more than groan. "Kyanna, where are the scrolls? We have to get them and get out of here."

Sweat broke out on his forehead, beaded his upper lip as he scanned the room. Enormous cracks snaked up the walls, exposing electrical wiring, raw studs, and brick. A window shattered, and he dove to cover her again, curling his arm protectively around her head as flying shards sliced at his back.

To hell with this. To hell with the scrolls. Her frail body wouldn't withstand the collapse of this building. Even now, noxious smoke was filling the apartment. He scooped her up just as the floor leveled once more. He pushed to his feet and bolted through the doorway and into the living room.

"Xander?" Her voice cracked, sounded nearly as bad as his own.

"Shh, it's okay." He pressed a harried kiss to her bruised brow. He noticed a quickly widening gap in the wall near the window. "I've got you."

A flaming beam of wood crashed to the floor halfway between them and the door. Cursing, he reared back, twisting to shield her as flames leaped high.

"The book," she gasped, coughed. "Have to. Get *the book*."

Xander peered down at her, frowning. "The scrolls?"

"Have to get. *The book*." She began struggling in earnest. "And the stone. Can't. Leave them."

The desperate drive to get her out of there battled with his sense of duty. "Where are they?"

"Second. Bedroom."

He carried her to the closed door.

"Put me. Down."

Bracing her, alarmed by the way she swayed on her feet, Xander sent up a prayer for the strength to protect her and the power to get her through this. Her face was as pale as the plaster dust clinging to her hair. But her jaw clenched with determination. In a reedy voice, she recited the incantation to lower the enchantments. At the same moment, she kicked one of the stones on the floor away with her bare foot, winced. Swearing out loud, Xander swept her up into his arms once more.

She'd been hurt. Again.

Just once. Was it too damned much to ask that *one* prayer be answered?

Dashing through the doorway, he swept the room. Bed. Dresser. Closet. Desk.

Lifting a trembling arm, Kyanna pointed at the desk. Xander rushed across the room and lowered her only enough for her to snatch up a slim, aged leather book. Clasping the book tightly to her chest, she curled into him.

"The stone," she whispered. He could barely hear her above the growing whoosh of crackling fire.

"Stone? You have the scrolls. I have to get you out of here. Don't worry about some damned rock."

She began fighting him, wiggling to be set free. "Need. The. Stone."

Damned obstinate woman. "Where?"

"Office." She was wheezing, inhaling too much smoke. Worry coiled around him, squeezing till he could hardly breathe himself.

"No time. Have to get you out of here."

"The stone. Must get." She began thrashing again.

Coughed so hard she gagged.

"Okay. Okay." He forcibly stilled her. His injured hand, where it hooked beneath her knees felt as if it were on fire. Dipped in Ralsha venom.

The building groaned around them, a God-awful sound that Xander felt to the depths of his soul. Whatever was going on, this building wouldn't take much more. Clutching her tightly against his chest, curling himself around her as best as he could, Xander hurdled the flaming beam in the living room, and flew down the stairs, his bare feet hardly touching a single step.

At the entrance to the office, he froze. The room was engulfed in flames. A complete inferno.

Once more, she began struggling. "Have to—"

"Leave it," he said, turning away. "Lower the enchantments."

"No. Sworn to—protect the—stone," she panted, shoving at his shoulder in a desperate bid to free herself. "Have to—" Coughing wracked her body, and still she fought.

Letting out a furious roar, he gently lowered her to her feet and braced her against the wall. He gripped her shoulders. "What's the stone look like?"

"Long. Cylindrical. Dark reddish." He remembered the rock she'd threatened him with that first time they'd met. "Desk."

"Stay here," he barked. Then, after pressing a fleeting kiss to her forehead, he turned to confront the conflagration.

Drawing in a ragged breath, raising one arm to shield his face, he threw himself through the doorway. Voracious flames licked greedily at him. Heat seared his skin. Black smoke curled through the white-hot, raging inferno. The scent of singed hair rolled his stomach. Blisters erupted across his flesh.

Sweeping burning ledgers from the desktop, he frantically searched for the rock. The skin on his forearms cracked in the heat, splitting open. He ripped drawers from the desk and rifled through them before dropping them to the floor. And then came a deafening bang. The building shuddered as if it were a living thing about to die. Xander's chest heaved. If the building started to collapse, could he get to her in time? He'd nearly made up his mind to say the hell with the damned rock and force her to open the enchantments when he jerked another drawer open. It was heavier than the others. Something rolled, clunking against the side.

Too late did he recall the damage that her precious ward stones had done to his hand.

Bracing himself for a fresh round of pain, he reached in and grasped the stone.

****

Kyanna blinked at the bright flames filling the doorway as the haze in her brain slowly cleared. Oh God. She'd sent him in there? What had she done? Tears poured down her face. How could she have put something else, an inanimate object, above Xander's life? It didn't matter what that stone was—what it was supposed to be capable of. Nothing was worth losing Xander.

The building shuddered. Her legs shook beneath her. The wall behind her, the one she was leaning on, began to buckle. A triumphant Xander burst from the flaming room, the stone clutched in his hand. He ran to her, thrust the stone into her hands and swept her up in his arms, barking, “Lower them. Now!”

More grateful than words could express, she threw her arms around his neck and hugged him fiercely. *He’s alive! He survived!*

An entire wall collapsed in a shower of roaring flames less than fifty feet away.

“Kyanna!”

“Sheptaé cali hwez.” She rushed to lower the enchantments and set them free. Syllable after syllable spilled forth.

The instant the enchantment dropped, horrific looking creatures began pouring into the building from every direction. Dozens of them. Terrifying screeches and hissing filled the room. And there in her arms, Xander morphed into the nightmare from the alley. His body growing taller, bulking up with bulging muscle, right beneath her hands. His skin turned blood-red. Wicked black horns sprouted from his head, and razor-sharp onyx claws sprang from the tips of his fingers. He roared. Jagged teeth filled his mouth. His chin and ears drew to points. And his eyes glowed, blazing-red.

But she clung to him and prayed there was still some semblance of the man she’d come to know buried in there somewhere.

A lethal plasma ball hurled from one of the monsters near the doorway. Xander juggled her, tucking her against his side while the other hand lifted, palm out. He caught the plasma ball in his hand like a baseball, then slowly closed his fist, extinguishing the pulsing sphere of raw heat.

“Cantartu eti zyph shamwin morte!” Xander’s voice was layered now, and so deep. As if many voices

spoke at once. And this time, the words shivered through her in the language she understood. The language of the angels. "Come and dance with death," he'd said.

As Xander spoke, many of the demon intruders shrank back. Fear radiated from them, a palpable thing. Until one stepped forward, regal as a king. He looked like a walking corpse, dressed in medieval garb. Extremely tall. Emaciated, gray flesh. Long, red dreadlocks knotted wildly around his head, and soulless black eyes.

Lifting his arms, he began a low chant. The intonations similar to those issued by Xander. A huge boom echoed through the building and the whole structure rocked. The floor shook once again, more violently than before. Hardwood buckled, erupting here and there in wild sprays of splintering wood. But Xander stood firm. Walls crumbled, toppling to the floor. And Xander grinned wickedly. Tipping his head back, he laughed, taunting the invaders. The sound sent ice through her veins.

Holding his free hand out at his side, palm out, his body stiffened. Thrum with energy. Light pulsed from his palm. Growing. Heating. Xander gave another roar, and it was if something inside him came unleashed. An unnatural evil.

She cringed and backed away. This was wrong. Something had gone very wrong inside him. But his arm tightened around her like a band of steel. Caging her to his side.

Four of the demons surrounding their dreadlocked leader exploded from within, blood and viscera splashed the room. The dreadlocked demon drew a deep breath and roared, expression livid, as though he were about to go crazy.

Screaming, Kyanna buried her face against Xander's chest. She felt him shift, and she glanced up. He stared down at her through flame red eyes. Blinked. Frowned. There was no light of recognition. No sign whatsoever that he knew who she was, or why she was in his arms. Kyanna saw him glance down between them. She followed his gaze, assuming he was looking at the book and the stone. Panic welled inside her. How was she to keep them safe, keep them from him, if he chose to take them by force in this state? And if he took them, then what? Would he leave her here to face her fate at the hands of these monsters alone?

But no, he wasn't looking at the book. Or the stone.

He was staring at the generous swell of her breasts, where they all but spilled from her spaghetti strap tank. A sound rumbled up from deep in his chest. A dark, wicked purr. The rumble of a lion. Her eyes widened when she realized the bulge in his pants was swelling. Huge and rigid as steel.

"Xander." Wedging the book more firmly between them, she lifted her shaking hand and cupped his cheek. "It's me, Xander. Kyanna."

Sweat trickled between her breasts, soaked the hair at her temples. The heat had become unbearable. Smoke was filling the lower floor now.

"Remember me," she coughed. "Remember what you were sent here to do."

His frown deepened and he shook his head as if trying to clear it. Then he drew in a sharp breath and looked around the building, took in the demons creeping steadily closer.

Kyanna was dizzy, and her vision had blurred. But suddenly, cool air washed over her. Fresh air. But Xander's heat still surrounded her. She tipped her chin to the sky. A canopy of leaves rose high overhead. Glancing back to him, she blinked in surprise. He was human once more. But his blisters, his wounds were…*gone? How?* Each and every last one of them completely healed. Aside from sweat streaked soot, he was utterly unscathed.

"We can't stop yet." His voice was still the same though. Still rough. Still hoarse. Still Xander's voice…no longer that deep layered voice of death. He palmed her head and gently pressed her face to his chest. His arms closed protectively around her. "Close your eyes."

Trusting in him, too weak to argue, she did as he instructed, even as she felt the bottom of her stomach fall away again. Like that first frightening drop on a rollercoaster. Long moments later, her feet landed on solid ground, and she no longer experienced that belly dropping sensation. He immediately let go of her. Her knees wobbled.

They were in a darkened kitchen. A plain, ordinary kitchen. Nothing fancy. The scene out the window gave her pause. No houses or stores nearby from what she could see, only an old barn in the dim circle of light. The dark shadows of trees danced in the distance, beyond a meadow of gently swaying grasses and flowers. It looked like an ordinary farm.

She turned back to him. Kyanna opened her mouth to ask where they were, but he caught her by surprise. Sinking his fingers deep in her hair, cupping the back of her head, he hauled her up against him. His left arm came around her waist and his lips slanted over hers, his mouth wide and devouring. He branded her. He tasted of sultry summer nights. Of sizzling fantasies come to life. Of untamed passions and of desperation.

Over and over his tongue plunged. His body was a granite wall of need against her, around her. She melted in to him. The book in one hand, the stone in the other, she wrapped her arms around his neck and accepted him, giving everything she had to the kiss, and to him. He released her hair, his hand sliding down her back. And then his hand was on her bottom. His fingertips digging in, squeezing, guiding her, rocking her up on her tiptoes as the solid length of his erection rode against her hip.

Xander groaned into her mouth. Slanting his head again, he took the kiss deeper still. His breath became hers. His need her own. His left hand fisted in the back of her shirt. His right hand pushed up her hip, bold, possessive, until the heat of his palm cupped her breast beneath her shirt, kneaded and stroked. Her body came alive in his arms. Deep in her core, a hollow ache grew.

Xander's hand flattened, splayed over her chest. Heat tingled there between them, just this side of pain. And he froze. Abruptly, he drew back, stepped away from her, dropping his hands to his sides. The kiss over as quickly, as impetuously as it had begun.

She staggered back without his support. Cradling the book and the stone, she caught herself on the edge of a counter. Her head was still spinning from his kiss. Alarm flared in her chest when Xander reached for the back of a chair, bracing himself, head bowed, panting.

Had he been hurt after all?

"Xander?" She moved forward, her legs slowly

steadying, and stretched a hand out to him. "Where are we?" Turning her head, she peered up at him through the darkness. "Did we shimmer?"

"Sebastian!" Xander yelled, ignoring her.

Okay. So they wouldn't be discussing *that* kiss either.

She stood immobile, unsure of what to do. What to say.

"What the hell, Slayer?"

Whirling, Kyanna gasped and then launched herself into Xander's arms. A man had materialized only a few short feet from them, from completely out of nowhere. Xander tucked her to his side, but he didn't tense, didn't morph back into the nightmare, so she took that as a sign this might be a friend. Feeling a bit foolish, she released her death grip on him. But his arm stayed anchored around her waist so she stayed put and observed the newcomer—presumably this Sebastian that Xander had called for. He reached over and flipped on the light switch. Kyanna blinked, squinting until she became accustomed to the light.

"We came in hot."

Sebastian's face hardened. His body tensed, as if preparing for battle. "How many are following?"

Shaking his head, Xander took a breath and drew himself up to his full height. His face wasn't quite so pale anymore. The lines around his eyes and mouth not so strained.

"Don't know. We bounced first," he replied.

"Well, if any have the balls to follow, we'll deal."

Giving a negligent shrug, Sebastian leaned back against the far counter, crossed his ankles, propped the heels of his palms on the granite on either side of him.

Fine hairs on the back of her neck prickled. He'd materialized—*shimmered,* she amended—just like she and Xander had. Was this another demon then?

Xander's friend was tall, extremely so. And very good looking. Tousled blond hair, white-blond stubble upon his jaw with a slightly longer goatee, and twinkling blue eyes highlighted a face beautiful enough to grace the cover of Maxim. His skin tone was several shades lighter than Xander's, but his body was lean and rippling with muscle and very naked to the waist. A well defined six-pack tracked down his abdomen, disappearing into the unbuttoned waistband of his jeans, tempting the lips to follow. He was sexy in a boy-next-door kind of way…provided your boy-next-door was the hunky stuff of highly erotic movies.

But something about the way he carried himself, something about the set of his jaw and the glint in his eyes screamed *hazardous to your health.* Strap a fur pelt and thick leather wristbands on him, put a battle ax in one hand and a shield in the other, and you had every woman's fantasy of a Nordic conqueror come to life.

"Put on a shirt," Xander growled.

"*You* put on a shirt." Seemingly unaffected by Xander's hostile attitude, Sebastian checked her out, appraising her with undisguised interest. His intrigued stare lingered on Xander's arm, the arm that even now tightened possessively, pulling her closer into his side. Sebastian's eyes gleamed as he pushed away from the counter. Holding his hand out, he offered her a broad, sultry smile.

"Hel-lo, beautiful."

Xander snarled. He actually bared his teeth and snarled.

"Shirt, Vengeance. Now."

He didn't wait for her to shake Sebastian's hand. Instead, he marched past Sebastian and through a doorway, pushing her ahead of him.

She gasped and scolded, "Xander."

On his way by, Xander snapped, "Sebastian, this is Kyanna. Kyanna, meet Sebastian, the Demon of Vengeance."

Sheesh. They were obviously going to have to work on more than "please" and "thank you."

"Nice to meet you, Sebastian," she called over her shoulder.

"Right back at ya, gorgeous. Make yourselves at home."

Kyanna surveyed the living room. Decorated with hunting-cabin flair, the area was cozy. A fire crackled to life in the fireplace. The overhead light blinked on. She allowed Xander to guide her to a long, plaid sofa. He sat down in the middle, then pulled her down beside him, making certain there wouldn't be room for anyone else on her other side. She tucked the book and the stone between them. In some ways, it comforted her, this possessive attitude of his. But it was also mildly irritating.

He was blatantly giving Sebastian the wrong idea about them.

But why?

As he sat down in an armchair near the fire, a shirt suddenly appeared upon Sebastian's person. A neon pink, puff-sleeved, silk shirt. With a ruffled collar. Kyanna blinked.

Whoa. How?

"Harsh, dude." Sebastian chuckled, glancing down.

He dropped his ankle on his knee and settled back in the chair. The pink shirt became a plain, white muscle shirt. Kyanna gaped. She glanced to Xander, who was now wearing a V-necked T-shirt.

Where'd that come from?

And then suddenly she, herself, was wearing different clothing. Gone was the smoke-stained, sweat-drenched spaghetti strap tank. Gone were her baby-blue, cloud patterned PJ bottoms with the draw-string waist. In their place, she wore baggy—ugly—dark blue sweatpants and an oversized matching sweatshirt. She even had a bra on now. Admittedly, the sweats were far more comfortable than the revealing PJ's, particularly considering the way Sebastian's gaze kept sliding to her chest. But this was the very definition of overkill. The only way she could be better covered was if she were wearing a snowmobile suit. Or a nun's habit.

"You know, Slayer, you're a real prude." Sebastian shook his head, clearly disappointed.

Sebastian seemed so normal. Had the book been wrong about everything?

Kyanna was seized with a bout of coughing, remnants of smoke inhalation, no doubt. A glass of water suddenly appeared on the coffee table in front of her. Without thinking, she picked it up and chugged. And then it clicked. Something else had just appeared from out of nowhere. She had to force the last swallow down.

Okay, wow. This was seriously going to mess with her head.

"Um, thanks?" She set the glass aside and watched Sebastian, who flipped his hands up in a *wasn't-me* kind of way before pointing a finger at Xander.

"How—"

"Later."

Really? Things were popping up right and left, clothing appearing on all of them from out of no-freakin'-where. And he thought *later* was gonna cut it?

"Ah, no. Now."

Sebastian's eyebrows shot to his hairline. A long, slow grin spread across his mouth, and a deep belly laugh rumbled up, spilling out.

Xander expressionless face slowly turned her way.

"Don't look at me like that," she snapped, causing Sebastian's laughter to intensify into hearty guffaws. Glancing over at him in irritation, she crossed her arms defensively. "My apartment—my business—is gone. Everything I own has probably burned to the ground by now. Rubble. Creatures the likes of which Steven Spielberg couldn't dream up poured into my burning storeroom like cockroaches…several of which, I might add, simultaneously blew up for no apparent reason, exploding blood and guts all over the place."

That last bit caused Sebastian's laughter to choke off. His alarmed gaze shot to Xander, who remained strangely silent at her side.

That was just fine with her. She wasn't through yet.

"I trusted you when you told me to, and I let you shimmer me here. Which, for a human, I'd like to point out to you, feels like falling off a damned cliff. And now stuff just keeps appearing"—she jabbed a finger at the water glass—"and starting with no one's help"—she gestured toward the fireplace—"and you think I'm gonna settle for *later*? Think again, buddy. So, one more time. How?"

"It is called conjuring," Xander explained, his

fingers brushing a loose strand of her hair back, tucking it gently behind her ear. “It works much like shimmering, but instead of transporting myself to a location, the object comes to me.”

Sebastian was now gawking at Xander. She ignored him, focusing on Xander. “How long have you been able to do this conjuring?”

Frowning, he replied matter-of-factly, “Always.”

Anger rose up, choking her. He’d had these powers and said nothing to her? She twisted in her seat to face him, glaring. “So yesterday, when I had to call Summer to get clothes for you, when she came over—” She broke off, heat scorching her cheeks as she remembered the box of condoms. “You could have just conjured them for yourself?”

“Wait…what was that? Why did you need clothing?” This from a grinning Sebastian, who seemed to be hanging on every word.

Perhaps she should have waited until later.

Xander shot him a quelling look, but he addressed Kyanna. “I was unable to use my powers at the time.”

She arched a brow, elevated her chin, and tilted her head. She was going to need a much better explanation than that.

Growling deep in his chest, Xander focused on her, blatantly ignoring Sebastian as well. “The enchantments you used on your building are far more powerful than any I’ve ever encountered. Something about them”—he shook his head, shrugged—“locked up my powers. Bound them. I couldn’t shimmer. Couldn’t conjure. Nothing.”

Xander cleared his throat and grimaced. He reached for her unfinished glass of water and downed the rest. Leaning back, he dropped his arm around her once more.

"Oh." Satisfied with his more detailed response, and the fact that he hadn't deliberately embarrassed her, she relaxed. Kyanna glanced up in time to see Sebastian gawking at Xander again. Like Sebastian no longer recognized him. Nibbling her lip, she watched Sebastian a little more closely as he watched Xander.

What was it about Xander's attitude—or was it his willingness to explain things to her in detail—that caused Sebastian to stare in blatant disbelief?

Stirring himself, Sebastian leaned forward, braced his elbows on his knees. "What about your gift?"

The way he'd said *gift*—the tone he'd used—sounded more like he meant *curse*.

"Still worked. Only thing that did." Xander ran a hand over his hair, shaking plaster dust loose.

"I wonder why?"

Xander tossed a shoulder in response.

"Gift?" Turning beneath his arm, she scowled. "What gift?"

"When we fell from Heaven, each of us lost our wings. As well as the one thing we were most prideful of." Xander stared at the fire. "As compensation, Lucifer *gifted* us—those who were the most powerful of our species—with positions high in his army, and a specialized power."

"What did you lose?"

"My voice," he replied simply.

When he said no more, Sebastian took over the tale. "Xander's voice was mesmerizing. He had but to speak, and those about him would fall under a trance, doing his bidding without thought. Without resistance, whether they wanted to or not. When he sang?" Sebastian shuddered, leaning back in his seat. "No angel in Heaven could compare. And so, when his wings were taken, the others—Gabriel, Michael, Seth and the rest—they all took great pleasure in destroying his voice too."

Filled with horror and sympathy, Kyanna impulsively laid her hand upon his thigh and gently squeezed, offering what meager comfort she could. Xander remained silent, expression completely blank. But the muscles in his thigh slowly turned to granite beneath her hand. His gaze slowly dropped to where her hand rested upon him, then just as slowly rose to pin her.

Kyanna forced a swallow. But somehow, she managed to work a little steel into her spine and she left her hand right where it was. For one slim moment, she tried to convince herself this was just one more social lesson she was trying to teach Xander, accustoming him to a compassionate touch.

Oh, who am I trying to fool?

She probably needed the contact more than he did. While the involuntary, initial touch may have been unplanned, she quickly became fascinated by the heat radiating through his jeans, and the sheer strength of his muscles.

Marshalling her thoughts, she scrambled to remember what they had been talking about. "What did you gain in return for following Lucifer?" She searched his face for his little tells. She couldn't find them. And that, more than anything, disturbed her the most.

"I can detect when someone tells a lie. My flesh feels as if a million insects swarm over me."

Grimacing on his behalf, she turned to Sebastian. "Do you mind if I ask what your loss was? What your gift is? Or the gifts of the others?"

"I won't speak for the others," Sebastian stated, polite but firm. "But as for me, my pride was my gift of listening."

Kyanna cocked her head, frowning. *He lost his hearing?*

"No, I see I've confused you. My hearing is fine. I lost my gift of listening to others' hearts. Of understanding their deepest wishes and desires. You see, just by being within a certain distance of someone, I could sense their most treasured dreams. In return I was *gifted* with my wings."

"Yours weren't taken from you? Gabriel and the others didn't—"

"Oh no. They ripped my heavenly wings from me. Laughed the whole time, bloody bastards." His eyes flickered black, just for a split second. Long enough for Kyanna to suck in a sharp breath. "I was given a new set of wings. The wings of Vengeance."

Was it too much to hope? "Figurative wings?"

"Literal wings. I am the Demon of Vengeance, after all." He grinned as she stared at him, baffled. He had no wings that she could see. "They only come out when I'm in demonic form," he explained. "They're quite impressive, if I do say so myself."

At that, Xander snorted. She glanced at him, lifting her brows. Pokerfaced, Xander lifted his hand, his thumb and forefinger measuring the span of an inch.

Her gaze flew to Sebastian. But he hadn't seemed to take offense. Instead, he offered a sympathetic smile. "You'll have to excuse him. Envy, you know."

Xander's eyes slowly narrowed. He popped his jaw.

Chapter Fifteen

Sebastian settled back in the cushions, making himself comfortable. "So, you wanna tell me why you interrupted my beauty sleep?"

"Gather the others."

Sebastian arched his brow at the imperious command.

"Please," Kyanna prompted, crossing her arms. The man could try the patience of a saint. "Honestly, it's one little word. Why do you have such an aversion to using it?"

Xander gave her his patented deadpan stare.

She glowered right back.

Sebastian, having witnessed the byplay, burst out laughing. Without another comment, he rose, drew a slim cell phone from his back pocket, and returned to the kitchen.

"Why didn't you tell me about your lie radar?"

Xander grunted.

Before she could ask any more questions, one of the fiercest beings she'd ever seen shimmered into the room near the fireplace. Clad head to toe in black leather, head shaved completely bald, he instantly filled the room with menace. Tattoos similar to Xander's stretched up the side of his neck, what she could see of it above his collar. He had a strong jaw, cleanly shaven, but a good portion of his face was heavily scarred. His eyes were pale green, and flat. As if nothing in life held any interest anymore.

"Mikhail," Xander greeted him.

Mikhail nodded. He glanced to Kyanna, and for one uncomfortable moment, she felt as if he were examining her soul beneath a microscope. Dissecting every decision she'd ever made, judging the depth of every sin. At length, he released her from his hypnotic stare and claimed Sebastian's vacated seat, letting out a deep breath. Kyanna nudged Xander.

"Mikhail, Kyanna. Kyanna, Mikhail, the Demon of War." His duty done, a sullen Xander fell silent.

Mikhail dipped his head on an abbreviated nod, then returned to studying the fire, one calloused finger tap-tapping on the arm of his chair.

Wow. And she'd thought Xander grim and uncommunicative.

Wait. Demon of War?

Why did that sound familiar? Hadn't there been something about him in the book? The urge to grab the book up and scour its pages for mention of the Demon of War burned through her. *Later,* she cautioned herself. Uneasy, she clasped her hands in her lap and stared at the fire too. An ominous sense of recognition tickled at her subconscious.

A few moments later, another demon shimmered into the room. He didn't appear nearly as fierce as Mikhail. His gaze immediately landed upon her. Only the phantom of curiosity reflected in his golden stare before he scanned the rest of the occupants.

She hadn't even been surprised by the unexpected appearance this time. Proud of herself, she offered him a tentative smile. The shadow of a roguish grin flitted across his mouth, gone in a wink of time. His hair was longish, tawny-gold, and curling wildly about his head, as if the only styling instrument that had touched it recently were his long, slim fingers.

His amber eyes held a striking intelligence that was impossible to miss, as were the deep bruises just beneath them. He looked as if he hadn't had a decent moments rest in too long to be healthy. His jaw sported several days' growth of whisker stubble, but it only drew attention to the perfect allure of his lips. His skin was sun-kissed, though his cheeks appeared a bit gaunt. His clothing was rumpled, his hair disheveled. He looked as if he'd exhausted himself in some woman's bed.

Lucky woman.

He inclined his head to her. "Ma'am." And then he dropped carelessly onto the loveseat.

"Hi," she replied, giving Xander an elbow when he offered no introductions.

A heavy sigh stirred the hair at her temple. Matted, smoke scented hair reminded her how badly she needed a shower. Dried sweat made her skin tight and sticky. And, thanks to the roaring blaze Sebastian had mysteriously kindled in the fireplace and the clothing in which Xander had dressed her, she was fast becoming unbearably hot. She pushed her sleeves up.

"Gideon, Kyanna. Kyanna, Gideon, the Demon of Temptation."

"Former. Former Demon of Temptation," he drawled absently, as if he'd repeated this fact so often he was losing hope anyone was actually paying attention. His voice caressed the senses. Husky sensuality thick with a Virginia gentleman's accent.

"It's nice to meet you, Gideon."

"Niklas will be here soon," Sebastian said as he returned to the room. The sofa bounced a bit as he dropped beside Xander. "So, Kyanna. How'd a little thing like you become a Guardian?"

Gideon's attention snapped back to her, pinning her to the spot. Mikhail's head didn't move, but his pale green eyes tracked to her as well. So apparently Sebastian hadn't told them everything. Talk about being dropped in the spotlight. She fought the urge to glance down at herself, just to make certain she wasn't sitting there in nothing but her underwear. All things considered, it wouldn't be completely out of the realm of possibility.

The air near the fireplace distorted before she could respond. Kyanna glanced up and immediately plastered herself to Xander's side. After the monsters she'd faced in her storeroom, the urge to scream was nearly more than she could control. A demon truly had arrived. A massive beast with black horns, vicious fangs, and jet black skin. Strange red runes glowed upon his flesh. His thighs were thick, his arms massive.

Xander patted his hand on her shoulder twice. "Niklas," he said quietly.

A moment after he solidified, the demon transformed into a man. Shoulder length dark hair curled at his nape. His jaw was smooth, his shoulders broad. His eyes were a stunning ice blue. The latest arrival peered at her in somber silence.

She nudged Xander, but apparently he felt his introduction duties were over.

"Um, hi? I'm Kyanna Hughes." She nervously tucked a wayward lock of hair behind her ear.

Niklas nodded.

"You must be the Seer," Kyanna murmured, remembering the information Xander had given her previously. Niklas arched an eyebrow in Xander's direction and promptly sat down on the only vacant seat left.

"Kyanna is the Guardian of the Arc Stone," Xander began without preamble.

Several voices all erupted at once, the least of which was her own.

"Arc Stone?" She peered up at Xander, filled with confusion. "I am custodian of the book. I don't—"

"Dude." Sebastian came to the edge of his seat, peering around Xander at her now as if she'd somehow tricked them. "The scrolls are—"

"The stone," Xander asserted.

"No, I'm not. You're not making any sense. This is just a ward stone, a really old, really powerful one. That's all." She rested her palm on the long, cylindrical rock that had been passed down in her family for generations along with the book. Bemused, she stared at Xander. How had he come to this insane conclusion? Arc Stone, indeed.

Gideon stared at the book, where it rested against her hip. "You sure?"

Xander turned to her, his expression asking permission. She didn't know where he was going with this, but she nodded assent, trusting him.

Xander lifted the heavy, cylindrical stone in his hand and extended his arm for all to see. He took the dagger from his ankle strap and, before anyone could react, drew the blade across his forearm, slicing deep.

"Xander! What are you—" Kyanna lunged forward

to stop him, but her alarmed gasp abruptly choked off. Almost before the blood could well, the cut sealed itself. And she suddenly remembered the blisters and cuts that had peppered his flesh when he'd first carried her down the steps of her burning apartment. Blisters and cuts that had mysteriously disappeared when he'd returned from her flaming office. Every eye in the room was glued to the rock in Xander's hand.

"It should have taken at least an hour for a wound that deep to heal for one of our kind," he added for her benefit.

"I-I don't understand." Frowning, she accepted the stone from him. She stared at the rock. Gnawed on her lip. "May I?" She motioned to Xander.

He lifted his brows but held the dagger out to her as he offered his free arm, obviously expecting her to experiment on him for herself. Instead of taking the dagger, she pricked her finger on the tip. Xander's reaction was lightning swift. He slapped it back in its sheath and scowled at her. Without warning, he grabbed her wrist, and yanked her hand in front of him. She held the stone up with her free hand, then twisted her wrist, showing the rest of the room her proof that he was somehow mistaken.

Crimson liquid welled from her fingertip. The small cut stung. And it wasn't healing. He'd proven nothing here.

Without explanation, Xander thrust her bleeding fingertip into his mouth. Held it there, lips sealed over her skin, tongue pressed hard to the cut. Confused, she stared at him, until she noticed that his gaze was locked not on her, but on Mikhail. Turning her attention to the others in the room, she realized they were all staring at

Mikhail. And, no one moved.

Each and every one of them behaved as if the slightest movement might provoke the Demon of War.

Subdued by the oppressive note of caution hanging heavy in the room, Kyanna slowly turned to Mikhail as well. He was rigid in his seat. His hands were locked on the arms of the chair. His knuckles were bleached white. His eyes flickered the deepest onyx. And not the flat black surface that she'd seen when Sebastian's eyes had changed. Mikhail's eyes were bottomless, black space. Freaky. Clenching his jaw, he visibly forced a swallow. By slow degrees, he began to relax. He uttered not a sound. At length, his eye color returned to their pale green color.

And everyone let out the breath they'd been holding.

"Well, I'll be damned." This from Gideon. "We have a relic."

"Why do you insist that it's a relic?" She glanced around the room, from one demon to the next, demanding an answer. Xander had released her finger from the distracting suction of his mouth. He glanced at the wound to make certain that blood no longer welled, then, apparently satisfied, he sat back, tucking her proprietarily against his side. All across the room, eyebrows lifted, yet no one spoke.

"I'm still cut," she insisted. "It didn't heal me at all."

"It wouldn't," Niklas responded. "You're human. Only a demon can conduct the real power harnessed within. Or an angel, theoretically."

"Her building shook like in an earthquake." Varying degrees of surprised frowns turned toward

Xander, but he offered no more.

"I know of only one demon capable of this. Agares." Mikhail spoke for the first time since his arrival, startling Kyanna. His voice was smoky and rippled across the senses. His pronouncement was met with stony silence and grim expressions. The name was completely unfamiliar to her. "Who is Agares?"

"Agares is nobility. A duke of Hell. He's capable of traveling between Earth and Hell, though, thankfully, he isn't strong enough to transport others." Niklas rubbed a hand down the length of his thigh. "He can create earthquakes. He's the only demon with that particular power over Earth. But he's also limited to disrupting localized areas only."

Xander nodded, supporting Niklas's comments, but remained silent now, letting the others do all the talking. She watched his face, searching for his little tells. The scrunched lines at the corners of his eyes. Dilated pupils. The bunched muscle in his jaw. The flattened lower lip. Heavens, even the tick in his eyelid. Anything at all.

But she found absolutely nothing. He was a blank slate. Unused to seeing him like this, so thoroughly closed off, she clenched her trembling hands in her lap, and turned her attention to the others.

"If Agares is involved," Sebastian was saying. "Then things just got a whole lot more complicated."

"A duke? This plot goes a lot farther up the chain of command than we assumed," Niklas added.

"But how far up?" Gideon glanced around. "Is it possible one of the princes might be involved?"

No one had an answer for him.

Absorbing everything she heard like a sponge, she

listened intently as Gideon discussed someone named Dimiezlo. He was an Animagi minion, they'd explained. A creature composed of a haphazard demonic mixture of human and animal parts, who'd been flitting all over the continent, half a step ahead of them in their search for the relics. Gideon had run into him time and again on his own unrewarding search for the scrolls. Dimiezlo was loyal to a Collector by the name of Ronové. Could he be the mastermind behind this whole plot to overthrow Lucifer? Gideon seemed to believe that assumption incorrect, as Ronové was a lower class demon, incapable of uniting the sheer numbers of demons necessary to overthrow Lucifer.

She also picked up additional information about each relic, what each was supposed to do. The Arc Stone, for example, must make its bearer less susceptible to injury, or significantly accelerate the healing process, and when wielded by the Chosen One, would make him or her completely impervious to physical harm. Obviously, it only worked for demons and, quite possibly, angels. Humans like herself were unaffected. Tentatively, she fingered the tender slice at the tip of her finger. Thankfully it was no longer bleeding. She peered covertly at Mikhail. The way he'd tensed the second she'd begun bleeding had been frightening.

Why had he behaved that way?

She recalled when Xander has laid his hand upon her chest and absorbed a portion of her essence from her. Did Mikhail feed another way? Could he possibly exist on blood? *Vampire* echoed in her mind. All things considered, would it really be so impossible?

"Have you had any luck with your leads,

Vengeance?" Niklas's words drew her back to the topic at hand.

"I gave up on the scrolls and started searching for the stone, as you know. I followed a promising lead to Scotland, which ended in failure. And then, barring all else, I finally contacted Asher. Paid an exorbitant fee for a twisted tip." Sebastian's grin darted in Kyanna's direction. "'The Guardian is of our world, but not one of us.' As we all can see, Xander snatched that one right out from under me."

Xander grunted. A distinct *na-na-na-boo-boo-on-you* sound if ever she'd heard one.

Kyanna, burning with curiosity and unable to keep quiet any longer, began peppering them with questions. And, surprisingly enough, they answered.

"Could anyone overthrow Lucifer with the sword, the stone, and the scrolls?"

"No," Niklas responded. "Only the Chosen One can harness them all."

"Who is the Chosen One?"

"No one knows for sure, darlin'." Gideon shifted in his seat, crossed his ankles as he laced his fingers over his abdomen. "But he'll have to be one powerful SOB to challenge Lucifer and win."

"Xander wears guard stones," she observed. "By rights, none of you should be able to be near them."

"We all have them." Gideon held his wrist up, displaying a heavy silver watch, turning it so she could see its face. It had been set with tiny chips of guard stones. Sebastian flicked a finger over the stud in his ear. Niklas held his hand up, displaying a ring. Again, the same stones were present. Her questioning stare traveled to Mikhail.

"Nobody knows where he keeps his, darlin'. Nobody wants to know badly enough to ask."

Mikhail's deadened stare locked on Gideon. Gideon arched a challenging brow, unfazed. Silence descended upon the room at once.

At length, Xander broke the silence, stunning them all.

"I believe Kyanna is of angelic descent."

Chapter Sixteen

She stared at Xander in disbelief. "What?"

Her question was echoed around the room.

"Kyanna is of angelic descent," Xander repeated.

"I sense no angel here," Gideon countered. The others shook their heads, murmuring their agreement with Gideon's assessment.

She blinked at him, bemused. Had she just been insulted, or complimented?

Seriously?

She twisted around to peer up at Xander. He was the only one in the room that wasn't staring at her as if she were likely to sprout a second head at any moment. Or a halo and white, downy wings. Somehow, the way they were acting, a second head might well be less threatening.

"I believe her line is generations old."

That seemed to explain something to the others. She could only wish it had been more informative for herself.

"Why do you believe this?" Sebastian propped his elbows on his knees, clasped his hands, and peered around Xander. He scanned her from the top of her head to the tips of her toes. Maybe he was still searching for that halo.

"Angels wouldn't give the kind of enchantments she was using to just anyone." Without looking at her,

Xander tucked his arm more securely around her, almost protectively, his hand settled on her hip. Yet his speech continued on, uninterrupted. Was he even aware of how possessive his actions might look to the others? Or how they felt to her? "Not only were the enchantments capable of blocking demons from entering the dwelling, but, once inside, they virtually nullified my powers. I've never encountered anything so powerful before. And the types of ward stones protecting the apartment? I've never seen those combinations before either."

Sebastian frowned. "Who gave the enchantments to you, Kyanna? And those stones?"

"My mother. And her mother before her. And hers before her."

"A matrilineal line?" Niklas demanded of Xander.

"There is more," Xander told them. Then, turning to her, he ordered, "Speak the words. Out loud. Say them."

Kyanna frowned at him. His demand went against everything she'd ever been taught. And yet she trusted him, so she spoke. *"Caéli ipi novena mar—"*

Xander suddenly clapped his hand over her mouth, silencing her before she could complete the phrases. When she'd begun reciting the enchantment, a tremor had shuddered through his large frame. All around the room, the others tensed, their bodies gone completely rigid. And yet the oddest expressions of wonder lingered upon their faces.

"The ancient tongue," Gideon whispered. And they all stared at her in open awe.

Lowering his hand to his lap, Xander nodded to Gideon. "I'm willing to bet that not only did the enchantments block demons, but they blocked angels as well, shielding her from Hell and Heaven both. It has to be how her line has survived this long."

"Survived this long?" Frustrated, she glared at Xander. "What do you mean?"

Xander squeezed Kyanna's hip, his attention finally focused solely on her. He cleared his throat again and grimaced, as if pained. "After the fall, angels were forbidden to mate with humans. Your line, I'm guessing, was seeded after the Fall." He studied her for a moment in silence. "By Gabriel's decree, your ancestors should have been wiped from the face of the Earth. You, your mother, your grandmother and all those that came before her, none of you would have been permitted to even be born."

Appalled, Kyanna chewed the edge of her lower lip. An *angel* had decreed this genocide? The very idea made her question where the line between good and evil really lay. Who was really on which side? And, perhaps more importantly, how could the line between the two become so blurred that an angel would decree the deaths of innocent babes? And yet demons fought relentlessly to save them? No sense whatsoever.

A nagging ache had begun to form at the base of her skull. She stared, unseeing, at the edge of the coffee table as she tried desperately to wrap her mind around all she'd seen and learned this night. Voices rose and fell around her. The words had become all but indistinguishable. She was only vaguely aware of Xander's hand sliding up, closing around the nape of her neck beneath her hair and kneading the stiff muscles. Lord, she was so tired. Worn thin, without the energy to even speak, let alone cry. Like a fading ghost.

Soon there would be nothing left of her at all. And still the others' conversation volleyed back and forth. She drew breath after breath. When would this all stop? When would she wake up from this nightmare? Would she ever?

How long would it take before she finally just melted into nothingness?

Across the room, Niklas cleared his throat. Silence followed. Xander's fingers continued their slow, hypnotic motions. How long had he been doing that? She trembled, from anxiety or as a purely physical reaction to Xander's touch she couldn't say. What she wouldn't give to make this nightmare all just go away. A thousand more questions circled her brain, but she kept her mouth shut, fearful that if she opened it, the only thing that might come out would be a scream. And if she started screaming, she might never stop.

"Do you need a blanket?"

Why was Xander asking her such an odd question? It must be a hundred degrees in here, between the roaring blaze in the fireplace, and the heat radiating from Xander. Not to mention, the stifling sweat-suit Xander had dressed her in. And yet, glancing down at herself, Kyanna realized she was shaking. And her hands were icy cold. Xander had released her nape and slipped his arm around her once more, and his hand was now banging awkwardly against her hip, the rapid beats firm enough to ensure she'd probably have bruises there tomorrow.

She shook her head. No. She didn't want a blanket.

She wanted to not throw up in front of a room full of demons.

And she wanted everyone to stop staring at her like

she were some damned curiosity. Or a threat that might sprout a halo and wings at any moment.

"Bathroom," she whispered.

Xander frowned down at her. "In the kitchen, the far door on the other side of the table."

Nodding, she pushed to her feet and crossed the room on wobbly legs. She could feel Xander's gaze following her from the room. Too distraught to coach Xander on his manners, she stumbled through the kitchen and gently closed the bathroom door behind her.

Her mind had raced in circles before, but now it had simply screeched to a halt, refusing to work beyond seeing to the most basic of her body's needs. Bending over the sink, she turned the water on and splashed some on her face. But that wasn't enough. She shoved the bulky sleeves of her sweatshirt up. But they only fell back down. Frustrated, frantic to get rid of the smell of smoke that clung to her skin, she whipped the shirt over her head and dropped it on the floor. After squirting liquid soap from the dispenser onto her palm, she worked the lather over her hands, wrists, and arms. Rinsed. Repeated. Then she spied a clean, dry washcloth hanging from the towel bar beside the utilitarian hand towels.

She wound her hair 'round and 'round, tucking it in on itself, forming a loose bun on the top of her head. Then Kyanna worked lather into the washcloth and scrubbed her face, neck, and chest.

She scrubbed and scrubbed and splashed more water on her face. Her hands shook. And suddenly the tears came. And they wouldn't stop. Grabbing a fist full of hand towels, she pressed them to her face and slid to the floor. Her back to the wall, she sobbed.

She'd taken all she could take. The loss of her store and home had been her tipping point. The final straw had been finding out that the very beings she'd been taught from the cradle to revere were indirectly responsible for her very existence. And then to learn that should they ever find out about her, they would undoubtedly try to kill her? Incomprehensible.

Deep down, all she'd ever wanted was to be normal. Some dark corner of her soul had always resented others—even her dearest friend, Summer, on some level—for being normal.

She would gladly go back to being "not normal" again. Happily. Gratefully. Not normal, but blessedly ignorant.

Nothing was ever going to be the same again.

Strong arms suddenly slipped around her. Startled, she jerked her face from the towels to stare at Xander. Without offering explanation, he scooted closer, lifted her onto his lap, and coaxed her to curl herself into his embrace. He pushed her head into the curve of his neck and rubbed her back as he cradled her to his chest. Silent. Warm. Solid.

Grateful, emotionally stretched to the breaking point, Kyanna snuggled into him, curling around him, and let the tears fall. Let the sobs wrack her body. Let the stress and the confusion pour out of her on a tidal wave of tears.

And all the while, Xander held her without saying a word, his cheek pressed to the top of her head. His arms were a protective circle where, for the first time in as long as she could remember, she felt truly safe.

Gradually, her sobs subsided. She was wrung dry.

Utterly spent.

And still he held her. At last, after sniffling into the remaining dry towel, she turned her face up to him. She knew she must look a sight, and so she was doubly surprised to see the strangest expression on his face. One she wasn't sure she'd ever seen before. He looked at her with…tenderness.

"Thank you," she said, just to break the silence. "How did you—"

"I'm not sure," he replied. "It just felt like this was where I needed to be."

Bemused, she blinked up at him, her breath catching on the remnants of a stutter-sob. "I'm sorry. I don't usually do this, give in to bawling like a baby this way. I don't want you to think—"

He silenced her with a fleeting brush of his lips against hers. "You are the strongest human I know."

That said, he reached into one of the drawers and drew out another hand full of small towels. He offered them to her. When she took them, he pressed a brief kiss to her brow and wordlessly transferred her from his lap to the floor before he shimmered himself from the bathroom.

Kyanna sat there for a few moments longer, absorbing what had just passed between them. How had he known she needed someone to hold her? No, not someone. Xander. She'd needed him. And just like that, he'd appeared. Baffling. Bracing herself against the wall, she slowly pushed to her feet. Kyanna rinsed away the tear tracks, unable to do anything about her puffy, red eyes. After drying her face, she pulled her shirt back on and leaned over the counter, hung her head, and dragged in one long breath after another.

She couldn't cower in here forever. That wasn't how she was raised. It wasn't in her.

****

"What are you going to do with the human?" Gideon's voice was laced with callous apathy.

"Her name is Kyanna," Xander replied. "And what I decide to do with her isn't any of your concern."

Xander watched the doorway, expecting her to appear any moment. But the doorway remained empty. She'd looked so fragile when he'd left her, and yet she'd held her chin up, proud and determined. He fought the urge to get up and go to her once more, just as he'd battled the strange emotion that had tugged through him earlier, that odd loathing to let her out of his sight. He deliberately turned his attention to the room, forced himself to focus on their common goal. Recovering the relics. Figuring out who else was hunting for them, who was trying to overthrow Lucifer…and stopping him.

Gideon, stone-faced, conjured a large, disposable coffee cup, lifted it to his lips and sipped. Mikhail, surrounded by his customary icy indifference, stared off into space, uncommunicative as always. Xander knew Niklas had read her aura before she'd left the room. Niklas had been given the gift of sight. The ability to see a human's emotions through a mystical swirl of color surrounding them. Part of Xander—a deep, foreign part—wanted to ask Niklas what he saw. Another part of him was just too uneasy to ask.

Confusion still warred within him. How had he known she needed him before, when she'd been in the bathroom crying? It made no sense. Was it some connection he'd unwittingly forged when he'd taken part of her soul? Maybe it was the restless hum of energy that lingered in his body. Did it somehow connect the two of them? The sight of her tears had done strange things to his insides. Twisted and tied him up in knots. Lord knew, his reaction wasn't normal. Why hadn't he been able to just walk away, like he'd done a hundred times—a thousand times—in the past?

Because Kyanna was different. *That's why.*

"When was the last time you fed?"

"A couple days."

Tilting his head, Niklas frowned. "How long were you"—he caught the Xander-stare and amended mid-sentence—"ah, a guest of Kyanna's?"

"A couple days," he reluctantly admitted.

"No wonder your eyes keep flashing red." Sebastian's grin quickly faded.

"I'll stay with your female if you need to hunt."

"I don't need to feed," Xander said, trying desperately to ignore the way his gut lurched at hearing Niklas refer to Kyanna as his female. "And she's not mine."

Creepy-crawlies slithered down his spine.

"She let you feed while you were a captive?"

"She is a Guardian," Mikhail countered, frowning at Gideon.

"Right," Sebastian addressed Gideon. "It's not like she'd break out a menu for him, order him up a nice tasty soul. Last I checked, you couldn't exactly phone the nearest Godfather's and order carry out or delivery for what we exist on, dude."

Ever the logical one, Niklas stepped in. "How did you feed, Slayer?"

Running his palm over his mouth, Xander reflected

on the strange energy that continued to hum though his veins even now. An energy that had never really abated after he'd taken part of Kyanna's essence into himself. Nor had the urge to feed overcome him as it should have by now.

He checked doorway. No sign of Kyanna. "I fed from Kyanna."

Dead silence met his claim.

Gideon dropped his foot to the floor. "But she's—"

"Still alive," Sebastian finished.

"It was only a partial feeding." He crossed his arms, setting his teeth.

Sebastian glanced to Niklas. "I've never heard of anyone only taking a partial feeding."

"No human could withstand that." Gideon shook his head. "It's not possible."

He turned to glare at Gideon. "Obviously it is."

"I've never heard of a human surviving a partial feeding before. Have you?" Sebastian asked Mikhail.

Mikhail shook his head. "Full blooded angels do not survive either."

Four pairs of eyes turned to the Demon of War, though he did not qualify his statement. A full measure of silence filled the room as each of them considered that last bit of information—and the possibilities of how he'd come by it—with raised eyebrows.

Shaking himself free of that alarming train of thought, Xander cleared his throat. They knew Xander had fed from Kyanna, he might as well spill the rest and have it over with. Maybe one of them could shed some light on the weird buzz still bouncing through his veins. "From the moment I fed from her, I've had a strange energy humming through me. It's like..." He struggled to come up with an explanation as the four of them stared at him like a science experiment that had gone wrong—badly wrong. "It's like the zing you get from an electrical shock. Only it hasn't gone away. And I do not feel the need to feed, though it's been well past time that I should."

"What does this mean?" Gideon looked around the room, his gaze landing on Niklas. "Did he somehow link himself to her?"

"How the hell should I know?" Niklas glowered. "I've never sucked half a soul from an innocent before." Seeming to remember his audience, he glanced toward Xander. "No offense."

Xander stared at him. Deadpan.

"Call Asher," Mikhail advised.

"What the hell do I need to call him for?"

"There is no end to what that dude knows, or what he can find," Sebastian said.

"Call Asher," Niklas agreed.

"Asher," Gideon repeated, throwing his two cents in as well.

What the hell was this? A Demonocracy? Were they all casting votes?

"Fine."

"Why in the name of Gabriel would you take part of her soul?" Sebastian shook his head, as if sorely disappointed.

"Didn't really have a choice at the time."

"Still, it wasn't very smart." Gideon glanced over. "No offense."

Oh, he was taking offense all right.

"I mean," Gideon went on, "what if you've bound yourself to her somehow. You better not let her too far from your sight, Slayer. For all you know, she could be your new Achilles heel."

Kyanna chose that moment to join them. A weight felt as if it had been lifted from his chest. Her eyes were swollen and red-rimmed. Her golden hair was caught up in some kind of messy knot on the top of her head now, revealing a long, slim neck. Her face was bright pink and scrubbed clean, reminding him of how delicate her skin had tasted against his tongue. How soft against his fingertips. He easily brought to mind the staggering curves hidden beneath the dowdy blue cotton sweat suit.

And those lips…

Lush lips that had yielded her passion to him and claimed a portion of his own soul in return.

"More than you know." Xander silently answered Gideon. "God help me, more than you know."

Trying to divert his focus from the woman lingering in the door, he turned to Niklas. "Have you discovered anything yet?"

For nearly a year, Niklas had been tracking Ronové. There'd been rumors he'd been sighted nearby.

The question was, why?

"Ronové's assembled eleven known minions. But he's playing it close to the vest, keeping them spread out, not letting them form a nest. I've seen a surge in demon numbers near a small town in Iowa, and the waxing moon is fast approaching. I think he's going to try to perform a summoning." Niklas shifted in his seat, crossed his arms.

"You think he's going to attempt to bring the mastermind behind this uprising to Earth?" Gideon leaned forward, dropping his elbows to his knees.

A nearly imperceptible nod.

"Well then, sitting around here flappin' jaws ain't gonna get the job done." Gideon vanished his coffee cup.

"You're still going to follow the lead Asher gave you on the Chosen One?"

Gideon gave a terse nod, then disappeared before anyone else could ask another question. It wasn't the lead—or more precisely the source of the lead—that had Xander worried. Asher, a rogue mercenary with loyalties to none but himself, had proven reliable time and again. He'd built himself a reputation nearly as fierce as that of the Fallen. Asher always got the job done, no matter what that job might be. And, though they'd never been able to figure out where he got his information from, it was always trustworthy. Always. You could stake your life on it. Heaven knew Xander had, more than once.

No, what had Xander worried was Gideon. The once charming and amiable Demon of Temptation had grown increasingly hostile and, at times, despondent. Volatile. No one else had voiced concern as of yet, but he knew they'd all noticed. Maybe it was time someone spoke up. Gideon was one of them. No one knew better than they the precarious line between good and evil he walked. If Gideon needed to be pulled back from the edge, so be it. Likewise, if he crossed that line…well, then action would need to be taken.

"It's getting harder for him to control the darkness," Xander observed.

A heavy silence filled the room.

"You think he's slipping?" Sebastian leaned

forward.

"You don't?" Niklas countered.

Mikhail grunted. Agreement or argument, who could tell?

"Are we supposed to start keeping tabs on him?" Niklas stroked his chin. He didn't need to voice aloud the rest of his thoughts. They all shared the same burden. Each was already battling his own inner darkness, each working toward his own redemption. Now they were fighting a common, faceless enemy. Add to that the weight of the possibility of having to put down one of their own? When would it all become too much for any of them to handle?

Sebastian shook his head. "He won't stand for it." He glanced around the room adding, "Would any of us?"

"He hasn't crossed the line yet," Niklas added.

"Space," Mikhail advised. "For now."

For now. Meaning that they'd deal with their comrade if, and when, the time came.

"All right." Sebastian stretched his arms. "On that happy note, I'm off to South America."

"We'll lay low at the cabin." Xander looked to Niklas and the others. "Go there if you find anything."

Sebastian glanced around the room, nodded when everyone seemed in accord, and then shimmered away. Mikhail waited for no one's permission, nor did he offer his own itinerary. He was simply there one moment and gone the next.

Niklas nodded to him, and then glanced once again at Kyanna. His frown deepened as he studied her aura once more. Xander had never asked about anyone's colors before. He'd never cared.

Now, it was all he could think about, what she was thinking. What she was feeling.

And Gideon's earlier words came back to haunt him. Kyanna had become his one and only weakness. His Achilles' heel. That left him with one driving question. What was he going to do about it?

Xander bit the tip of his tongue as he considered Niklas. Niklas had leaned forward, as if to speak, but he paused for a moment, studying the air surrounding Kyanna once more. His brow puckered, and a muscle bunched on his jaw. From the corner of his eye, Xander saw Kyanna turn her head. She was watching him now, and her expression changed infinitesimally. And at that moment, Niklas's eyes widened. Shaking his head, Niklas rubbed the back of his neck. A sure sign that something he saw troubled him. With one last alarmed glance at Kyanna, Niklas turned his full attention to Xander.

"Huchtaé ma'k, locti'vars," Niklas said in Demonic, his voice deep and layered. *Choose your battles wisely, my brother.*

And then he shimmered away, leaving Xander alone with Kyanna.

Chapter Seventeen

Slowly, Kyanna returned to her seat beside him. "What now?"

He resisted the urge to wrap his arms around her. But only just. She was pale, and that worried him. She was silent. And that worried him more. What was going in inside that beautiful head of hers? And that, too, worried him.

And that he worried…worried him. All this worry. *Bah!*

"Now they'll continue the search." He reached up and brushed a stray lock of hair from her brow, tucked it behind her ear. "The more relics we find, the less chance this mastermind has of succeeding."

"Don't you need to continue searching as well, Xander?" Kyanna asked quietly. Her expression was pinched. Her hands were clenched tight in her lap.

"My duty is to guard you and the stone."

A tiny frown creased her brow, but she glanced away without a word. Kyanna nodded but remained silent.

He pushed to his feet. Beside him, Kyanna stood as well, subdued.

What had Niklas meant by his last comment before he'd left? *Choose your battles wisely.* He'd already chosen his battle. He'd never return to Lucifer's side.

Slowly, he turned to face Kyanna. She looked so

fragile. So overwhelmed and dazed.

"Come." He held out his hand, bracing himself for her arguments.

Kyanna surprised him. Offering no resistance, she stepped into the circle of his arms. Laying her palms flat upon his abdomen between them, she dropped her forehead to his chest. Her shoulders sagged on a weary sigh.

It tore him up to see her this way. He couldn't resist pressing a quick kiss to the side of her head. "Are you ready?" He asked against her hair.

She gave a tiny nod, her head bumping his lips.

"Close your eyes," he whispered.

"They already are." Sweet Mary, she sounded exhausted.

Relieved they'd only have to shimmer once because they were leaving a secure location, he let out a long, tired breath of his own. Turning his focus inward, he brought to mind his cabin in the Rockies. The fresh scent of pine was immediate and soothing. Gentle rays of sunlight spilled in through the east windows above the sink as the sun began to peek over the treetops. Even though they'd already completed shimmering, he couldn't bring himself to release her.

She must not have minded, because she continued to stand, docile, in the circle of his arms.

Slowly, he stroked his hand up and down her back. Pleased when she relaxed and leaned into him, he pressed another kiss to the crown of her head. He slid his free hand up until he cupped the back of her neck. Xander began moving his fingers in tentative circles, experimenting with pressure and motion until he heard her sigh, just as he had earlier. The last of the tension ebbed from her shoulders, and her hands slipped downward and crept around his waist.

From the moment he'd first met her, she'd been fearless. Challenging him at every turn. Stirring his passions like no other before her. To see her like this, vulnerable and nearly too weary to stand, shook him, igniting a firestorm of protective instincts he never knew he possessed. He wanted nothing more than to hold her and protect her. To comfort her. To reassure her and convince her that he'd never let anything or anyone ever hurt her again.

But the words wouldn't come. He had no experience with this kind of thing. These emotions. Asking Kyanna for guidance while she was so upset seemed wrong. But standing here doing nothing while she so obviously needed him wasn't an option, pride or no pride.

"What can I do?" He whispered the words against her temple as his hands continued to caress her.

"I'm sorry." Her voice was so soft against his shirt that he had to strain to hear her. "I'm just so tired."

"Let me take care of you." Reaching down, he swept an arm beneath her knees, lifting her high against his chest. "Let's get you to bed."

"No." But her arms crept around him, and she nuzzled her cheek into the crook of his neck. She felt so right, snuggled in his embrace. As if she'd been born for no other purpose than to belong to him. "I need a shower, or a bath. Something. Can't"—she stifled a wide yawn—"can't sleep like this. I feel so grimy."

He skirted the rustic, log furniture in the living area. The heavy echo of his boots crossing the polished hardwood was temporarily muted while he tread over the thick fur rug on the floor in front of the huge, rough-cut stone fireplace. He scanned the room as he headed toward the bathroom. At least it was clean. After all, he'd been here a little over two weeks ago, though he hadn't planned on returning quite so soon.

The place wasn't huge by any means. The main floor contained nothing more than the living area on one side with its open kitchen nestled in the back corner on the other side flanked by a small pantry, and a full bath. The second floor was actually a large loft that spanned the width of the cabin above the kitchen area and was separated from the rest of the space by nothing more than a rough-hewn wooden railing.

His home in the Rockies was his private retreat. His one and only comfort. Much like the farmhouse in Minnesota was Sebastian's haven. He'd made it clear to the others that this was the one place they were not to bother him, not unless the world was coming to an end. Even then it was a questionable.

But having Kyanna here didn't bother him. In fact, he'd never felt more right about anything in his life.

Once in the bathroom, he was brought up short. She was dead on her feet. He doubted she'd be able to stand through a shower. But could he trust her not to drown in the bath? Glancing down at her, he winced. She looked breakable right now. And the only thing she'd requested of him was to be able to take a shower or bath. He could conjure her clean. It would be a damned sight easier. But she wanted a bath.

By all that was in his power, if she wanted a bath, then a bath she would have.

In short order, he had steaming water running in the large, claw foot tub. Remembering his shower in

Kyanna's bathroom, he conjured thick towels and bottles of floral-scented soaps and shampoos, just like hers. He even conjured a giant bottle of bubble bath. Bubble bath and women seemed to go together, right?

He sat down on the side of the tub, resting Kyanna on his lap. Sighing, she readjusted her hold on him, snuggling close once more. Something deep in his chest swelled to uncomfortable proportions—some sensation so foreign it caught him so by surprise that he nearly dropped her. He reached over and began pouring the bubble bath into the water. But how much? Shrugging, he dumped some in, then dumped in some more. When nearly half the bottle was gone, he gave a satisfied nod as a towering wall of bubbles began to form.

While he waited for the tub to finish filling, Xander stared down at her. She was all but asleep in his arms. Her face so innocent. So trusting. His heart seized in his chest.

How could he, even for one greedy moment, ever think he could deserve one such as her?

With a mental twist of the knob, he shut the water off, just as he shut down that torturous train of thought. He stood and lowered Kyanna to her feet, then gave her a little nudge.

"The bathwater is ready."

"Okay," she mumbled.

He slowly released her, keeping his hand out, ready to grab her should she fall. Blinking woozily up at him, she began to wrestle her sweatshirt over her head.

"Will you be all right?"

"Hmm? Oh. Yes. I'll be fine."

Her words, already beginning to slur, were nearly lost in the folds of her thick sweatshirt. "You're going to drown if I leave you in here alone," he accused.

Wriggling her arms down, she peered at him through a tunnel of blue cotton, giving him the look, one of her frustrated, don't-be-ridiculous glances that he found oddly reassuring. And then she pulled the sweatshirt over her head, leaving him salivating over the sudden display of lace and delectable flesh.

"Go. Away."

Dismissed, he stood there, unsure of what to do. Her attention had already returned to the tub, her hands were reaching behind her for the clasp on her bra.

Throwing his hands up, palms out, he shimmered from the room. Walking wasn't fast enough. If he'd lingered even a moment longer, he would have helped her with her bra. And the rest of her clothing. He'd have climbed right into that tub with her and helped himself. To her.

Mentally kicking those images out of his head, he conjured himself clean, dropped down on the sofa, and pulled out his phone. Speed dialing number five, he settled back and, crossing his ankles, he waited.

He didn't have long to wait. Three rings earned him a gruff, "What?"

"I need information."

"It'll cost you," Asher said.

"Doesn't it always?"

"What information?"

"Theoretically, if a demon fed from a human and only took a part of the soul, how would it affect the demon…and the human?"

A long pause followed. Then a dubious, "Theoretically?"

"Yeah."

Another long pause. "I'll get back to you."

And the line went dead. Unsurprised by Asher's abrupt manner, Xander snapped his phone closed and tucked it into his pocket. With a concentrated thought, a roaring fire blazed to life in the hearth, burning the chill from the air.

Abruptly sitting upright, he swore. The furnace in the cabin hadn't been run in two weeks and it was quite a bit cooler up here in the mountains. She was probably freezing in there. If she hadn't already drowned. Instinct had him concentrating on the bathroom, preparing to shimmer. But then he stopped. She was in the bathtub. Naked.

Naked!

Sweet Heaven above.

Sweat beaded on his forehead despite the cool air. How was he supposed to check on her if she was naked? Or, more precisely, how was he supposed to not take advantage of her being naked?

Kyanna. Naked.

Sweet Mary and Joseph, he had to get that word out of his head.

He crossed to the closed bathroom door and stared at it for a long moment, bracing himself, before knocking. "Kyanna?"

No response. Frowning, he knocked a little harder. "Kyanna?"

Again nothing. Fear poured through him in icy waves. She'd drowned. He just knew it. He'd turned his back for five damnable minutes, and she'd drowned.

Without a second thought, he opened the door and pushed his way inside.

There she lay, head tipped back, arms draped along

the rim of the tub, eyes closed. Her hair, freshly washed, snaked over one shoulder and dipped into the water, fanning out between her breasts in an island of bubbles. One knee broke the surface of the water and rested against the side of the tub. Her chest rose and fell in a steady rhythm. He watched, mesmerized, as a bead of moisture trickled from her temple down the side of her face, before skimming along her neck to pool at the base of her throat. And once that sweet hollow had filled, the water spilled over, tracking down, down the deep valley between her plump breasts, disappearing into more bubbles.

Every ounce of spit in his mouth dried up.

His body went instantly, painfully rock hard.

Her head lolled to the side and her foot slipped along the tub until her knee disappeared. She started sliding down. When her chin hit the surface of the water and she didn't even stir, Xander jumped forward, panicked. His hands clenching and unclenching at his sides. He couldn't touch her. He didn't dare touch her.

Oh God, how he wanted to touch her.

"Kyanna," he called hoarsely. "Kyanna, wake up."

"Xander?" Turning her head, she blinked, smiled. And then she went back to sleep.

Gritting his teeth, he dug deep for control. Xander snatched up a towel, and somehow managed to coax her up out of the water, all the while keeping his eyes carefully averted. Not an easy task when the woman he was trying to keep his hands *off* was soaking wet and limp as a noodle. This was his penance for lusting after her. Reparation and punishment. And he didn't want to falter. But the urge to take care of her, to see to her needs in her exhausted state wasn't as strong as his lust.

And the blasted towel kept slipping. The sooner he got his hands off her, the better it would be for both of them.

Oh, to hell with good intentions. Where had they gotten him anyway?

Xander conjured her dry and clothed and shimmered them to the loft.

"Are you hungry?" he asked, desperate to get his mind off the memory of her in her bath.

"No. No food." She gave a lusty yawn and swayed on her feet. "And no sweats."

"What?"

"Can't sleep in a sweatshirt and sweatpants," she complained. "Too hot."

"It's cold in here," he protested. And that was when he made a colossal error in strategy. He looked at her. Her hair was still slightly damp, clinging to her neck and shoulders. Her cheeks were flushed a rosy hue, like the dew-kissed petals of a rose. Her eyes were heavy-lidded, just like he imagined they would be in the deepest throes of passion. And her luscious mouth begged to be ravished. She looked like a goddess just risen from the sea. The scent of her wrapped itself around him and wouldn't let go.

"More blankets. No sweats."

He blinked down at her, lost. *Blankets? Sweats*? What the hell had they been talking about?

He forced a swallow, dragging his mind from the king-sized bed that filled the room and presented way too much temptation. As if the woman before him wasn't enough temptation on her own already. "What do you want to wear?"

"T-shirt."

Groaning, he silently vanished the dowdy clothing he'd dressed her in and seamlessly replaced it with an oversized T-shirt.

She immediately frowned, opening her eyes to blink drowsily up at him. "No bra."

Sweet Mother Mary! She'd be the death of him yet.

He licked his lips and vanished her bra. His control, already stretched to the limit, suffered a thousand tiny fissures at the sight of her hardened nipples thrusting against the soft white cotton.

She wound her arms around his neck and leaned into him, tugging his head down. A contented smile curving her lips. "Thank you." And she pressed a soft kiss to his cheek. Those tiny fissures widened into irreparable cracks.

The feel of her breasts pressed against him took his breath away.

Just like that, his control snapped. Sinking his fingers deep in her damp hair, he dragged her head back and fastened his mouth over hers. His free hand rode the ridges of her spine down, down until he cupped the soft curve of her bottom, squeezing, lifting her to the tips of her toes as he ground his throbbing erection against her soft belly. Moaning, he sank his tongue inside the sweet, silky heat of her mouth. Over and over, Xander thrust his tongue against hers. He groaned aloud when she slid one knee up his leg, hooking her thigh around his.

His body engulfed in need, he gripped her generous bottom in both hands and picked her up. Xander's body quaked when she wrapped her long legs around his waist. Kyanna's arms tightened around his neck. She angled her head and kissed him back with enough need, with enough demand, to make his knees shake. She set fire to his blood. He took an unsteady step toward the bed, convictions and good intentions rapidly falling to the wayside in a pile of ash. Single-minded determination drove him. In minutes, he'd lose himself inside her. Nothing else mattered.

The phone in his back pocket suddenly began screeching. It took several long seconds for the sound to penetrate the haze of lust fogging his mind. The noise hadn't seemed to catch up to Kyanna, however. Her mouth continued to slant over his, her deft tongue dueling with his. And all the while she wrapped herself around him, rubbing her full breasts against his chest, grinding the juncture of her thighs along the ridged length of his throbbing erection.

Cursing himself, Xander tore his lips from hers. His chest heaved as he stared into her dazed eyes and battled to regain his senses. He'd been moments from spilling her onto the bed, stripping them both naked and plunging himself inside her sweet body until both of them were mindless.

He'd been in way over his head, and he hadn't even realized the danger until it was too late.

He watched as she blinked at him. Her pupils were dilated. Whether from passion or exhaustion, he couldn't tell.

No. Not like this.

He took a mental step back, then slowly settled her on her feet. When—no, *if*, not when, as when implied determined certainty—if he took her, he wanted her wide awake. Fully cognizant of what they were doing. He wouldn't leave room for doubt for either of them later. He had enough guilt to live with as it was. Taking advantage of her in her weakened, emotional state might not be the lowest point in his existence. But he had a nagging suspicion it might well be the one act that truly haunted him for the rest of eternity.

"I have to take this call." He could barely get the words out. Xander took Kyanna firmly by the shoulders, and nudged her back a step, giving them both some much needed space. "Get into bed. Cover up."

Before she could speak, he shimmered to the living area and sat down on the sofa once more. His body shook with his need. His erection was so painful, he gritted his teeth against the urge to stroke it himself just to relieve the pressure. He refused to do that though. The pain was his penance for slipping, for giving into the lust.

He snapped into the phone, "Speak."

"It's only been done once before that I've been able to learn about," Asher cut to the chase, taking up the conversation as if it had never been interrupted.

"And?"

"It didn't go well. For either of them," he qualified.

"Explain."

"By absorbing only a portion of the soul, the demon inadvertently bound his life force to the human. Another demon found out, captured the human, and killed him. The demon's own life force withered and, no matter how many times he fed, he died not long after."

Xander swiped a hand over his mouth in a vain effort not to burst into a fit of wild ranting and swearing.

"Doubtful the human would have survived

anyway."

That brought him up cold. "Why?"

"A few hours after the partial feeding, the human began to sicken. Seems they don't thrive well with only half a soul." Asher's tone left a careless *go figure* hanging at the end of his pronouncement.

Panic clenched an icy fist in his chest, but he did his best to calm himself. A matter of hours, Asher had said. It had been well over twenty-four hours, and Kyanna hadn't displayed any sickness yet.

She's strong. She'll be fine.

But worry niggled again. He'd never seen her so tired as she was tonight. He'd never seen any human that worn down. Maybe it was a delayed side effect. Panic began to blossom inside him once more, clutching his chest in an icy fist. What if she was displaying the first signs of the side effects of his feeding? "What if the human was of angelic descent?"

"A Halfling?" Asher was definitely interested now.

"Very diluted, but yeah. A Halfling."

"Theoretically speaking?"

"Just spit it out." It took everything in him not to crush the phone in his hand before he got the information he needed.

"Impossible to say. That, to my knowledge, has never been done. Ain't too many Halflings running around, you know. Could be the same effect. Could turn out in the end to have no effect on either party." Asher was quiet for a moment, and then he added, "Man, one thing's for certain, theoretically speaking, whatever fool it was that did something so stupid had better be finding a safe place under a lock and key for that Halfling. Just in case."

"What do you mean?"

"Halfling dies, demon dies. That's an awfully big damned risk to take on a maybe. Anything else?" That was Asher. Always cut and dry. Always closing the deal, ready to move on to the next contract.

"No," Xander muttered before snapping the phone closed. Dropping the phone to the sofa beside him, he tipped his head back against the cushion and ran both hands over his head, scrubbing.

What in the name of Saint Peter have I done?

Still painfully erect, he stalked to the counter and, resting his clenched fists on the edge of the sink, he stared out the window, restless. Itchy inside.

I should be out there hunting. I've got more important things to do than play babysitter to a Halfling that means absolutely nothing to me.

Creepy-crawlies skittered down his spine.

He wiggled his shoulders in a vain attempt to shake them off.

Damn it. The cabin was the one place he wasn't supposed to have to worry about his curse. There wasn't supposed to be anything here to intrude on his peace of mind or his confidence in the path that he'd chosen for himself.

Out of all the places in the world he'd ever been, this small cabin in the woods—this quiet oasis on the side of a mountain—was where he'd always been able to find his center. Right now, at this very moment, he'd never been more off balance. He didn't have to turn and look over his shoulder to see the source of his troubles. He knew she was still up there. Asleep in his bed. He felt her presence in his bones. Deep in his soul. Just like the seemingly permanent hum her essence had given him.

He couldn't be with her, not like he wanted. He'd chosen this path for himself. He'd walked this path for two centuries. And yet he couldn't walk away from her either. For more reasons, if he were being totally honest with himself, than because her soul might somehow be connected to his. No, he didn't think he'd be able to walk away from her, even if it meant facing the fires of Hell once again. Or greeting Oblivion without a sword in his hand.

If he were being honest, he'd admit she was more than a bump in his road. Somehow, she'd become the destination on every road sign.

He didn't like it. Not one bit.

And that wasn't the only thing bothering him. He owed her something. She had a right to know what he'd done to her that first night. How he'd absorbed a portion of her soul. Oh sure, he'd told her he'd absorbed some of her *essence*. But he'd been deliberately vague. She deserved the whole truth, even if she ended up loathing him for it. She certainly couldn't hate him any worse than he hated himself. Nothing he'd done in his long existence had ever weighed upon him as did that one single event. Suppressing it, ignoring it wasn't helping. Not knowing what his impetuous actions might do to her, what harm he may have caused her only compounded the issue. The guilt was eating him alive.

Filled with dread, he shimmered to the loft, sat down in the log rocker in the corner. Kyanna was curled up in a little ball in the middle of his king sized bed, dead to the world, the covers pulled up around her ears. His gaze slid to his nightstand, came to rest on the tattered Bible. He reached over and picked it up. He ran his fingers over the worn, embossed cross, desperate for guidance.

He'd pray for direction and place his trust in the Lord's word, just as he'd been doing for the past two hundred years. After flipping the book open, he dropped his finger randomly on the first page he came to and silently read.

For where your treasure is, there your heart will be also. Luke 12:34.

A sucker punch to the gut wouldn't have stunned him more. He gingerly closed the Bible and returned it to its place. Xander rubbed the palm of his hand over his chest, just above his heart, as he settled back in the chair and swallowed. Hard. At length, he braced his elbows on the arms of the rocker, laced his fingers together, and pressed his joined fists to his lips.

And he watched her sleep.

Chapter Eighteen

Unable to cope with the unsettling emotions seething inside him, Xander shimmered to the boulder on the edge of his meadow. Perched cross-legged on the top of the massive stone, he clasped his hands in his lap and tipped his face to the rising sun. He closed his eyes and drew a deep breath, released it slowly, deliberately emptied his mind and let it all go.

He let the scents and the sounds wash over him. Evergreens swayed in a gentle breeze. Their pungent aroma, mixed with the crisp fragrance of morning dew drying on fading mountain grasses, seeped through him, familiar and welcome. The meadows vivid colors were so bright they hurt his eyes. Crows squabbled in the distance and flew away. Blue jays and sparrows cart-wheeled and swooped through the skies, perching on trembling branches, calling to their mates in trilling cries or chirp-chirping at intruders who ventured too closely to their nests. Tiny creatures scurried through the underbrush, stockpiling for the winter. Bees hovered and darted, industriously flying to and fro, tending their queen's dying gardens. Long wisps of white streaked across the pale blue sky. All around him life flourished, indifferent to his quandary.

By rote, he bowed his head and recited the Lord's Prayer. But when it came to the line about God's will being done, he paused.

What is your will, Father?

Would he ever find the missing piece to the puzzle? Once he'd turned his back on Lucifer, he'd never questioned his path, never wavered. Not once. He'd steadfastly battled evil on every front and diligently practiced celibacy. He'd aided the innocent whenever the opportunity arose. He'd sacrificed, he'd prayed, he'd repented.

And still, he hadn't found forgiveness. Just one more battle.

Always one more battle.

Was this to be another trial then? Had Kyanna been sent to test his dedication?

If he caved, if he took what he so desperately wanted, would he throw away all he'd worked so hard for, forever damning himself? Was he already beyond redemption?

If he *didn't* take Kyanna, would he be wasting his one and only shot at Heaven here on Earth?

But could *she* be happy with *him*?

All these questions were tearing him up inside. It took everything he had, every ounce of his vaunted self-control, not to rage at the sky. Not to leap to his feet and curse God at the top of his lungs, so great was his anger, so great his confusion. He clenched his fists at his side in effort to quell the plasma balls that wanted to spring free and level this peaceful meadow. Darkness swarmed below his calm surface, waiting, biding its time to rise up and destroy. And yet, he wouldn't let it win, couldn't let it free. Not out there in the world of man. And not here. Not in his meadow.

He'd come here countless times before. Through the centuries, he'd watched tiny seedlings grow into stout, soaring behemoths. He'd observed that river over there winding its way through the hills as it carved a path for itself. In the beginning, it had been nothing more than a tiny, trickling brook. He'd watched it swell to a raging unstoppable force of nature and dry out to almost nothing. And now look how many of God's creatures came to its banks, depended upon its swift flowing, crystal clear waters. Though none were brave enough to approach him, generations of those creatures had become inured to his presence.

This meadow was the only temple allowed to him. This boulder was his altar. The scent of pine was his incense, the wind his confessor. This sanctuary was the one sacred place he could commune with his creator.

But now it all seemed to mock him. He'd come here to worship. To renew his faith.

Instead, he only found more questions. A sly sense of injustice slithered through him, and was quickly squashed.

His mind turned, unbidden, to the woman asleep in his bed, and he reflected back over the short time he'd spent with her. Granted, some of it had been eye-opening and, admittedly, horrifying, even for a demon. He flashed back to their shopping trip. Xander shuddered and rubbed his fingers over his temple, forcibly ejecting those thoughts from his mind. Instead, he thought of her store. A plethora of sentimental junk stacked here and there. Old furniture and doodads that she'd put such stock in. He remembered the way she'd carefully taken the small statue of Mary from his hand, remembered her soft, gentle smile. Her voice had been so soothing as she'd spoken of its value. Not monetary value, but the value one found in one's heart. And her happiness had enthralled him.

Those things were all gone now. He grimaced. She'd lost so much because of him and his kind. How could he ask her to stay with him? How could he ask her to give him her future when he'd already taken so much of her past?

That's not all I've taken, now is it?

The image of a laughing Kyanna sitting on the floor in the library, draped with little boys, swamped him, tugging at something in his gut. And the way she'd tossed her head back and let laughter pour forth when that old man with the cane had begun spouting dirty jokes left a warm sensation swimming in his chest. It had been all he could do not to crack a smile then. Or now at the memory. In truth, he'd mentally recited his old fall-back, "The Slayer does not smile," so many times that afternoon he'd begun to feel like a broken record.

And when that pansy of an ex-boyfriend of hers had showed up at her store, flowers in hand and pretty words on his lips? It had been all Xander could do not to turn him inside out. Literally.

He'd known Kyanna for such a short time, only a few days, and yet he couldn't remember anyone ever making such a forceful impact on his life. For the love of Saint Christopher, he'd even tried to comfort her when she'd grown distraught during their meeting with the others. That whole mess had felt awkward. Truth be told, he was completely inept at comforting, having had zero experience with the act.

He saved the innocent, and his duty was done. He never, never stuck around to offer comfort. The human got weepy and that was his cue to disappear. And yet when Kyanna had blinked up at him with glassy eyes, when she'd trembled and looked so lost, he hadn't been able to help himself. He couldn't stand to see her like that. It had shredded him. Panicked him in a way he'd never experienced before.

And he didn't like that at all.

The Slayer didn't offer comfort.

And the Slayer sure as hell did not panic.

What is wrong with me?

****

Kyanna yawned and stretched. She blinked and sat up. It took a moment of squinting around the room before she remembered where she was. And why she was here. Her store was gone. And her home. She had nothing left.

She gasped. *The book! The stone!*

She'd had them when they'd shimmered from the farm. But she could remember very little after that. She had a hazy memory of a hot bubble bath.

Her breath came a little faster as she picked her memories apart, scrambling to remember what had transpired since Xander had brought her here. The bath, yes. Her eyes widened even more. She'd been dead on her feet, but that was no excuse. And when he'd dressed her in sweats and she'd requested—

Oh, my God! She quickly glanced down. Yes, she wore a plain white T-Shirt, which was presently twisted around her waist. And no bra.

She hung her head.

But the memories of the night past weren't through with her yet. He'd kissed her. Oh boy, what a kiss it had been.

Heat crawled into her cheeks and her lips formed a

small “o” as she recalled throwing herself into his arms and all but forcing herself on him moments before he’d set her away from him and disappeared.

She caught sight of the deep red stone resting on the nightstand and relaxed. Beside the stone, there on the nightstand, was the book. *Xander,* she thought. He could act so cold and unfeeling at times. And yet he’d known she would panic until she knew the book and the stone were safe. He was such a contradiction.

Turning her head, she peered down through the railing, down toward the windows on the far side of the fireplace in the living area. Deep magenta streaked the navy skyline above the treetops. The room below was shrouded in darkness. It was nighttime? Already? She’d only just fallen asleep, hadn’t she?

How could she have slept an entire day away?

All was quiet below. “Xander?”

“I’m here.”

Gasping, she pressed a fist to her chest and whirled back around, peering into the inky blackness filling the corner. He sat in the rocker. She caught a flutter of motion, then shielded her face as golden light winked on, bathing the area around the nightstand.

Slowly lowering her hand, she took a good look at him. Tiny lines fanned his eyes, the way they did when he was deep in thought. Whisker stubble darkened his jaw. Other than to turn the reading lamp on, he hadn’t moved a muscle. Indeed, the way Xander sat watching her reminded her of one of those Mutual of Omaha episodes chronicling the way a lion holds perfectly still as it stalks its prey, right in those few breathless moments before it pounces.

She pushed up farther in the bed, wiggled the T-shirt down over her hips, and tucked her legs beneath her before shoving her tangled hair over one shoulder. And then she noticed the way the muscle in his jaw was bunched. Something was bothering him.

"What's happened? Are the others okay? Did they find something?"

He was silent for so long, she'd begun to think he hadn't heard her. Or, if he had, that he didn't intend to answer.

"They're fine," he finally responded.

"Did they find another Guardian?"

"No."

"Then why are you so grim?"

"I had a decision to make." Had. Past tense. Then he'd already made up his mind about whatever it was that was troubling him. And, apparently, his decision didn't sit too well. He tilted his head slightly to the side. "Now I see I had no choice at all."

"I don't understand." The determined, almost angry tone of his voice unsettled her. Frowning, she clutched the blankets and tugged them up, closer against her chest. "Can I help?"

Xander huffed out a breath. A tiny crease suddenly appeared in one cheek. It was a line she'd never seen before, and it threw her concentration off for a moment. Enough that when he suddenly leaned forward, the motion startled her.

"Your cooperation is appreciated, though I'm honestly not sure it's a requirement anymore."

"What are you talking about, Xander?" He slowly rose from the rocker. She caught herself scooting backward, away from him, and forced herself to hold her ground. "What are you doing?"

Suddenly, unexpectedly, he grinned at her. A wicked grin that set her stomach to trembling. The sight of it took her breath away. His teeth were even and white. Deep grooves dug themselves into his cheeks on both sides of his mouth. She could only stare in wonder.

"Do you remember what I told you, about how things are in my world?" He eased closer to the bed, every step reminiscent of that stalking big cat. "How when a male finds a female that he wants for his own, he pursues her, would do anything to obtain her? Would fight to the death to keep her?" His thigh came to rest against the edge of the bed. "And that once he has her, he would never let her go?"

Kyanna bobbed her head. Her heart was lodged firmly in her throat, preventing speech all together. Speech? Hell, she couldn't even breathe.

"I've decided."

"What?" She croaked, cleared her throat and tried again. "You've decided what?"

"What I'm going to do with you." His eyes burned with an intensity she'd never seen before. His grin fell away, and his expression became deadly serious, leaving no room for doubt that he meant exactly what he was saying. Every. Single. Word. "You were always supposed to belong to me. I'm keeping you."

"Keeping me?" She squeaked as he snagged the edge of the blanket and began drawing it away. Kyanna tugged right back, fisting the blanket in a death grip. Just like that, the blankets vanished altogether. "Knock it off," she ordered, coming up on her knees in the middle of the bed. Her temper took hold and she pointed a threatening finger at him. "That's not fair. I don't go disappearing things on you."

His T-shirt was suddenly gone. “There.” He smirked. “Now we’re even.”

Her mouth went dry and her lips parted on a long, shuddering breath. She didn’t know how to deal with him. This was an entirely new side to him, one she’d not witnessed before. He was—*grinning, for Pete’s sake!* She stared at him, devouring the feast of naked flesh suddenly on display. The muscles of his abdomen rippled and tightened as he put one knee up on the bed. The mattress dipped beneath his weight, and he balanced himself with his knuckles.

Bringing his other knee up, he began slowly crawling toward her on his hands and knees, stalking her across the huge bed. She scooted away, her mind suddenly racing. Was this actually happening? Was this what she thought it was? Or was she, somehow, still asleep? Lost in an erotic fantasy?

His body language certainly indicated he had every intention of making good use of this bed. And sleep was nowhere on his agenda. He was sacrificing two hundred years of celibacy.

Oh God, that’s a lot of expectation to live up to.

A shudder worked its way through her system. He hadn’t been with a woman in two hundred years. She’d always thought herself worldly. She was certainly no innocent. But the intensity on his face, his single-minded focus, the tension in his body gave her pause. Maybe this whole situation was more than she could handle. Maybe *he* was more than she could handle.

She’d scooted as far as she could go. Her spine hit the railing. She darted a glance toward the foot of the bed and freedom. Xander snaked his arm out and he hooked his hand around the back of her bent knee.

"Xander," she whispered, barely able to draw breath. A warning. A plea.

She should argue with him. Should at least attempt to make him see reason. He was throwing away so much for this one moment of passion. Centuries of self denial, lost in a heartbeat. And yet she could barely find her voice. How was she ever to argue with him, stubborn granite wall that he was? Shaking her head, she braced her hands against his chest as he straightened before her. His skin was smooth, and so hot to the touch. Her fingers curled and dug into muscle. Slim inches separated them now. The hand he'd anchored on her lower back burned through her thin T-shirt. The hand he'd hooked around her knee slid up the back of her thigh and came to rest on the curve of her hip, beneath the hem of her shirt. He searched her face.

"*For where your treasure is…*" he murmured.

Dipping his head, hauling her up tight against him, he captured her lips so forcefully that her back bowed. It was all she could do not to moan her surrender. His lips moved over hers insistently. Rubbing. Nipping. Demanding a response. She was incapable of resisting. He sucked her lower lip between his and gently held it there between his teeth. His tongue swept over the sensitive inner edge. His hands boldly cupped her bottom and squeezed.

Startled, she gasped. Xander took advantage of her surprise, sweeping his tongue inside her mouth. This time she *did* moan. He swallowed the sound and angled his head, deepening the kiss, taking her even further under before she had time to surface. His heat surrounded her. His strength caged her. His mouth made her burn.

Leaving one hand on her bottom, he swept the other up her back, beneath the T-shirt, catching the hem on his wrist, baring her belly in the process. Skin met hot skin, and she sucked in a sharp breath. Desire deep in the pit of her stomach fluttered and clenched tight. His callused palm sent goose bumps over her back. Xander splayed his hand between her shoulder blades. And still he worked magic with his mouth. Her insides trembled. She was suddenly giddy. Short of breath. Achy with need. She couldn't get close enough to him.

His lips left hers. His teeth nipped their way along her cheek and down the side of her neck. And there he played, flicking the tip of his tongue over the pulse point beneath the ridge of her jaw. When she was physically shaking, her fingers digging in to his shoulders, drawing him closer as she arched her neck for better access, he suckled her earlobe.

"I need you, Kyanna," he whispered, his breath hot against her ear. "God, help me. I need you."

This demon who never needed anyone, needed her. The knowledge left her reeling.

Unable to help herself, she laced her fingers in his short hair and drew his face to hers. She peered into his eyes for one long moment, and then she claimed his lips. For a few moments, he let her be the aggressor. Let her control the kiss, sink her tongue inside his mouth and suck his tongue into hers. He let her press herself against him. She wrapped her arms around his neck.

With a muffled groan, he shifted his hold on her, sank his fingers in her hair, and dragged her head back. His lips seized her throat, sucking and laving until she moaned his name aloud. He made short work of her T-shirt, whipping it over her head and tossing it away. Xander leaned back for a moment, allowing a few sparse inches between them, and his gaze swept over her. She didn't have time to be shy about the way her breasts had swollen, or the way her nipples had hardened, thrusting toward him. She didn't have time to be embarrassed about kneeling on the bed in front of him in nothing more than a pair of lacy panties.

A heated oath slipped from his lips, and then she was suddenly flat on her back, pinned beneath the erotic weight of him. Anxious to ease the ache, she skimmed her knees up the outside of his thighs. Suddenly, his pants were gone. The coarse hair on his legs tickled the arches of her feet. The searing heat of his thick erection pressed against her belly. His hand slipped between them to cup her breast. His tough fingertips flicked and massaged her nipple until she arched her back and whimpered. Only then did he lower his mouth to sooth her. Xander drew her nipple into the wet heat of his mouth and rubbed his tongue over it. Suckled. Circled. Rolled the tip with his tongue. Paying homage to first one and then the other.

And while he did so, his hand flattened on her belly. His palm slid down, down, down, until his fingertips slipped beneath the lace of her panties. And still he kept going, until he covered her, pressed, and began a slow, sensuous, circular motion.

Gasping, she arched her hips.

"Tell me," he whispered, nibbling back up her chest, along the ridge of her arched neck. "Tell me what you want."

"Oh, God, Xander, please," she panted. Her head thrashed to the side.

"Please, what?" Just the tip of one finger slid through her silken wet folds. Retreated. And she groaned her disappointment. "This? Is this what you want?" His finger returned, this time to circle, circle, coming so close to penetrating her, and yet not quite dipping in. She nodded weakly, could have cried. He was ruthless. Pushing her to respond. Not letting her hold anything back.

"Yes," she cried. "Touch me."

Her legs moved restlessly, her heels digging into the bed as she lifted her hips in demand.

His lips seized hers and he thrust his tongue against hers in a taunting mimicry of lovemaking. And then, so slowly she could have screamed, he began to penetrate her with his finger. Her sheath clenched tight on him. She cried out, grateful, and yet still needing more.

"More," she begged. "Please, Xander. More."

Her hips thrust up in demand, lifting his weight as well. He vanished her panties finally and angled his hand, thrusting a second finger inside her, working it, grinding his palm against her. His movements were less than gentle now, his breathing ragged, and it made her even hotter.

Panting, she tossed her head to the side. Her body shook with sensation. And then Xander slid farther down, wedging his shoulders between her thighs, pushing her knees wider as he slid his hands beneath her bottom, lifting her up. One long, hot lick nearly sent her over the edge. Nearly. But not quite. Setting his mouth to her, he used his lips and his tongue and his teeth to urge her higher and higher.

Kyanna stretched one hand up, bracing her palm against the headboard. The other slid across the sheets, grabbing, twisting, fisting the material as she called his name in sheer desperation. He'd set her on fire. He'd abraded every nerve in her body and stroked them to bliss. And still he pushed her, driving her higher. His tongue—*oh sweet Lord, his tongue!*

Her body shattered, and still he continued to worship her, driving her ruthlessly up peak after peak until she sobbed his name in sheer, mindless abandon.

****

Xander finally released her and sat back on his heels. She sprawled before him, panting. She stared blindly at the ceiling. Her body was limp. One hand was plastered to the headboard, the other was tangled in the twisted bedding at her side. The taste of her honey was the most intoxicating aphrodisiac he'd ever experienced. His body was strung out, rock hard, and aching. He couldn't get enough of her.

He'd meant what he'd said before. This was meant to be. She was always meant to belong to him. But there was one thing he hadn't told her yet.

He was *never* going to let her go.

Xander prowled up her boneless body, and eased himself on top of her, bracing his weight on his elbows on either side of her head. He captured her lips in a long, slow, yet demanding kiss. Her arms came around him, and she raised her knees, dragging her feet up the backs of his thighs. The feel of her limbs wrapped around him, her pliant body soft beneath him, her tongue tangling with his drove him crazy. He fought not to lose control. It was the hardest battle of his life. He wanted to savor every moment, every sensation.

The pace of her breathing began to pick up again. Her legs lifted higher as she moved beneath him, lifting her pelvis, rubbing against him; her passion rapidly rekindled. Xander eased his hips back, then shifted forward until he slid his erection along her drenched, silky cleft. Torturing them both, he rubbed back and forth at a snail's pace. The friction made him shudder and tremble in her arms. She writhed against him now, whimpering, urging him on. Her body was telling him she needed more, begging him for more.

And he needed more.

He drew his knees up beneath her bottom and slipped a hand under her lower back. He slid his free hand beneath her shoulders and pulled her up with him until he was kneeling on the bed with her straddling his lap. She locked her ankles behind him and wiggled closer. Xander gripped her hips between his hands and, holding her steady, he lifted her higher, until the tip of his throbbing erection nudged her entrance. Tipping his head back, he watched her face, watched as she gasped, and she stared back at him.

Only then did he lower her down his throbbing length. One long, slow, torturous inch at a time.

"Xander," she moaned.

Her silky sheath slipped over him, tight, hot, squeezing him, making him groan. Wrapping his arms around her waist, splaying his hands on her sides, he began to lift, lower, lift her, smooth and steady, until she whimpered low in her throat, her eyelids sliding closed as she tipped her forehead to touch his.

"Oh God, Xander, don't stop," she begged. "Don't ever stop."

The sound of his name on her lips at the pinnacle of her passion stirred possessive and elemental instincts until he felt he would burst with it. Anchoring an arm around her, he leaned forward, lowering them both to the bed.

He'd meant to be gentle. Meant to go slowly and draw this out. But the way she took him in and urged him on with wild abandon shattered his restraint. Over and over he plunged, each thrust faster and more forceful than the last. He pushed his hands up behind her, hooked them over her shoulders taking some of his weight off her, anchoring her in place. He leaned down and seized her lips.

She tasted so sweet. If he had but one moment to take with him, only one moment to remember for the rest of his eternal life, let it be this one.

Her body began to tense beneath his. Her nails dug into his back, and the burn was exquisite. Her whimpers were frantic now. He branded openmouthed kisses down the side of her neck, gripped her shoulders and rolled his hips, rocking into her with such force the bed frame shook and groaned. Over and over. And once again Kyanna screamed his name. Her sheath contracted on him and her nails scored his flesh. Xander pressed his mouth to her neck, felt her pulse pounding beneath his lips. He growled aloud as he emptied himself deep inside her.

He lay there for long moments afterward, still joined with her, thunderstruck, as her breath rushed across the side of his temple. He couldn't move. Couldn't think. Couldn't fathom the intensity of what had just happened between them.

Without a word passing between them, Xander rolled to his side. He curled his arm possessively around her, carefully turning her, and drew her back, tucking her securely into the shelter of his body. She was boneless against him, snuggling close with a contented sigh. Xander conjured thick, soft blankets to cover them. He rested his cheek against her hair and drew the scent of her in deep, pleased when her breathing grew slow and even. Well over an hour passed as he lay like that, holding her. An hour of pure contentment, the likes of which he'd never known, not even as an angel in Heaven. And when he fell asleep, he did so with one enveloping thought on his mind.

He'd kill anyone or anything that tried to take his treasure from him.

Chapter Nineteen

"Please, Xander," she pleaded. "I'm going stir crazy in here. I need to stretch my legs. We're in the middle of nowhere. Nobody is going to find us here. You can even come with me if you're that worried."

Xander lowered the can of soda and rested his elbow on the arm of the sofa. That there-and-gone-again groove in his cheek flirted from his cheek and his heated gaze swept over her. "I would have thought you'd gotten enough exercise last night."

Heat flooded her face, and she ducked her head. He'd laid siege to her defenses and claimed her body no less than four times over the course of the night. Hard and fast. Slow and easy. Rough, gentle, and every degree in between. And when she woke up cuddled in his arms this morning, he'd kissed her senseless and ravished her yet again.

He utterly baffled her. He was still quiet. Still…Xander. But the smoldering, knowing glances he kept sending her way left her shaken to the tips of her toes. As if he were remembering the way she'd screamed his name in the throes of every bone-melting climax. Or the way she'd clung to him, writhed against him, and begged for more.

She was a woman who'd always made sure her relationships were clear cut. For obvious reasons, she couldn't afford for there to be room for mistakes. But this thing she had with Xander? She had no clue. It was an uncomfortable sensation, being on the fence like this. Were they a couple now? Had it just been a one-time thing? Had last night been a lapse in judgment for both of them? Had it been a product of extenuating circumstances? What did he feel for her? What did she feel for him? The whole situation made her edgy. But she couldn't bring herself to broach the subject with him. She felt vulnerable and the risk was more than she cared to consider. So she let things ride.

For now, at least.

Ignoring the heat in her cheeks, she crossed her arms and peered out the window over the sink. There were still several hours till sunset. They could take a nice hike through the woods. She'd never needed the big city to thrive. But, truly, the inactivity was beginning to get to her. Then again, maybe it was being virtually locked up in such a small space with all this unresolved tension hanging in the air.

"Just for a little while?"

"It's not safe, Kyanna."

"I put enchantments around the book and the stone, just as you asked. And you have your ward stones around the cabin. They'll be fine."

"I'm not talking about the book and the stone. I'm talking about you." He downed the last of his cola and vanished the can. Funny how she'd become accustomed to this little quirk of things appearing from out of nowhere, and then disappearing just as quickly. "I found this place once. Anyone else can too."

"I trust you to protect me." She bent down to take hold of his hands and drew him to his feet. "Please?"

"Half an hour," he grudgingly agreed.

Before she had time to blink, she was suddenly wearing a warm sweatshirt and comfortable hiking boots. Touched by his consideration, she grinned up at him. "That's handy."

"I'm faster at taking them off." He arched an eyebrow, his gray eyes sparkling with temptation. "Wanna see?"

Her lips twitched. He was a sneaky one, all right, trying to divert her from her goals. And if anything could do it that would be it. "After our walk."

Kyanna spun on her heel and hurried to the door, beckoning him forward before he could change her mind. The air was crisp and so fresh she could have made a small fortune bottling and marketing it. Several yards from the cabin, she threw her arms out and spun around, drinking in the scenery. This surely had to be one of the most beautiful places on Earth. No wonder Xander chose this spot as his haven. Glancing over her shoulder, she offered him a wide, encouraging smile. He followed at a much more sedate pace. Finally, frustrated that he wasn't moving fast enough, she took hold of his hand and pulled him onward.

They wandered through the woods, with Kyanna chatting incessantly and Xander responding in his customary monosyllables and grunts, until they came to a meadow. He hesitated at the edge of the small clearing. And then, seeming to square his shoulders, he took the lead and guided her to a massive stone. Without a word, he grasped her waist, lifted her up to the top of the boulder. He perched beside her and drew her against his side.

"It's so beautiful here," she whispered, awed.

Xander was silent. Turning to look up at him, she

caught the strangest expression on his face. He looked peaceful. She'd never seen him like that.

Okay, well, to be fair, she had. Several times last night, and again this morning, in fact. Every time he'd lost himself deep inside her. Each and every time he'd—

Heat and hunger flooded her body at the memory. Clearing her throat, she sternly mastered her thoughts.

She laid her hand on his knee. "What is this place?"

"I come here to pray."

She didn't know what surprised her more, that he had a special place like this or that he would share it with her. She blinked up at him, completely at a loss as to what to say. This was deep. He was allowing her to see an important part of himself, something she was sure he'd allowed no one else to see. The realization warmed her to her toes. He tucked her more firmly against his side and wrapped his arm around her, sparing her from having to respond.

"I found this place by accident shortly after we renounced Lucifer." He laced his fingers through hers. "I built the cabin and I come here whenever I need to focus." He was quiet for a moment, before adding, "Whenever the path becomes unclear."

"Wait." She tipped her head back on his shoulder so she could see his face. "You built the cabin?"

He nodded.

"With your bare hands?"

The groove in his cheek peeped at her. "I might have used a few tools now and then."

"Why didn't you just conjure it, like all the other stuff?"

He leered down at her. "Sometimes I like to work with my hands."

She nudged him. "Seriously!"

He shrugged. "I do like to work with my hands, building things, you know? It's therapeutic. Besides conjuring can be very draining. The size of *what* we're conjuring also plays a factor in how much energy we expend. For small stuff—a can of soda, a shirt—it's really nothing. Not unless we're severely injured, or after morphing from one shape to the other. Though it affects everyone differently, going demonic—or coming back from it—is very disorienting and taxing on the system in general. Niklas, for example, can get raging migraines. For Sebastian…it's a lot like a human with a severe hangover. So conjuring isn't always ideal. That's why we try to keep necessities on hand. Just in case."

"Some of those timbers are huge."

"The others help out on occasion, for a price."

"A price?"

"They get to use the place whenever they want, as long as I'm not already here." He urged her head back to the curve of his shoulder. The sound of his voice rumbled against her ear, and the steady beat of his heart echoed throughout her entire body. "They don't come here often though. Sebastian prefers his farm, and Gideon has a place down south."

"And you mentioned Niklas has a flat in Paris."

"Yes."

"What about Mikhail?"

"No one really knows exactly where he spends his time."

"Hmm." That sounded about right. From what

she'd been able to gather, Mikhail seemed to be the ultimate recluse among the bunch, not that any of them appeared to go out of their way to share company. But he gave new meaning to the term *lone wolf*.

Before she'd placed the book and the stone in a small chest in Xander's loft bedroom, she'd done a quick search for the Demon of War. While the book had a lot of valuable information, it also contained frustrating holes and obvious misinformation when it came to identifying demons. However, she'd been able to safely determine one thing. As one of Lucifer's devoted followers, Mikhail had been one ubber-bad SOB. Any time—every time—there'd been a battle between good and evil, especially if it'd been a particularly bloody conflict, Mikhail had always been up close and personal, leading the charge. The book even speculated that he'd had some sort of influence over the wars that broke out amongst mankind as well.

It was silly, really—she didn't lend much credence to the connotation, thought it more superstitious babble like what she'd read about Xander withering the crops in the fields—but one of her ancestors had hinted that the Demon of War was, perhaps, one of the Four Horsemen of the Apocalypse.

Nonsense. Uneducated, medieval, superstitious conjecture.

Then again, was it?

Putting those disturbing thoughts aside, she took a mental tour of his cabin and marveled over the details. "Everything is so modern."

"It's a work in progress. I've updated it over the years."

"What about the electricity? How did you—"

"There's a big generator in that shed attached to the well house out back."

Kyanna let her thoughts race. The logistics were mind boggling. They'd been wandering in a wide circle around the cabin, and she hadn't seen even the faintest hint of a road. "How did you have the furniture delivered? The sofa, and the bed—"

Before she could say more, a massive bed identical to the one back at the cabin suddenly appeared in the middle of the meadow. Startled birds squawked and took flight. Her jaw dropped. Of course. His nifty little conjuring ability. How could she have forgotten that?

He tipped his head close and whispered in her ear. "Wanna see if it's as comfortable as the other one?"

She couldn't help it, she laughed out loud. Xander stared down at her, his expression an odd mixture of bemusement, consternation and tenderness. Without warning, he leaned in and captured her lips with his. The kiss was slow and so incredibly sweet, her heart fluttered. Once he released her, she glanced back at the clearing. The bed was gone. All was as it should be.

She thought about the things he'd told her, and one comment stood out.

"What did you mean earlier when you said, 'whenever the path becomes unclear'?"

The light in his eyes dimmed. His attention turned to the meadow, and he drew a deep breath. Tension invested his frame.

"I've been earthbound for two hundred years, Kyanna." He drew away from her, propped his elbows on his raised knees and clasped his wrist in the opposite hand. She felt the emotional distance far keener than the physical withdrawal. "Two hundred years of fighting the very thing I became when I fell from Heaven." He popped his jaw. "Two hundred years is a long time to fight for something that will probably never happen."

The bleak acceptance in his voice startled her. He truly didn't think he would ever earn redemption. And yet he continued to seek it.

It hurt her to see him so dejected. The instinct to offer comfort was more than she could deny. Slipping her hand down his thigh, she leaned into him, rested her chin on his bicep, and stared up at him. "What you do, you and the others, what you do makes a difference. You have to believe that."

The muscle in his jaw bunched. He suddenly leaped down from the boulder and paced away. Unease filled her. She hopped down and chased after him.

"You do believe that, right? Xander?"

He drew up short and she smashed into his back. He turned in time to catch her before she fell down.

"Right?" She tucked a loose strand of hair behind her ear and insisted, "What you do is important."

He didn't exactly snort in disbelief, but the deadpan look he gave her spoke eloquently of his skepticism. He released her and stormed away.

"Damn it, Xander." Her patience gone, she stood her ground and yelled at him. "Turn around and look at me."

He stopped and slowly turned on his heel, obviously unable to believe she'd just taken that tone with him. She marched right up to him, took his face in her hands, and pulled his head down so she could glare him right in the eyes. "You save people, Xander. Not innocents. *People.* Just like Mr. Dobbs." At his blank look, she heaved a put-upon sigh and elaborated, "The old man at the gas station?" Recognition dawned, and she went on. "You save lives, like Gina Taylor's little boys. I'm telling you, what you do matters. Do you understand me?"

He didn't say a word. He neither accepted her point, nor denied her claim. Instead, he reached up and grasped her wrists in his fists. She didn't give him the chance to pull away again. Kyanna went up on her toes, and she kissed him. She had to get through to him, somehow. It was imperative that he understand he was important too. And not only in the greater scheme of things.

He was important to her.

"What you do is amazing, Xander. You matter."

He drew back to stare at her, clearly shocked. He looked as if she'd just sucker punched him. He opened his mouth, closed it. His hands gripped her shoulders. Shaking his head, he released her and stomped away. Some thirty yards away, he stopped in his tracks. He propped his laced fingers on the top of his head, his back still to her as he began to speak.

"Look, Kyanna. There's something you need to know. Something I should have told you long before now," he said as he turned to face her. "That first night, when I—"

He froze. His attention seemed focused slightly to the left of her. Turning, she gasped. A man stood there in the meadow with them, only a few short paces from her. Where had he come from? He wore a long, flowing white robe. His expression was serene. His eyes were the color of the springtime sky. What stunned her immobile and speechless were his massive, flowing, snow-white wings. He was beautiful.

The angel looked from her to Xander and back. His gaze was piercing, enthralling her. Beckoning her. He held out his hand, and she was filled with the longing to take it. To let him lead her wherever he chose.

"Kyanna! No!" Xander yelled. "Don't let him touch you."

"I only want the book," the angel said, his voice like warm silk. His words sank through her, alluring and soft. Compelling. "You want to give me the book, Kyanna."

"The hell she does. Stay away from her, Gabriel, or I'll rip your wings off and feed them to you."

She couldn't move. She was dimly aware the angel was moving closer to her, just as she was dimly aware that something was very wrong. But she just couldn't quite put her finger on it. All she wanted to do was float in the warm, wispy cloud of contentment surrounding her right now. Her periphery vision tracked Xander as he raced to her side. The angel whipped around to face off against Xander, and as he did, the tip of one of his white wings sliced across her forearm, cutting through the sweatshirt like a razor-sharp sword. Beautiful, but deadly. The cut wasn't deep, but it burned like hell, startling her from her daze.

Sucking in a sharp breath, she dodged away from the angel and threw herself into Xander's open arms. The bottom of her stomach dropped as the world around her spun. And suddenly they were standing in the middle of the living room back in Xander's cabin.

"Call the enchantments. Now!"

"But—"

"Now!" He held her so close, wrapped tightly—protectively—in his arms, she could barely breathe. His wary attention darted around the cabin.

"Xander, you'll be rendered powerless again."

"Do it, woman. Now! Before he tracks us and finds you again."

Kyanna quickly recited the incantations. She felt them the moment they surrounded the cabin. A warm fuzzy blanket of reassurance.

Only then did Xander release her. He swore, ripe and long, as he paced across the cabin, paced back. Something warm trickled over her wrist and down to her fingertips. Struggling to understand what had just happened, she glanced down and stared blankly at the blood soaking her shirtsleeve and running down the back of her hand.

"Damn it!" Xander exploded, and she jumped.

He flew across and seized her wounded arm. He snatched up a towel from the counter and pulled her sweatshirt over her head. Xander gently wrapped her forearm, applying pressure. His fierce expression so at odds with his solicitous actions.

"Was that an angel?"

He grunted affirmation, led her over to the sofa, and sat beside her.

After unwrapping the towel, he inspected her wound. The bleeding had already slowed, but the gash was long. It would take some time to heal. Swearing, he pressed the towel to it again. "This is all my fault. I should never have put you at risk like that."

"By going outside?" Baffled, she peered at him, trying to understand where all this guilt was coming from.

"I shouldn't have let you go out, unprotected."

"Xander, you can't expect me to stay locked inside

this cabin the rest of my life."

He turned to stare at her, but he chose not to comment. Instead, he changed the subject. "Why does he want the book?"

Chilled bumps rippled along her skin. Cursing softly, Xander shot to his feet, ran up the stairs, and returned a spare moment later with a T-shirt. Very carefully, he helped her into it and sat beside her.

Pressing her lips together, she glanced away. His finger curled beneath her chin, drawing her face up to his. "Why does Gabriel want the book, Kyanna? There has to be more in there than incantations and a few recipes."

Still she vacillated. It wasn't that she didn't trust him, but it had been drilled into her to keep the contents of that book secret at all cost.

"Damn it, I can't protect you if you won't trust me. I can't keep you, the stone, or the book safe unless I know what's in there."

"All right," she finally agreed.

Feeling as if she were betraying every ancestor that had come before her, she rose and, cradling her injured arm, she went up to the loft to retrieve the book. On heavy feet, she returned to his side, clutching the object of contention in her hand. Kyanna dropped to the sofa and stared at the worn leather cover. She trusted him. She kept telling herself that, but it didn't make this any easier. Her loyalties divided, she chewed on the inside of her lower lip and finally handed the book over.

He frowned at her, clearly confused, so she leaned closer and opened the front cover. "This section contains the angelic enchantments. It also contains incantations to repel demons and protect homes, reinforce ward stones and guard stones, that sort of thing." She thumbed through a few pages, then came to the next section. "These pages are listings of the healing properties of certain plants and herbs, and prescribed remedies for injuries and ailments." Again, she turned a few pages as her unease grew.

"This section is a listing of demons my ancestors have had some contact with. They recorded as much information on those demons as they could gather. Some of it seems spot on. Some is little more than narrow-minded superstition." The pages crackled beneath her suddenly trembling fingers. "And this section…this section contains the record of angelic lineage."

His gaze snapped to her face. "Ancient lines, like yours?"

She slowly shook her head. "Not all of them are ancient. Most of the ones listed in here are. But there are several that are newer. Within the last century. There's even a new line originating less than twenty-five years ago."

"A first-generation Halfling," he breathed. Then his gaze cut to her, direct, probing. "Why were you given this list?"

"To protect the Halflings when possible. To provide assistance, should the need arise. To give them the enchantments one day and to teach them how to avoid detection."

"Have you had contact with the first-generation Halfling?"

"No. Not yet. My mother." She stopped, swallowed as grief surfaced. "My mother watched over the Halfling's human mother while she was still pregnant. I found Mom's journal mixed in with some of her things. I didn't even know she kept a journal. Anyway, she didn't write in it religiously, but she did mention a Clarisse Michaels several times. Unfortunately, Clarisse disappeared shortly before giving birth. Mom thought maybe something might have spooked her. Maybe an angel or a demon had made contact, she wasn't sure. Only that Clarisse had suddenly packed up, quit her job, and disappeared. Anyway, Clarisse was gone, and it was only later that Mom learned that Clarisse had died in childbirth, and the baby had been fostered out. She managed to track the child, ah, Margaret was her name, but she kept falling through the cracks of the DHS system. If I remember correctly, I think she ended up in some kind of placement facility. Oh, what was it called?" Kyanna frowned, struggling to remember. "Stone, stone, stone," she muttered, tapping her fingers to her forehead. "Stonebridge Academy!"

"Where are your mother's journals? Is it possible there might be more information there?"

"There may have been, but they were in my apartment. They're gone now."

Something dark flickered over Xander's face, but he turned away before she could tell what it was exactly.

"Mom did tell me once, that in order to minimize the risk of discovery I'm only supposed to contact any Halflings once, to teach them the enchantments, to teach them about the ward stones and about your world. But then I'm not supposed to have contact with them again, not unless I become aware of a mortal threat to them. The idea is to help from afar and to keep all contact to a bare minimum. Emergencies only. So that if one leaf falls, the whole tree won't follow."

Xander was silent for a moment, his brows pulled together.

"What's wrong?"

"How did your mother know about Clarisse and her child? How did she find out there was a new Halfling?"

That gave Kyanna pause. This was a touchy subject. One her mother had only ever spoken about once, long ago when Kyanna had been very small.

"My mother was a Guardian for the stone, and a custodian for the book. But she was also a Keeper. To my knowledge…to *her* knowledge, there are but a slim handful of Keepers in the world."

"And what's a Keeper?"

"A Keeper of Secrets. When an angel fathered a child with a human, obviously they couldn't watch over that child for themselves lest other angels, let alone demons, find out about it. So they made contact with a Keeper, and charge him or her with watching over their Halfling offspring."

"So your mother actually had contact with an angel?"

Kyanna nodded, recalling even after all these years the way her mother had trembled and gone pale when speaking of the incident.

"Did she mention *which* angel?"

"No. But I know, whoever he was, he scared the living hell out of her."

Xander was silent for a moment. He lifted his eyebrows. "Can I?"

Nodding, she settled back on the sofa and watched as he rose and made his way to the table. Xander dropped onto one of the chairs, laid the open book on the table, turned carefully to the first page, and bent his head over the brittle pages. Minutes ticked by. Half an hour. And still he read. Growing drowsy, Kyanna laid her head on the arm of the sofa and let the voices drift around her.

Chapter Twenty

"So it's like a Halfling family tree?" Sebastian hopped up to sit on the counter in the kitchen area. Leaning forward, he braced his weight on his palms.

"There are four lines listed." Xander pushed the book toward Gideon.

Gideon skimmed the list. "I don't see a Hughes family listed in here. I thought you were certain Kyanna was of angelic descent."

"She is." Satisfied with his pronouncement, Xander leaned back and crossed his arms.

"But her family isn't listed in here," Gideon repeated.

"It wouldn't need to be, would it?" At end of the table, Mikhail adopted a similar pose as Xander. "She'd hardly be expected to keep track of her own line in a book like this, would she?"

"Either way, that thing is dangerous." Sebastian reached over, took a can of soda from the fridge, popped the top and took a long draw. "If it fell into the wrong hands—"

"Those lineages could be eliminated," Gideon finished.

"Or exploited," Mikhail added. That verdict led to a long, heavy silence.

"Gabriel knows about Kyanna. He knows she has the book. And he wants it." Xander waited for the ramifications to sink in.

"Well I sure as hell wouldn't be sittin' around, waitin' for him to come knockin' if I were you."

"What do you suggest?"

Gideon scrubbed a hand over the bristly shadow on his jaw. His hair was wild, all but standing on end. His eyes were shadowed, his clothing even more rumpled than the last time they'd seen him. "Take the bull by the horns."

"Meaning?" Sebastian prompted.

"Capture an angel," Gideon tossed out, as easy as if he were suggesting fried chicken for supper. "Gabriel, if possible. Assess the level of threat against your woman."

Xander looked to the sofa where Kyanna lay sleeping. This time he didn't even try to deny it. Not to the others, and not to himself. Without giving it a second thought, he got up, crossed the room, and drew a blanket over her. He tucked it tightly around her, covering her all the way up over her ears like she seemed to prefer. He returned to his seat, ignoring the incredulous glances Sebastian and Gideon were shooting him. At least Mikhail could keep his thoughts to himself.

"And once we have him, what the hell are we going to do with him?" Sebastian glanced around the room. "Gabriel won't talk. It's not like we can torture the truth from him—or kill him when we're done."

"Did you read any of these incantations, Xander?"

"Yeah."

"This is some scary stuff. There's one in here that might be useful." Gideon's long finger traced a path over a line in the book. "It compels demons to tell the truth. Pointless for you, I know. But damned handy for the rest of us."

"Gabriel might be a pain in the ass at times," Sebastian snorted, "but in case you haven't noticed, he's not exactly a demon."

"The wording could be altered, but the effect should still be the same." Gideon tapped his fingers on the table. "We still have the cuffs Asher used to bind that last demon. We capture Gabriel, slap the cuffs on him, and use the incantation to coerce him into telling the truth."

"While we have him, we could find out if the angels know anything about the Prophesy," Sebastian suggested. "They may know where the other Guardians are."

Xander waited, but no one else seemed to see the fly in the ointment. "And then?"

"Then what?" Sebastian frowned, draining the last of his soda before setting his can aside.

"Then what do we do with him?"

When no one responded right away, Gideon closed the book and leaned back in his chair. "We let him go."

Sweet Mary, why weren't any of them waking up to the big picture? "You think he won't be the slightest bit pissed off? You think he'll just happily fly off on his merry way? You think he won't call the full force of heavenly wrath down upon our heads?"

"There's a charm in here to incapacitate a demon. And another to make them forget their purpose, at least short term," Gideon said, laying his hand on the book. "It's only temporary, but if altering one incantation works, we should be able to do it on any of the others. We could use it, take him someplace, dump him and split before he comes to. Before he realizes what happened."

"You're just full of bright ideas," Xander snapped. Ideas that had disaster written all over them.

"It's better than sittin' around here, wringin' my hands and frettin' like a bunch of old women," Gideon snapped. His flickered red for a moment.

Xander stared at him, grim and assessing. He didn't like what he saw. Gideon had been walking a tightrope lately, playing it fast and loose, taking greater and greater risks every time he went off on his own. Word was starting to spread, slowly filtering back to Xander and the others. Gideon had begun showing a cold-blooded brutality he hadn't had since the Great Fall.

A cold, efficient part of Xander—a part that was also more than a little saddened by the fact—began to wonder how long it would be before they would be forced to hunt the Demon of Temptation and put him down like the rabid dog he was obviously becoming.

That day might come sooner rather than later if Gideon was suggesting using Xander's woman as bait like Xander thought he was.

Sebastian, ever the diplomat, stepped in to the tense silence. "It could work, Xander."

Xander didn't back down. "You're forgetting one sticking point. How do you intend to lure Gabriel out into the open?"

"Bait the hook with somethin' he can't resist." Apparently, Gideon didn't realize how close he was to meeting his end. That or he was just too stupid to care.

"And what would that be?" His fists clenched, and his body went rigid, preparing for a fight. Hungry for one.

"Me."

Xander's gaze flew to the sofa. Kyanna was sitting up now, a blanket clutched around her shoulders. Her attention focused on them.

Damn it. How much had she heard?

Slowly she rose, dropping the blanket to the sofa, and crossed the room. She drew the chair beside his from the table, sat, and stared at Gideon. "That's what you're talking about, isn't it? For this to work, I need to be the bait?"

"No," Xander barked, coming to the edge of his seat.

Ignoring him, Kyanna continued to stare at Gideon, waiting for an answer.

"You or your book, darlin'."

She shook her head. "I can't risk him getting his hands on that book."

"And Gabriel getting his hands on you would be better?" Xander snarled.

"Will I alone be enough to draw him out?" She continued to ignore his outburst, refused to even look his way. Fury boiled inside him. He clenched his teeth so tightly it was little wonder they didn't shatter. She stared hard at the Demon of Temptation. "Gideon?"

"Yes. You could draw him out."

Xander exploded, shoving away from the table. "Hasn't anyone been listening to a damn thing I've been saying? You're of angelic descent, Kyanna. If he gets his hands on you, he'll kill you. To him, you're an offense against nature. A genetic flaw, a disease that must be stamped out before it's allowed to spread. To him, you're no better than us." He swung his arm around the room in a sweeping gesture.

Kyanna turned to stare up at him. Her face was too pale. But her expression was grim. And determined.

"Xander, it's the only way to draw the angels out." Clasping her hands together to still the trembling he'd already seen, she pleaded with him. "It's necessary. I can't hide anymore. He already knows about me. He's going to start actively hunting for me now anyway, won't he?"

Xander met her question with stony silence. Not if he had anything to say about it.

"Exactly," she nodded, even though he hadn't agreed with her. "And how long before he finds one of the Halflings? I can't hide here forever with my head buried in the sand. I have to help those Halflings, especially the newest one, in whatever way that I can."

"You are the Guardian of the Arc Stone, not some damned Halfling protector."

"Yes, Xander, that's exactly what I am. It is my job, just as much as it is yours, to protect those that cannot protect themselves."

"And what if we draw more than Gabriel here? What if he brings an army with him? What if those demons that were after you—Agares and the others—manage to track you here too?" He braced his knuckles on the tabletop and loomed over her. "You could spark another battle between angels and demons, this one right here on Earth."

Alarm flared in her voice. "Are you talking about the Apocalypse?"

"No." Frowning, he drew back. "Not that. Not with Lucifer still trapped in Hell. But it'd be damned messy."

"Then we have to risk it." She glanced to Sebastian and Mikhail, obviously seeking their support. But they continued to stare at him, waiting for his decree. She turned to the Demon of Temptation, clearly desperate. He could all but see the cogs turning in her head. Gideon was the one who'd come up with this plan, the least he could do was back her up here. Sure enough, she pressed, "Gideon? Help me out here."

He, too, stared at Xander. But his gaze was far less passive.

"It's worth the risk, Slayer." He conjured his customary cup of carmel macchiato and sprawled negligently, hooking an elbow over the back of his chair.

"The hell it is. This is *my* woman you're willing to sacrifice," Xander roared.

Kyanna leaned back in her chair. Color flooded her cheeks. But she didn't deny him which was a very good thing. He didn't know what he would have done if she had. "Xander." Quietly, calmly, she informed him, "I'm going to do this."

And the look on her face was the final straw. She'd made up her mind.

"Oh, no, you're not." His hand clamped around her wrist. He stared at her for one long, hard moment, and then he swore aloud. Her enchantments were preventing him from shimmering. He wasn't going to stand here and argue with her like this in front of the others. Instead, he dragged her from her chair and towed her behind him to the bathroom.

****

"What are you doing?" Kyanna gasped, jerking at her arm, digging her heels in. It was no use. He was an unstoppable force, dragging her along in his wake.

He tugged her inside the bathroom, their momentum hurtling her to the far wall as he turned and slammed the door. The moment he released her, she spun around and backed away, glaring her displeasure at him. "What was that about?"

"I can't shimmer with the enchantments in place," he reminded her.

"So you drag me around like a caveman?" She rubbed at her forearm, and his expression was immediately contrite. Wait. She blinked, probing her arm now, examining it closely. It was the same arm that the angel had cut with his wing. But it was completely healed. How had he managed that? When? She hadn't felt a thing.

"What did you do to my arm?"

He reached out to take her wrist, but she batted his hand away. He shouldn't have dragged her behind him like some recalcitrant child—she didn't care if he'd been too pissed off to think straight or not. How dare he, for one moment, imagine she would tolerate that sort of behavior?

"Did I hurt you?" Again, he reached for her. Again, she batted his hand aside. He scowled and tried once more. Grasping her hand before she could elude him, he gently but firmly tugged her arm forward for his inspection.

"No, it's not hurt, not at all in fact. Not even where the angel cut me. What did you do?"

"I had Mikhail heal you while you slept."

That brought her up short. The same Mikhail that had freaked out when she'd pricked her finger and dripped a tiny bit of blood? And what, exactly did he mean, heal her while she slept? How?

"I'm trying to talk some sense into you," he interrupted her thoughts.

"In the bathroom?" She glared up at him, finally managing to tug her arm free.

"It's the only place inside the cabin with any privacy. And I can't exactly shimmer you outside, or anywhere else right now for that matter."

"I've made up my mind, Xander." She waved his explanation away. "Now step aside and let me go."

He shook his head, continuing to block the doorway. "Do you have any idea the kind of monsters that are out there, just waiting for you to do something stupid like this? Do you realize what they would do to you? They may be angels, but they are far from harmless."

"I didn't exactly expect them to invite me to afternoon tea."

He blinked at her. His face slowly turning red as the muscles in his jaw bunched. He popped his jaw. "I'm not joking, Kyanna. They'll—"

"I know what they'll do. Or, at least I have some idea. But I have no choice, Xander. I'm a Guardian. This is what I was born to do. I have to protect others of my kind from—

She stopped abruptly, caught her breath. She hadn't meant to draw comparisons, but it was too late.

"From others of *my* kind," he finished for her.

"No," she corrected, suddenly filled with hope, despite the grim set of his face. They were so very different, the demons that hunted her and the ones that protected her. They might share some of the same physical traits, the same abilities, but they weren't at all alike, not in the ways that truly mattered. "No, those demons like Agares are not *your kind.* You're nothing like the demons I've been raised to hate. Nor are they anything like the angels I was trained to revere. I don't think those beings even exist outside the pages of that book." She took a step closer, daring to try one last time to make him see reason. "I have to do this for me, Xander. I need to do something that matters too."

He stared at her for a long time, his gaze bleak. But then, just as she'd begun to think she'd convinced him, he shook his head and adamantly informed her, "I'm not going to allow you to do this."

Frowning, she didn't immediately comprehend. And then she did. She tipped her head down and glared up at him.

"You're not going to allow me?" She drew in one impossibly deep breath through flared nostrils. And then another. "You're not going to allow me—"

"I won't let you be hurt."

Without warning, he jerked her into his arms and ravished her mouth, stealing her breath, shocking her into momentary compliance. But then she realized what was happening. He was trying to get around her. Shoving at his shoulders, she attempted to twist her head to the side, attempted to break his hold on her. He clamped both his large hands on either side of her head, trapping her, holding her immobile as he ravished her mouth and overwhelmed her senses.

His tongue thrust into her mouth as his lower body came up against hers, pushing her back, maneuvering her until he pinned her against the cabinets. The hard ridge of his erection rode her hip. And still he held her head in a painless vise, plying her mouth with sensual heat, melting her resistance by slow degrees. And soon her body followed. No longer did her hands push at his chest, or wedge between them to feebly pry for some safe distance. Instead, they gripped his hips, fingertips digging in, pulling him in tighter. No longer did she try to twist her head away. Instead, her lips sought his, clung. Her tongue mated with his, urging him on.

Chest heaving, he finally released her head, his hands falling to her shoulders, sweeping down to her waist as his mouth continued to master hers. His fingers slipped up beneath the hem of her T-Shirt, seeking flesh. With a muffled oath, he leaned back long enough to wrench the cotton up her body and over her head before tossing it on the floor. His shirt and her bra met the same fate.

"I'll die before I see you hurt again." She'd never seen him so determined. "You are my treasure. Wherever you are, you carry my heart with you."

His lips seized hers once more, and soon he filled his hands with her breasts. Cupping them, molding them. Teasing her aching nipples, pressing them against his own chest.

She struggled to think beyond the sensations. His treasure? And suddenly everything clicked into place. He wasn't trying to get around her. He was afraid for her. He was afraid of losing her and was doing everything in his power to see that that didn't happen. Even if it meant fighting dirty.

But the one realization that rocked her to the depths of her soul? He had feelings for her. Deep feelings.

The last shreds of her resistance fell away, and she gave herself up to him. She still had every intention of playing an integral role in capturing that angel. But this, what was happening between them, was driven by far more than motives and deceptions. This was pure emotion. A connection that would not be denied. Everything else outside of this room and what was happening between them fell away into nothing.

His lips slid across her cheek and down the side of her neck, leaving a trail of fire in their wake. He nipped at her collarbone as his nimble fingers worked the button on her jeans free. Desperate hands tugged at her zipper, dragged her jeans and panties over her hips and down her legs. She moaned low in her throat as his hot, hungry mouth found a taut nipple. Kyanna's head fell back as she sank her fingers in his hair and her mouth fell open on a gasp. Hot spears of pleasure pierced her body. The feel of his hands on her was exquisite. And the sensation of his lips and tongue and teeth teasing her breasts was driving her crazy.

"Oh God, Xander," she begged. His name was a ragged plea upon her lips. Her body was on fire.

He rose, shucking his own jeans on the way. In one smooth move, he wrapped her leg around his hip and thrust deep inside her. He captured her startled cry in his mouth as she shattered in his arms.

But it wasn't enough. Not for either of them. Capturing her by the hips, he lifted her until she wrapped both legs around his waist and locked her ankles over the tight muscles of his butt. Cupping her bottom, Xander carried her a few short steps and then pressed her up against the door. He pinned her between the unforgiving wood and his hard, hot body. One large, strong hand fisted in her hair, dragging her head back. He fastened his mouth over hers and Kyanna moaned aloud as he began thrusting himself inside her. Deep.

Hard. Over and over. Filling her to the depths of her soul. Shockwaves of delight rocketed through her. Already the coil of another climax began tightening deep in her core.

Kyanna wrapped her arms around his neck and accepted him. Took every violent thrust and demanded more. Trapped as she was between the door and Xander, she couldn't move much, and so she used what little movement that had afforded her to her advantage. Her legs clamped tight. Her arms held him close. Her tongue dueled with his. And her inner muscles clenched and unclenched, squeezed and released.

"Kyanna." He groaned into her ear. "Baby, don't do that. I can't," he panted, then sucked in a sharp breath as she bore down, clenching her inner muscles tighter than before. He gasped aloud. "I'm not going to be able to hold back much longer if you do th—"

Smiling with sheer rapture, she did it again.

"Kyanna!" He slammed himself into her and exploded, igniting her own stunning orgasm. And it went on and on as he continued to thrust inside her. Slower now, languidly prolonging the friction.

Drawing a shuddering breath, Kyanna pressed a gentle kiss to his lips as he leaned into her. His legs were trembling. His whole body was trembling, but she didn't fear he would drop her. And he didn't.

Xander gently untangled his fingers from her hair and slid his arm around her back. Taking an unsteady step back, careful to keep himself firmly embedded inside her, he turned. With his shoulders against the door, he slowly slid to the floor. Kyanna straddled his lap now.

Xander kissed her, unhurried now. The sense of

urgency tempered now by the connection they'd forged. His hand cupped her jaw. And, with measured ease, he rocked his hips, guiding her smoothly, tenderly up and down his still hard shaft.

Surprised, she drew her head back and peered at him in surprise.

"You're so beautiful," he whispered. "So pure. I won't lose you. I'll never let you go."

Somehow, she knew he was talking about more than the color of her eyes, or the luster of her hair and the curve of her breasts. When he looked at her like he was now, she *felt* beautiful.

Xander was the embodiment of sheer, raw power. The strength of him—wrapped around her, moving inside her—amazed her. And yet, at that moment, he held a vulnerability she'd never seen before.

Cupping his face, she leaned in and brushed butterfly kisses across his lips. Without breaking the rhythm their bodies craved, she whispered, "I'm still going to help capture that angel, Xander. But," she hurried to add when it became obvious he was becoming tense and upset all over again, "I promise I won't take any unnecessary risks." She pressed a gentle kiss to his mouth and then smiled at him. "I trust you not to let anything happen to me."

"I'm not going to change your mind about this, am I?" He continued the steady, smooth thrusts, even though a frown had formed between his brows.

She shook her head no, softening the denial with a sad smile.

He let out a deep, resigned breath. "And I can't keep you locked away forever, can I?"

Again she shook her head.

"I don't like this," he grumbled, though he never stopped rolling his hips beneath her. His hands smoothed up and down her back.

"I know."

"You'll do exactly as I say, the moment I say it?"

Her lips twitched. "Within reason."

His arms tightened warningly around her.

"Within reason," she reiterated.

His put-upon sigh would have knocked her over had he not been holding her so tightly. Like that treasure he kept mentioning.

"I won't let anything happen to you," he vowed, moving his hips with renewed purpose.

She wrapped her arms around his neck, tipped her forehead to his, and whispered, "I know."

A short while later, as the last shudders of her orgasm left her weak and trembling, Xander clasped her to his heaving chest. The door behind him suddenly rattled beneath the weight of a fist.

"Hey, you two might want to finish up in there," Sebastian called. "Gideon found something in Kyanna's book."

"What'd he find?" Xander asked, his hold tightening on Kyanna when she made to move.

"A key."

Chapter Twenty-One

"You're sure this will work?" Xander watched Kyanna set the last stone in place, forming a perfect circle around Sebastian, Gideon, Mikhail, and himself. "We'll be able to break free of the stones when the enchantment is lowered?"

Glancing up, she nodded, offering him a reassuring smile. "The stones are the same as those guarding your cabin. They won't hinder you, but combined with the enchantments, they should effectively shield you from the others. Both sides."

"I don't like this," he repeated for what had to be the hundredth time. No one seemed to be listening. Ever since they'd found a tiny key they'd speculated belonged to some kind of a strong box, Kyanna, Gideon, and the rest of them had begun making their precious plans. The key had been replaced in the spine of the book for safe keeping until they could follow up on it later. And now here they were, ready to throw Kyanna to the wolves.

Maybe he'd feel better about this if Niklas was here too. Having an extra set of hands on their side would have improved the odds. Maybe if he'd had the chance to talk to Kyanna, to tell her about taking part of her soul…

And even if the creepy-crawlies hadn't swarmed over his neck, he'd still have known that last to be a lie.

Hell, who was he trying to fool? Absolutely nothing about this situation was going to make him feel good.

Besides, he'd had the chance to tell her the truth, many of them in fact. He'd just been too much of a coward. He drew a deep breath and resolved that as soon as this was over, the very moment he got her alone again, he'd tell her the truth. All of it. No more excuses. No more delays.

Niklas had reported in just a few hours ago that he'd tracked down a solid lead on the summoning in Iowa. It appeared it was a summoning of some magnitude, and it was happening very soon. Niklas was closing in and believed he had discovered the location. For that reason alone, he wasn't here. Thwarting the summoning would put a serious crimp in the rebellious mastermind's plans. Things were finally starting to turn around for them. In addition, a reliable source, namely Asher, had found evidence of a descendent of the slain Guardian who'd been charged with protecting The Sword of Kathnesh. A lead Sebastian would soon follow.

Xander had a bad feeling in the pit of his stomach. He couldn't believe he'd let Kyanna talk him into this. Gideon and the others had decided the best place for this confrontation would be the meadow, away from the cabin. Away from civilization. But still a home field advantage, so to speak. The woods were silent around them, almost as if it somehow sensed an impending battle. Gideon, ever the strategist, had insisted that the best course of action would be an ambush. Sebastian and Mikhail had latched on to the idea like terriers with a juicy bone.

And so Kyanna, in her misguided eagerness to

help, had somehow convinced him to allow her to be the bait. She'd formed a circle with her stones and would, in a few short moments, recite the enchantments. He'd been having second and third thoughts—hell, fourth and fifth thoughts, for that matter—about this whole disaster in the making.

As she straightened, he grabbed her wrist and tugged her into the circle of stones. Right in to the circle of his arms. "You don't have to do this. We'll find another way."

She laid a hand softly against the side of his face, went up on tiptoe, and gently kissed him. Drawing back, she whispered, "I'm not worried. You'll keep me safe."

Well, that was fine. Just dandy. She wasn't worried. Yipee. Goodie for her.

Because he was scared out of his freakin' skull. He, the Slayer, was shaking inside like a little schoolgirl.

Before he could argue, she stepped back, and began the incantation. He felt the barrier descend between them, and that fear for her turned into a claustrophobic, clawing rage. Everything in him screamed this was wrong. His woman was out there, outside the circle. Unshielded. Unprotected and vulnerable.

His body began to change, bulking up. Going demonic.

She was the one taking all the risk. How could he have been so stupid as to allow this to happen?

As if sensing his turmoil, Sebastian laid a hand on his shoulder. "She'll be okay."

Rounding on his compatriots like a feral dog with rabies, he snarled in that layered voice, "She better be."

His burning gaze sliced to Gideon. “Because if so much as a single hair on her head is harmed, I’m coming after you. And I don’t care if you have suddenly developed a death wish. I’ll make your death so damned miserable and painful that living would seem like a better option.”

No one responded. Because each one of them knew he meant every word he spoke. He turned to watch her walk through the trees until she was out of sight. He could still hear her as she made her way toward the boulder. He drew in the lingering scent of her upon his own body. Used it to calm his fraying nerves.

“I’m fine, Xander.” He heard her reassuring whisper on the breeze.

Please God, if you never answer another of my prayers, please answer this one. Please, please, let her stay that way.

Xander’s fingers flexed as he readjusted his grip on his dagger. Motionless. Silent. Ten minutes passed. Fifteen. He drew in a breath to call out to her, just to make sure she was still there, still okay, when he heard voices.

“Where is your guard dog, little human?”

“Not here, obviously,” she replied tartly. “You’re Gabriel, right?”

“I see the demon traitors have educated you.”

“And I see you’ve brought friends. Were you so afraid of one little human that you needed to bring along bodyguards? Really, Gabriel. Am I so scary you need six more angels with you?”

She was feeding them information now. Making sure that they didn’t shimmer into the meadow blind. She was the one in imminent danger, and yet she was protecting them.

This was killing him. He could hear them, hear every bloody word. But he couldn't see them at all. Mikhail had chosen their hiding place a little too well. No one could see them from the clearing for all the trees and undergrowth. Nor could they see anyone in the clearing. Seven angels were out there with her. Seven threats to her safety. And he couldn't tell which ones had come. Michael was known to be a bit impatient and more than a little hotheaded. Was he out there too? Or Paul? Had Raphael come? He, at least, would listen first and draw his sword later. What about Samuel? Could he be persuaded to hear them out? Or would he view them as Gabriel obviously did? As traitors, and nothing more.

He'd warned Kyanna over and over on their way out here not to let Gabriel come too close. And to never let him or another angel get their hands on her, no matter what. She'd taken additional precautions so that Gabriel couldn't put her under another trance like before, but if they managed to get their hands on her, they could flash her back to the Heavens, the one place Xander could not follow. How could she possibly keep track of all seven of them?

Please, let her have taken his warnings to heart.

Another thought occurred to him, and his blood ran cold. What if Zachariel had come with Gabriel? Zachariel's primary duty was to control memories. What if he made Kyanna forget all they'd shared together? What if he made her forget that she even knew him? Or that Xander wasn't fighting for the side of evil anymore?

What if Zachariel made her forget who she was?

He thought then of how he'd thrust his hand into

the enchantments and moved the stone in her burning apartment. He'd do it again now, in a heartbeat, if need be. In fact, he was already considering the stone directly in front of him.

"Why are you here alone?" Gabriel sounded suspicious.

"I came out to clear my head. Get a bit of fresh air."

"Your watchdog wouldn't let you out of his sight."

"He thinks I'm napping."

"Why are you really here?"

"Maybe I was hoping you'd show up."

"You wish us to take you to safety?" Xander could hear the interest in Gabriel's voice and his fury flared.

"No," Kyanna quickly corrected him. "I want information. I'm perfectly safe, right where I am."

"Where is the book?" Displeasure crackled in Gabriel's demand.

"It's safe." He heard movement. Grass rustled. A twig snapped. "And that's just about close enough," Kyanna warned. The sounds of movement stopped. "If you harm me, you'll never get that book. It'd be such a pity if it ends up in the wrong hands, now wouldn't it."

Damn it, what the hell did she think she was doing, taunting Gabriel this way. And even as he cursed her, a part of him was proud of her courage, of her audacity.

"I know of your bloodline," Gabriel coaxed. "Would you not like to hear from whom you are descended?"

"You called me human before. Not Halfling."

"Your bloodline is so diluted it hardly matters to us anymore."

Creepy-crawlies skittered over Xander's flesh. Oh,

her bloodline mattered to them all right. Shaking the bug-crawling sensation, he concentrated on their conversation, waiting. He motioned to the others that the angel had just told his first lie. Beside him, Mikhail silently drew a wicked looking sword from its sheath.

"Why do you want the book so badly?"

"Why do you want to keep it?" Gabriel countered.

"I've been charged with keeping it safe."

"By giving it to a band of demon traitors?"

"That's the second time you've called them that. One more time and this conversation is over. As far as I can tell, Xander and his brothers-in-arms have done more to save this world than you and all the rest of your kind."

A seething silence followed, and Xander tensed. Had she just pushed Gabriel too far?

"You shouldn't trust that demon trai—the Slayer, or the others. They will lead you down the path of destruction."

"I trust Xander with my life. I trust him with my soul," she replied evenly, speaking with cool disdain for Gabriel and unwavering confidence in Xander. That confidence was like shards of glass raking through his conscience. Anxiety over her safety already rode him hard. Guilt choked him now. In a strained tone, Gabriel queried once again, "Do you not wish to know the origination of your line? I can tell you."

"And what would the cost be?" *Smart girl,* Xander thought.

"Come with us, willingly. And the book, of course."

"Of course." Another moment of silence stretched on. Then, "You know, I'm not really interested in that information. Nor am I interested in going anywhere with you. How about this, instead? You give me some information that I do want first, on good faith. And, in return, I'll give you the book. And I'll stay right where I am."

Xander scowled at the trees surrounding them. He couldn't see a damned thing, and it was killing him.

"What sort of information?"

"Tell me about." She paused, drawing the tension out. "The Prophesy."

Gabriel waited a beat before replying. "What Prophesy would that be?"

"You know exactly which Prophesy to which I refer." Her tone snapped, indicating she wasn't willing to waste any more time fencing. She wanted answers. Now. Xander closed his eyes and focused on the meadow. On the boulder, on the exact location in which he'd told her to stay. He kept the dark magic seething just beneath the surface, harnessed and ready so that the second the enchantments dropped he'd already be shimmering to her side. "The Prophesy about the Chosen One and the relics."

Another beat passed. And then another. One beat too long. "I know of no Chosen One, no relics."

Lie, Xander's creepy-crawlies screamed.

"Give us the book and we will let you go, unharmed, back to your demon."

The creepy-crawlies swarmed through his system so powerfully, he nearly retched.

"You have nothing to—what is this?" Anger filled Gabriel's voice. "What trap is this?"

Xander looked over his shoulder to the others in his group. All were accounted for. Who, then, was Gabriel talking about? He needed to be out there. Now.

Suddenly Kyanna's voice rang out, filled with fear. The first few lines of the enchantment echoed in the distance. But, just before she could finish the incantation, her voice was cut off, choked silent on an explosion. The enchantments still firmly in place. Another, smaller explosion rocked the ground beneath them, followed by another, and another.

Panicked, he yelled for Kyanna and bent to reach for the stone by his feet. His fingertips began to burn. Her voice suddenly called out again, shaking and terrified, but she finished the incantation and the shield dropped. Xander and the others shimmered to the meadow.

Right into the middle of an apocalyptic scene.

Demons swarmed the small clearing, at least two dozen, with angels wading into the fray, fighting as if called by God himself to defend this tiny, isolated glade. And in the middle of it all? His small, defenseless female, ducking plasma balls, dodging lethally sharp wingtips and swinging swords.

Xander had shimmered to the boulder, right where she was supposed to be. But Kyanna wasn't there, because the boulder was no longer there. It lay all around, scattered and broken. Exploded into a million irreparable pieces. He tracked to her, where she ducked another plasma ball and rolled away from the arc of a glowing sword of flames. In a heartbeat, he was at her side. He scooped her up in one arm, even as he conjured his own sword and raised it in defense. Forged from Quïnï, a specialized composite of cursed metals infused with Ralsha poison, his blade deflected the flames of an angel's blade in a shower of sparks.

Xander shielded Kyanna with his own body.

With half his attention on the angel currently trying to gut him, he quickly assessed the battlefield. Gideon, now in fully demonic form, was holding his own with a group of demons and an angel. Mikhail, also in demonic form, stood upon a growing pile of demon ash, his sword slicing and dicing its way through another group of demons. Shadows moved over the ground, deflecting sunlight like man-shaped clouds, and he shot a fast glance skyward. A fully demonic Sebastian swooped through the skies, cart-wheeling and tumbling, soaring and slashing, as he battled three angels. One angelic blade swept too close to Sebastian for comfort. His massive black wings swept forward, wrapping around his body protectively, and the angel's sword was repelled in a spray of sparks as metal skidded over metal.

Satisfied that Sebastian seemed to have things well in hand, he turned his attention to the others. On the far side of the clearing, the angel Gabriel went toe-to-toe with the gray-fleshed Agares. Nearer to them, closer to the stream, the angel Samuel fended off three demons.

Another angel attacked, drawing his attention. This one was unknown to him, but he fought with a dedication and viciousness Xander found admirable. If the angel hadn't been trying his damnedest to behead him, thereby placing Kyanna in jeopardy, Xander may well have applauded him.

Just then, another demon shimmered behind Samuel, lifting a black sword high to deliver a death blow. Xander sucked in a sharp breath. And even as he did so, he knew his yells—even if they were heard—would come too late. Nor could he shimmer Kyanna back to the cabin and safety and return in time to save Samuel. With no other alternative available to him, he shimmered himself and Kyanna to Samuel's side. Xander wedged Kyanna between Samuel and himself, and threw his blade up, blocking the downward slash.

Just as quickly, he thrust his dagger forward, slashing across the demon's exposed belly. When the demon faltered, Xander took his head, already looking for his next victim. He shot a glance to Samuel and the two remaining demons, and he absently noted the surprise on Samuel's face. Surprise quickly followed by first puzzlement, then consternation.

Samuel's lips parted, but Xander shoved him aside seconds before a demon sword would have taken his head. That was twice in as many minutes that he'd saved the angel's life.

Another demon shimmered near them and engaged Samuel. Kyanna plastered herself to Xander's side. Her eyes were huge, her breathing ragged as she stared all around her. Xander cursed to himself as he disemboweled another demon. He hadn't ever wanted her to see this kind of violence. Hadn't wanted her exposed to this carnage. She must be terrified.

Across the way, two angels battled wings-to-wings against a swarm of horned, burnt-orange demons. One of the angels fell to one knee and his head was taken. Every angel in the clearing jolted, all focus swinging to their fallen comrade even as their swords continued to clash and crash. Xander remembered that marrow-deep connection, one he'd once held with these same soldiers of God.

Out of habit, Xander took stock of his own men. Mikhail had moved on to another group of demons newly arrived. He didn't give them a moment to acclimate. Instead, he hacked his way through their numbers with very little resistance.

Gideon had leveled his demon adversaries, and now dueled with an angel. Xander thought to yell a warning, thought to caution him not to kill the angel, even by accident. He even took a step in their direction, but then hesitated, slowed by Kyanna's presence. Gideon had a wild look about him. He looked as if he no longer knew where he was, or who he fought. His goal had simply become to kill anything within reach.

He wouldn't let Kyanna get anywhere near Gideon just now.

Worried over Gideon's excessive rage, Xander searched for Sebastian. The Demon of Vengeance had brought his battle to the ground. And Xander immediately saw why. His left wing was hanging at an odd angle, its tip dragging on the ground. But still he fought on, wounding another angel in the arm. Again, Xander thought to call out a warning not to kill the angel. But instead of taking advantage of one angel's slip in defense and beheading him, Sebastian brought the grip of his sword down on the angel's temple, rendering him unconscious before turning on the other angel. The glint of flaming steel caught his attention, and Xander ducked as a sword thrust at his own head. He swung his blade up to fend off the next anticipated blow, but it never came. He glanced over in time to see Sebastian grab hold of an angel's wing and give a brutal twist. The angel screeched in pain as his wing was broken.

Broken, but not torn from his body.

Xander didn't know if he would have been able to

exercise such restraint were he in Sebastian's shoes. Kyanna muffled a shriek against his side as an angel suddenly vaulted into their path.

No, not just any angel. Gabriel himself.

****

Kyanna couldn't look away from the vengeful countenance of the angel before them. His blade arced through the air, missing Xander by slim inches. So close she could feel the heat of the flaming blade sizzle in the air.

All around her, she witnessed monstrous creatures battling one another, mutilating and killing one another. Beautiful angels fought with vicious, cold-hearted resolve. Resolve that, she knew, would eventually turn her way. Fear swamped her. She wasn't ready to die yet.

She'd watched as the boy-next-door Sebastian had morphed into a terrifying monster. His skin had become the color of smoke and ash. He'd grown nearly a foot taller than the angels around him, his muscles—everything about him—bulging to three times the normal size. Great, thick horns sprouted from the sides of his head, spiraling up and back. His eyes were black as coal, chilling her to the bottom of her soul. Monstrous fangs flashed every time he opened his mouth to roar. He'd assured her once that he had wings. And wings he most certainly had. With a great shudder and a flexing of his shoulders, massive, black wings had unfurled behind him. They glinted in the sunlight like polished, feather-shaped, metallic plates. And what's more, he'd actually flown.

The wings of vengeance…

She'd watched Gideon shift into a wild, feral

creature with reddish-orange skin, and flickering red eyes. His long black claws glinted as he swiped his way through yet another demon's body with little to no help from the sword he held in one hand. He was still lean, still tall and muscled. But now, instead of the façade of a southern gentleman, what she saw scared the bejeepers out of her. He looked utterly rabid. As if he'd turn on friend or foe alike with no warning whatsoever.

And Mikhail—

She could scarcely wrap her mind around what he'd become. The nightmare of all nightmares. Kyanna turned her face into Xander's side and she prayed for this to all be over soon.

Xander continued to battle in his human form, and she wondered if he was doing that to spare her more fear. Gabriel slashed and thrust, his face a determined mask of hatred. Xander parried and dodged, striking back lightning quick, but never dealing the death blow that even she could see should be coming. Why was he holding back? Why wasn't he ending this?

A frightful looking demon suddenly appeared behind Gabriel, and Kyanna suddenly remembered him. It was the demon that had led the invasion in her storeroom. The one with red dreadlocks and gray skin. He held his arms up, an evil grin stretched wide over wickedly sharp teeth, and his lips moved silently. The ground buckled beneath their feet, shaking violently. Several lost their footing, angels and demons alike, including Gabriel. Caught by surprise, the angel went to one knee, his sword swinging wildly to deflect the blow from Xander that never came. Instead, Xander anchored a protective arm around Kyanna and leaped to the side.

It all happened so quickly, and yet it all seemed to

go in slow motion. The dreadlocked demon reached out to grasp the angel's wings. The angel, now aware of the additional threat, twisted but couldn't get away as the Earth below him trembled and heaved. Xander thrust her behind him and slashed out with his own sword, severing the demon's hand from his body, the hand that had latched on to Gabriel's wing.

The dismembered hand tumbled to the grass and burst into ash. Screeching in agony, the dreadlocked demon—*Agares*, she now recalled—cradled his handless arm to his chest and vanished. Rolling to his feet, Gabriel stared at Xander, wary. Watchful. His sword at the ready.

"What trick is this?" Gabriel watched them carefully, but he didn't attack. Not yet.

Kyanna wanted to run her hands over Xander, wanted to visually search his body, make sure he hadn't sustained any wounds while trying to protect her. She was a liability to him right now. She knew that. That was why she didn't resist whenever he pushed her or pulled her this way or that. She couldn't risk distracting him, not even for a moment.

"This is no trick," Xander panted, swiping his forearm over his sweating brow, even as he pushed her behind him once more, keeping a defensive arm between her and the angel. "I don't want you dead, Gabriel. Despite what you may believe. This is a warning. For all of you. Come near my woman again, try to harm her in any way, and I will kill you, angel or not."

"The law was given. Her kind are not allowed to live."

"The law was made by you and by Michael."

Xander lowered his sword and his dagger, though he remained tense, ready to explode into action at the slightest threat. "And we both know why."

Gabriel bellowed and launched himself at Xander, sword swinging, bloodlust in his eyes. But before he could engage in lethal combat, another pack—or horde or nest or whatever it was that Xander had called them—of demons appeared all around them. Xander scanned them, even as he spun about to wrap both arms around Kyanna.

Xander growled, "Dimiezlo."

Kyanna stared at the bizarre creature. It looked like a mishmash of eclectic parts. Goat legs, a bald horned head, furry arms, and a snake's tongue. He carried an unconscious woman over one shoulder. Her hair was long, flowing nearly to the ground behind him, and she wore nothing but a sheer white robe. One of the other demons that had arrived with him took one look around the embattled meadow and snarled, "Stolas didn't say nothing about fighting no damned angels." And then he disappeared.

"Stolas!" Xander swore aloud at that pronouncement.

Just as the bottom of her stomach began to fall away, she felt Xander jolt in her arms, his back arched and he hissed in a sharp breath. And then everything around her went gray, and her stomach dropped.

Chapter Twenty-Two

Kyanna stumbled back as Xander's weight sagged against her. Then he righted himself, giving her the chance to look around them. This place was completely unfamiliar to her. It looked medieval. The walls were damp gray stone with rusty iron rings and chains nailed into them at sporadic intervals, the floor beneath her feet dirty rock. The air was musty and dank. The scene was complete with flaming iron torches anchored to the walls here and there.

"Are we in a dungeon?" she whispered.

Xander's chest heaved, and she realized he was struggling to catch his breath. Panic squeezed her in a death grip.

"Are you all right?" he ground out.

"Xander, are you hurt?" Her hands flew to his chest, skimmed his sides, and drew back covered in blood. Horrified, she stared first at her splayed hands, then up at him, unable to form a coherent sentence. "The stone…we have to get you to the stone!"

"Damn it, are you all right?" He gripped her shoulders. She could only nod in response, and, once she did, his body sagged. Relief slackened his features for a moment. And then he tensed, yelling out in a hoarse voice, "Asher!"

"Xander," she insisted, holding her hands up for his inspection. "You're bleeding! You have to—"

“Slayer?”

Gasping, spinning around, Kyanna gawked. Another demon had shimmered into the dungeon with them. Not quite as tall as Xander, he was as yet unarmed, but still packed with solid muscle and more than a little intimidating. And Xander was hurt. She was frantic. She fumbled and wrenched the dagger from Xander. She jumped in front of him and shoved the blade up threateningly at the newcomer.

“Just stay back,” she warned.

He raised a jet-black brow and regarded her with deep chocolate brown eyes, obviously amused. The torchlight glistened on the sheen of sweat coating his mocha-colored skin. He wore black fatigues, combat boots, and a snow-white muscle shirt.

“You better put that thing away before you hurt yourself, baby girl.”

At the same moment, Xander reached around her and gently closed his hand over hers on the hilt, forcing her arms down. “Asher is a…friend,” he gasped against her ear, hesitating only the slightest bit on the last word.

Once the blade, as well as the sword, were tucked away and vanished respectively, Asher crossed his arms. “Why did you come here?”

“Need a favor.” Xander cut to the chase.

“You couldn’t pick up the phone? You had to invade my space uninvited?” He wasn’t happy, and he wasn’t shy about letting them know it.

“No time,” Xander breathed. And once again, she was reminded of his injuries. How severe were they? How long would it take before he began healing?

Why wasn’t he healing already?

“The favor,” Xander prompted.

"What is it?" Asher stroked his goatee with one hand, adding, "You know I don't work for free."

"You must guard Kyanna. Keep her safe at all cost. You must swear to me no harm will come to her. And after the battle is over, take her to Sebastian."

"You keep me safe," Kyanna insisted, whirling around to glare at him. She didn't like the looks of this situation. Or this demon.

"No time," he told her. "I have to go back. Now."

"What? No, you're hurt. You can't—"

"The others need me. Can't abandon them."

Even as that statement stung, she knew he was right. She'd seen how swarm after swarm of demons kept appearing. How viciously those angels had fought. And Sebastian was already hurt. In the time they'd stood here talking, had another of his friends been wounded? Or worse yet, been cut down?

Asher regarded him with obvious annoyance. "I'm a little busy right now. It'll cost you more."

"Don't care how much," Xander rasped. His grip on her tightened when she began to object.

Asher weighed Xander's words. Then a wholly evil grin worked its way across his face and he flashed even white teeth. Apprehension balled in Kyanna's gut. Something frightening was going on behind those dark, dark eyes. And she suddenly wasn't sure this was such a good idea. In fact, whatever this demon would ask for was going to be, most assuredly, way too costly.

"I will come to you one day and ask for your help. And you're going to give it to me. Without qualification, without hesitation. You will do everything in your considerable power to help me." An ancient parchment appeared from nowhere, hovering in the air near Xander. “Do we have a deal?”

Kyanna frowned up at him, shaking her head. But he’d already swiped his hand over his bleeding side. Before she could stop him, he slapped his bloody handprint to the parchment, and then the parchment disappeared.

“Xander, no.”

“Too late,” he said. “It’s done.”

He turned her into his arms and pressed a kiss first to her mouth, then to her forehead. His attention focused solely on her. He appeared so serious, stared at her so intensely, it was as if he’d completely forgotten Asher was in the room with them.

“How do you feel?”

“What?”

“Damn it, Kyanna, answer me. How do you feel? Do you feel weakened at all? Dizzy?”

“No. I feel fine.”

Again, his expression was relieved.

“Xander, what—”

“You’re going to be just fine,” he cut her off, his voice filled with relief.

“I’m not worried about me. I’m worried about you. You’re hurt—”

“I’ll be fine too.” He did that shivery-shrug thing he did whenever his lie radar went off. She’d picked up on that tell too. Worry swamped her. His fingers tightened on her shoulders when she opened her mouth to challenge him. “You have to go with Asher now. I’ll come for you, just as soon as I know the others are okay.”

And then he did that shiver-shrug thing again. He didn’t believe he would come for her. He didn’t think he was going to make it.

Before she could argue, he pressed a quick kiss to her lips. Too fast it was over, and he was pulling away, urging her toward the demon she didn't know. The demon she didn't want to go with.

"You better come for me," she warned him, struggling to force courage into her threat. "Or I'll come after you and curse you with the worst enchantment I can find."

Those seldom seen but much loved grooves dug into his cheeks. Beside her, Asher did a double take. There were so many things she should have told Xander before now. Before she could give in to the urge to run back into his arms, Asher's hands closed over her shoulders. Strong and unyielding. And suddenly, the air near Xander wavered.

Kyanna sucked in a breath, choking on a scream, even as the demon beside her began swearing.

"You led an angel here, Slayer? That's gonna cost you extra."

In that same moment, Xander spun, drawing his blade. But he was too late. Gabriel's sword was already in hand. She struggled with all her might, sobbing his name. But Asher's grip was unrelenting. The last thing Kyanna saw before Asher shimmered her away was the sight of Gabriel's flaming blade thrusting into Xander's stomach and exiting his back.

****

Stolas slammed his fist into the granite wall. Dust plumed, and the Great Hall shook. He roared, raking his extended claws over the surface, leaving behind deep gashes. The other occupants in the room quaked, but still they remained on their knees, heads bowed, arms crossed, trembling fists pressed to their shoulders.

Only one stood among them. Agares cradled his mutilated arm and watched this unbridled display of fury, his expression impassive. If he'd had any sense, he too would be on his knees…or not have shown his face this side of Hell for the next millennia. They had failed him yet again. All of them.

He overturned the table on the raised dais. The one designated for his Earthen treasures. But his anger was such that he no longer cared. Trinkets and weapons flew through the air, scattering across the floor. Some bounced. Some shattered. The small, clear bottle exploded, splattering precious scented liquid across the floor. The loss of one of his favorite offerings only fueled his fury.

He picked up the lightweight gun, he crushed it in his fist, uncaring whether or not it contained holy water. Liquid dribbled down his wrist and forearm. But no burn. And that too added kindling to his fire. If they were going to bring him a damned weapon, the least they could do was bring a useful one.

And then he came to music-makers. All of them broken. Smashed into tiny, shiny pieces. He roared once more, turning his fury on the closest Charocté. Flames erupted from the cowering demon's eyes and poured from its mouth choking off the tortured screams. In seconds, the demon vaporized, rupturing from within.

Not nearly satisfying enough. Another servant exploded. And another. And still he couldn't contain his wrath. The Guardian—a Halfling that may have been strong enough to conceive and carry demon spawn to term—had eluded them. The relic was gone. The Slayer had escaped him once more. And, adding insult to injury, his minions also had a shot at the rest of the Fallen. He could have had all five of them in one fell swoop. The Seer, the Slayer, Vengeance, Temptation, and War. But his worthless followers had failed.

And, not only had they failed him, but they'd also given up his identity. Dimiezlo was certain the Slayer had heard one of his minions utter his name aloud. His enemies now knew that he was the one staging the greatest coup in history. If Lucifer found out—

Two more Charocté exploded.

"That's going to get awfully expensive," Agares calmly intoned.

Spinning about, he hissed. "You—" He was so livid, he could barely form coherent words. "You had an angel's wings in your hand. Not only did you lose the wings, but you lost your own hand as well, you worthless *gnaéchtoïrapta*. I should send you to Oblivion. I should—"

"Ah-ah, cousin." Agares tsked, shaking his head. "A few missing Charocté are hardly noteworthy. However, should one of his Generals suddenly disappear, you can be sure Lucifer will most definitely start asking questions. Lots of very uncomfortable questions."

Another Charocté exploded. Just to make a point. Stolas refused to let this weakling intimidate him or blackmail him. Neither was he ready to give up on his aspirations to overthrow Lucifer. He'd been born to rule. Born to walk the Earth and enslave all humanity. The Fallen might have managed to get their hands on one of the relics. But the scrolls and the Chosen One were still fair game. Besides, he still had the sword.

And he'd heard rumors that the Demon of Temptation was slipping toward the abyss. Perhaps, with the right…persuasion, Temptation might be made to see the benefits of a new regime. It would be to his benefit to have a spy amongst the Fallen. It would certainly make things much easier when the time came to get his hands on the Arc Stone.

Yes, this could work. The Fallen might have won this round, but they would not win the war.

"Get out," Stolas barked. "All of you. Get out now. All"—he qualified, pointing his claw-tipped finger at Dimiezlo—"but you."

Chapter Twenty-Three

Kyanna stood at the sink, staring despondently out the window. Blurs of brilliant color made her blink, but she stared anyway. Reminders of him were everywhere. So much bittersweet longing filled her. The raw pain, the devastating grief was still so fresh she found it hard to function at times. At those moments, she often found herself staring out this window. How many times had Xander stared out this window? Had he, when building this cabin, deliberately positioned the window because of this exact view? Every time she thought of him, every time something reminded her of him in any way—which was nearly everything—it felt like a dagger were ripping through her chest. But she couldn't ignore the memories or the pain, and she couldn't pretend she'd be fine…someday.

She missed Xander.

The sudden sound of movement behind her barely perked her interest. "Gideon." She sighed. "I don't want to go anywhere else, so please stop asking. I told you yesterday and again a few hours ago. I haven't changed my mind."

Silence met her request.

She appreciated Gideon's concern. His attitude might be a bit surly at times, but certainly no worse than Mikhail's on a good day. Still, he and the others didn't need to keep checking in on her like this. The angels hadn't bothered her since the battle in the meadow, nor had the demons.

The battle in which she'd lost everything important to her…

"Kyanna."

Everything inside her froze. *Great!* Now she was hallucinating.

Unable to stop herself, knowing she was only setting herself up for crushing disappointment, she slowly pivoted.

The coffee mug slipped from her fingers, shattering on the tile at her feet. She paid the shards no heed, nor the coffee pooling at her feet. For a moment, her vision wavered as she stared at the ghost before her. She groped blindly for the counter and braced herself as her knees turned to mush.

"Xander?" she whispered, afraid the figment of her imagination would disappear if she so much as blinked.

He looked so real, real enough to reach out and touch. Heaven help her, her sanity couldn't take much more of this. Xander was gone. Lost to her with an angel's sword buried deep in his belly.

The others hadn't been able to offer her hope. An angel's sword, a Blade of Justice, was deadly to a demon, though they did say he had a slim chance of surviving.

A slim chance.

Night after night of loneliness had convinced her that "a slim chance" hadn't been in the cards for them.

Day after day of heartache—and that shiver-shrug tell of Xander's—had convinced her Xander knew he would not make it. And he'd sent her away rather than let her stay with him at the end.

A slim chance.

Well, she didn't believe it. There was no way he could have survived that. No way at all. And the loss of him had shaken her faith. Sebastian, having dropped in unexpectedly on what was to be the first of innumerable drop-ins, had prevented her from burning the book and hurling the Arc Stone into the river. And he'd gone one step further, surprising her to no end. When she'd broken down, sobbing for Xander, Sebastian had simply held her until she'd cried herself out.

She'd stayed on at the cabin. She had nowhere else to go. Summer had tried to convince her to come back to Isle when Kyanna had phoned her to let her know she was all right. She'd tried to talk Kyanna into staying with her and Duff since her business and home had inexplicably burned to the ground.

But Summer didn't understand, didn't know the danger Kyanna would bring with her. And so she'd begun distancing herself from those she'd come to know and love in Isle, choosing instead to live like a hermit in Xander's cabin. She'd kept the book. Kept the stone, as was her duty. She protected them with enchantments and ward stones, just as she had always done. She'd had no other choice. Gideon and the others had refused to take them, though they continued to shimmer to the cabin to check on her now and again.

That was why she hadn't been startled by the unannounced visitor. She'd figured it was Gideon, or one of the others, though Gideon had just made his daily check-in a little over an hour ago. His attitude toward her seemed to have softened, though there was a certain hollowness in his eyes. He'd even been known to sit down and watch a few sitcoms now and again.

Strange pastime for a demon, but there it was.

She'd even had one brief, wary visit from an angel named Samuel. He'd appeared one day, just outside the cabin door, and called out to her, tried to assure her that she would come to no further harm at the hands of the angels. She'd believed that about as much as she'd believed Xander would come back from the dead. After all, it had been an angel, not a demon, who had taken Xander from her. And so she'd told the angel, in no uncertain terms to get lost and never darken her doorway again.

Shaking her head, she blinked when Xander's mirage smiled. A full blown, teeth showing smile, grooves in his cheeks and all. And that was what convinced her this was all a figment of her imagination. Xander did not smile. Well, at least he hadn't until toward the end. She squeezed her eyes closed. Counted to ten.

Miracle of miracles, when she opened them, he was still there.

Anguish clogged her throat. With a sob, she deliberately blinked again, almost hoping he'd be gone. She couldn't take this. This was some cruel trick her mind was playing on her. Nothing more.

But he was still there.

"Kyanna—"

Her muffled sob interrupted him. Pressing one trembling hand to her stomach, and a fist to her mouth, she shook her head again. *Not real. Not real,* she chanted in her mind.

"Not real," she whispered aloud.

A frown creased his brow and he stepped forward.

Gasping, sucking in one desperate lungful of air

after another, she bent over at the waist as the room began to spin. And suddenly he was there, his strong arms surrounding her, lifting her up, his warm body supporting her. His familiar scent surrounding her.

With a cautious finger, she reached out and poked him in the middle of the chest.

Solid. He was solid. Warm. Flesh and blood.

"Xander?" she sobbed weakly, then threw her arms around him. Babbling, bawling, she peppered his smiling face with wet kisses.

His lips finally found hers, captured them, and, angling his head, he deepened the kiss until her knees shook. Trembling, she jerked back, pushing him away.

"You died." She shook her head, backing up another step, fingers pressed to her tingling lips. She reached out, her hands hovered over his chest, but not quite touching. It didn't matter, he held on to her arms, refusing to release her.

"You *died*!" she insisted.

"No. Well, yes. Maybe. But I'm back," he clarified in that same raspy voice she'd come to know and love—come to miss more than she could have ever imagined.

"I don't understand," she whispered, staring up at him. His image through a thick veil of tears.

"You need to sit down. You look like you're about to fall on your face. Do you want a drink or—"

"I don't want to sit down," she snapped, suddenly furious. Oh Lord, was she angry. Slapping a hand against his chest, she pushed at him and demanded, "I don't want a damned drink. I want an explanation. What the hell happened to you? Where have you been all this time?"

"All this time?" Now he was the one scowling. "How long have I been gone?"

"Six days."

"Six—" He released her, took a deep breath, and ran a hand over his jaw. "Of course, I didn't think—"

Frustrated, she glared at him. "Of course, what?"

Taking another deep breath, Xander snagged her by the wrist and dragged her to the couch. He put his hands on her shoulders and, more or less, pushed her down onto the couch. He sat beside her and drew her cold hands into his.

"Let me explain."

"I really wish you would."

He gave her a stern look, and she gritted her teeth, pressed her lips together.

"There's a lot for me to explain, so bear with me…please. I owe you an explanation, and an apology. Where do I even start?" He shook his head, clutching her hands like a lifeline. "I did die," he began. "When Gabriel stabbed me, I died. He didn't take my head, but the Sword of Justice—never mind all that." His expression filled with wonder at this point. "I returned to Heaven, Kyanna. After all this time. I returned. And that was because of you."

"Me?"

Now guilt, unmistakable and heavy, flooded his features. "That first night, when I laid my hand upon your chest and—" He broke off, licking his lips. "You asked me what I did to you."

"You said you took part of my essence."

"Yes. That was true, but not—I think—in the way you believe."

She went very still. "What do you mean, Xander?"

He drew a deep breath. "I took a part of your very soul."

"My soul?" Kyanna cocked her head, eyes narrowed. "My *soul*?"

Xander nodded.

Kyanna's mind raced. What did that mean? What did it *really* mean? Absorbing part of her soul?

"How much did you take?"

"I, ah, I don't really know." His face was so serious, and so filled with anguish, she couldn't bring herself to yell, or burst from her seat in a fit of anger. She couldn't see past his misery. Or her own happiness at having him back.

Besides, he had to be wrong. She felt fine. Normal. Certainly no different than she had before he'd burst into her life. Well, other than the all-consuming love she'd developed for him, of course.

"Will it grow back?"

He blinked, as if startled by her question.

"No," he said cautiously. "Souls don't grow. They tarnish and blacken with evil thoughts and deeds." But then he cocked his head. "But they can be redeemed too…hmm, I guess, on second thought, maybe it is possible." He gave a helpless shrug. "No one's ever done anything like this before. Only taken part of a soul."

Her mind muddled around his explanation. It was hard to be angry when she'd come so close to losing him. Every day, every moment since she'd lost him, she'd pleaded with God, bargained to do anything, give up anything to have Xander back?

Was this the price she was to pay?

She stared deep into those turbulent gray eyes

rimmed with thick black lashes. It seemed a fair enough price to her. Heaven knew there were too many others out there who'd be willing to do the same to get a loved one back, only they hadn't been given this second chance. Who was she to naysay it?

"You said you went to Heaven because of me. How?"

"As a demon, when I died, I should have gone to Oblivion. I should have had a soulless death." His thumb began rubbing circles over the backs of her knuckles. "But ever since I absorbed that portion of your soul, I haven't felt the need to feed again. Not like I should have by now. There's been this strange…hum of energy constantly inside me now." He reached up and cupped her cheek. "It was that part of your soul inside me, sustaining me. *Saving me*. Because of that bit of your soul, I was drawn to Heaven, rather than fading to nothing. Because of that bit of your soul, I was given another chance. *You saved me*."

Kyanna caught her lower lip between her teeth as she searched his eyes. This was too good to be true. This didn't happen in real life. A portion of her soul for the man she loved. She'd pay it again, twice over, if it was required of her.

He gave her a strange look. "Why aren't you furious with me? Why aren't you shouting and cursing me?"

A tremulous smile curved her lips. She reached out, taking his face between her hands. "Because, if it means saving you, I'd do it again in a heartbeat."

His smile was blinding. He swooped down and captured her lips in a tender kiss. But remembering that not all her questions had been answered, not knowing how long she had left with him, she pulled back. "What about the rest?"

Her emotions were on a rollercoaster. She was so grateful to have him back. So confused over his presence when he should, by all accounts, be dead. And she was so angry at being left in the dark for nearly a week. A week filled with nothing but unmitigated, crushing grief.

"I was given a choice." He looked as if he couldn't quite believe it himself. "I could remain there, an angel once more. Or I could return here, to you. Less than a demon, but more than a man."

Frowning, she struggled to take it all in. He'd gone to Heaven? Then why was he here with her?

"But you're here? What about Heaven? I thought…all this time, you've been trying to go back. You've worked so hard and—"

"And none of that mattered when I realized if I stayed there, I couldn't have you."

She tugged her hands from his, confusion, guilt, hope overwhelmed her. "But—"

"I told you how it is in my world, Kyanna." He took a firmer grip on her hands, refusing to let her put physical distance between them. "I will always come for you. And I will never, *never* let you go."

"But a *week*, Xander?" she reminded him. "It took you that long to make up your mind? I mean, I didn't exactly expect you'd flip a quarter or something. But *six days*?"

God help her, but she couldn't keep the sudden anger and the pain from her voice. He'd left her. Abandoned her without explanation. First sent her away, and then stayed gone for days without thought to how that would make her feel. How was she supposed to not take that personally?

"It's not like that, Kyanna. Didn't the others explain?"

"Explain what?" She finally succeeded in jerking her hands from his and pushed to her feet. Crossing her arms defensively, she paced to the far side of the fireplace.

He rose, but when she took a hasty step back, he remained in place. "Time passes differently in Heaven, just as it does in Hell. A few minutes in Heaven can be days on Earth. A few hours on Earth are, in turn, days in Hell. It's all relative."

Struggling to wrap her mind around that, she raked her fingers through her hair, paced away, paced back, and wrung her hands together.

Finally she stopped, and peered up at him. "Why?"

"Why what?"

"*Heaven*, Xander. You gave up *Heaven*?" Then, her mind made up, she forced a swallow, firmed her resolve, and crossed her arms. Lifting her chin, she said, "You have to go back."

"What?" His incredulous expression spoke volumes.

"You have to go back. I'm sure it's not too late. With everything you've done, all the innocents you've saved, God has to give you another chance…" Her voice trailed away as he shook his head.

"I'm not going back." He went to her then, drew her resisting form into his arms. "At least, not right now, anyway. Why did you stay here? When you thought I was gone, why did you stay?"

She clenched her teeth, not wanting to answer. But

he wouldn't be denied. He squeezed her, gave her a little shake.

"Being a Guardian doesn't come with a hefty salary, you know." She struggled, pushing against his chest. But still he held her, caged her in his arms. "I didn't have anything to go back to, if you remember. Someone burned my store down."

He stilled. Frowned. Then, shaking his own head, he pressed. "That's not why, and you know it."

But she refused to admit aloud that she couldn't bear the thought of leaving this place behind. Of losing that last tenuous tie with him.

As if he'd read her thoughts somehow, he smiled again—a truly unnerving sight—and he ducked his head to kiss her. But she pulled back at the last moment. Shaken. What if something like this happened again? What if he didn't come back the next time?

"We both want this. I know it, and so do you." He growled, low in his chest. "Stop resisting and give in. Let me love you."

Those were the wrong words.

Struggling in earnest now, she forced him to release her lest he hurt her. She'd had six days to second guess everything between them. Six days of grief to twist her emotions into a million tiny knots. Six days to doubt herself. And him.

"You sent me away." She pushed her hair back as she stomped across the living area, stopping only when she had the safety of the heavy couch between them. "Love, Xander? You don't love. *The Slayer* doesn't love. You don't know what love is."

Scowling, he opened his mouth, but she hurried to cut him off. "Love is standing beside each other, all the way to the end. Trusting in each other to stand firm. Not sending the other away when things get tough. This, what's between us, is just…sex. It's just sex."

She wouldn't survive the loss of him again, and so she pushed him away, the only way she knew how.

"The hell it is," he exploded. In one swift move, he sent the couch flying and he was in her face.

"Go back, Xander. There is nothing for you here."

He scowled as he took her by the shoulders. "I came back for what is mine. *You* are here. *You* are mine."

"No, not any longer," she denied, though the words left a hollow ache in her chest.

"I'm not your wuss Jack. I'm not civilized. I won't walk away because you're too afraid to face your feelings."

"Afraid." She gasped, her mouth hanging open. Words jumbled in her mind, but she couldn't get them to pour out.

"Afraid," he repeated forcefully. "You believe I will leave again. But I won't. You have given yourself to me. You've given your body to me. You've given your heart to me. You love me. You. Are. Mine."

She glanced away, unable to look him in the eye with the lie bitter on her tongue. "No. You're wrong. You did walk away. And you'd do it again if you thought it was the right thing to do. You made your decision. A decision that we should have made together. A decision you know I would never agree to. What we had was nothing more than sex. I don't love you. Not anymore."

"It was more than sex," he growled. He shook her, forcing her to look at him. "You love me still!"

"Stop it! Stop using your lie radar on me."

"I'm not reading you. I can't read you anymore. I can't read anyone anymore. I am a half-mortal now. And you do love me still. I can feel it. Here, I can feel it." He slapped her hand to his chest, held it there when she resisted. His heart beat strong beneath her palm. Xander lowered his head, his lips mere inches from hers. "Because I love you too. Tell me again that you don't love me. Look at me and tell me that you don't want me. I've given up everything to be with you. Given up my immortality, given up Heaven. To be with *you*. Look me in the eyes and tell me that it was all for nothing," he said, his voice growing hoarse.

Her mouth fell open as the truth of his words finally hit her.

"You won't leave again?"

"Never again," he vowed solemnly.

On a sob, Kyanna launched herself into his arms, tears streaming down her face. "Tell me. Tell me again."

"I won't leave."

"No, the other," she said between kisses.

"I love you." Laughing now, he wrapped his arms around her and spun around. "I'll love you forever, Kyanna Hughes. And no one and nothing will ever keep us apart again."

"I love you too, Xander."

He lowered her to her feet, his mouth on hers, stealing her breath, stealing her inhibitions. Hands fumbled, tugged, and pulled stripping clothing away in a frantic rush.

"I need you," he whispered against her lips, "I need you so badly, Kyanna."

"Now, Xander! I can't wait any longer." He didn't give her time to make any further comments. He sealed his lips over hers, vanished their clothing, and lowered her to the thick rug in front of the fireplace. Dancing orange flames roared to life in the grate, as greedy flames of desire licked through her body. His hands swept over her, spreading those flames, stoking them, fueling them into a raging inferno. And all the while, his lips moved over her, branding her flesh.

"I'm yours, sweetheart. For as long as you'll have me," he whispered in her ear. "And longer still."

"Forever. I won't take less than forever."

She caught her breath as he wedged his knee between hers. Kyanna moaned aloud as he settled himself in the cradle of her thighs and rubbed the length of his throbbing erection against her. His mouth scorched the length of her throat.

"Forever," he groaned as he slipped inside her.

His mouth sealed over hers, angled, deepened the kiss as his body began moving upon hers, moved powerfully inside her. Xander guided her legs around him as he rocked, slow and steady, deep into her.

As their bodies strained toward release, Xander stared down at her. "I love you." He dropped a kiss to her lips, adding, "You're never getting rid of me."

And then he drove them both over the edge.

Epilogue

Niklas stepped back into the shadows, lifting the champagne flute to his lips as he watched the happy couple kiss. Again. For the bazillionth time. Maybe he should have gifted them with a lifetime supply of lip balm instead of a month-long honeymoon in Maui.

He tugged at the collar of his monkey-suit. Wearing fine silk adorned with lace and seed pearls, Kyanna was stunning. Xander didn't look half bad in his own monkey-suit either. For a besotted fool, that was. Though it had been a small—*very* small—affair, Kyanna had insisted she wasn't getting married while half the wedding party was dressed in combat gear. As far as Xander it was concerned, whatever Kyanna wanted, Kyanna got.

They still hadn't quite figured out all the nuances of Xander's return. Not that Xander had given them much time to work out all the kinks. He hadn't allowed himself to be away from Kyanna's side for more than a few hours at a time. They had figured out that Xander no longer needed to siphon human souls to exist. He could still shimmer and conjure. He could still form plasma balls. But he'd lost the ability to call forth Hellfire. They were still testing the parameters of his abilities. However, when injured, he healed at the normal rate of a human—therefore, he could be mortally injured. Something Kyanna, of course, was not happy to hear. Especially when he'd revealed his life span was now tied directly to Kyanna's, thanks to the portion of her soul that he'd absorbed. He would age as she did. And when she died, he would follow. Unfortunately, to Xander's dismay, the reverse was true as well. One half could not survive without the other.

Perhaps more than anything, what bothered Niklas the most was Xander's unwillingness to be parted from his female. While Niklas had grown—fond, he supposed was the right word—of Kyanna, he still couldn't understand how Xander could have given up all he had for one human woman. Immortality? Heaven?

For a woman?

It just wasn't logical. There was no strategy involved, no gain that he could see. And yet, he'd never seen Xander like this.

Happy. Or as happy as the Slayer could get. And that itself was just freaky. The Slayer…happy.

Deep shades of pink and crimson surrounded not only Kyanna, but Xander as well. Niklas had never seen colors of any kind surrounding Xander before, or any of the other Fallen either. And to see pink, the colors of love—and red, the color of lust—around the once cold and emotionless, colorless, Xander? Yep. Freaky. Besotted was definitely the right word. Shaking his head, he downed the last of his champagne and then vanished his glass. Love. Lust. It all equaled stupidity.

Vulnerability, a dark inner voice echoed disdainfully.

Whatever the hell it was that Xander had become afflicted with, Niklas wasn't getting within ten feet of it. He didn't have the time or the inclination for that crap. Never mind the fact that he could potentially live forever. He had more important things on his plate.

Never in a million years did he ever figure he'd be fighting to once again keep bad old Lucy in power down under, but that's exactly what they were doing. In a roundabout way. Galling as hell was what it was, actually. Drawing a deep breath, he straightened and caught Mikhail's eye. Getting the nod from Mikhail, he flicked a glance first to Gideon, and then Sebastian. The last scowled.

Sebastian might be too well mannered to cut out early, but he wasn't. Neither was Mikhail. One could always count on Mikhail to be the ultimate lone wolf. He did what he wanted, when he wanted, where he wanted. No one in his right mind would try to stop him. And those not in their right mind? Well, they weren't in any shape to object for long. Of course, lately, Gideon wasn't much better.

They'd discussed assignments earlier in the morning after they'd gathered to share intel. The plan had been to depart in the morning for their various destinations. Mikhail had volunteered to head up the search in Maine. Gideon was headed to the jungles of Mexico. Sebastian was on his way to Michigan. And Niklas was off to Iowa, of all places.

Now was as good a time as any to leave. Frankly, he'd personally had about all the PDA he could stomach. All this mushy, emotional stuff was giving him the creeps. For the love of all that was holy, Xander had even smiled. More than once. *Freaky!* It was time to get back out there and hunt the rest of those relics down before they lost anymore to Stolas.

Without saying goodbye, he shimmered himself to

his flat in Paris.

Space.

That was what he needed. Unfortunately, he wouldn't be getting enough of that in the near future. Asher had turned up information on another nest, and a larger than normal surge in demonic power in northern Iowa. In a matter of minutes, Niklas conjured himself into his customary attire. Black pants, combat boots, T-shirt, and full arsenal. Niklas grabbed a bag he kept packed for personal convenience, but then he hesitated. He needed to get the hell out of Dodge, but his gut was telling him something about this next mission was going to get sticky.

Grim, he went down on one knee and reached under the bed. Energy transferred through the handle and hummed up his arm as he pulled the trunk out. Might as well go loaded, he figured. And ammo—at least ammo in a fight against his own kind—didn't get any more powerful than what he had stashed away in this trunk.

He shrugged on a long trench coat, slid his shades up the bridge of his nose, grabbed up his bag and trunk and headed for the door. He had places to go, relics to find and demon ass to kick.

A word about the author...

Brenda Huber lives in Iowa with her husband, her two children and her very spoiled dog Sam. You can learn more by visiting her on her website (www.brendahuber.webs.com) or follow her on Facebook (http://on.fb.me/1F4VsNc).

Look for these titles by Brenda Huber
Now Available:

Paranormal Romance
Mine
Cravings
Shadows

Romantic Suspense
Queen's Chess

Historical Romance
Texas Bride
Texas Blaze

Chronicles of the Fallen
The Slayer

Coming Soon:
The Seer

Thank you for purchasing
this publication of The Wild Rose Press, Inc.

For questions or more information
contact us at
info@thewildrosepress.com.

The Wild Rose Press, Inc.
www.thewildrosepress.com

To visit with authors of
The Wild Rose Press, Inc.
join our yahoo loop at
http://groups.yahoo.com/group/thewildrosepress/